D0209095

LEAH'S CHOICE

LEAH'S CHOICE

Pleasant Valley
BOOK ONE

MARTA PERRY

BERKLEY BOOKS, NEW YORK

THE BERKLEY PUBLISHING GROUP
Published by the Penguin Group
Penguin Group (USA) Inc.
375 Hudson Street, New York, New York 10014, USA
Penguin Group (Canada), 90 Eglinton Avenue East, Suite 700, Toronto, Ontario M4P 2Y3, Canada
(a division of Pearson Penguin Canada Inc.)
Penguin Books Ltd., 80 Strand, London WC2R 0RL, England
Penguin Group Ireland, 25 St. Stephen's Green, Dublin 2, Ireland (a division of Penguin Books Ltd.)
Penguin Group (Australia), 250 Camberwell Road, Camberwell, Victoria 3124, Australia
(a division of Pearson Australia Group Pty. Ltd.)
Penguin Books India Pvt. Ltd., 11 Community Centre, Panchsheel Park, New Delhi—110 017, India
Penguin Group (NZ), 67 Apollo Drive, Rosedale, North Shore 0632, New Zealand
(a division of Pearson New Zealand Ltd.)
Penguin Books (South Africa) (Pty.) Ltd., 24 Sturdee Avenue, Rosebank, Johannesburg 2196,
South Africa

Penguin Books Ltd., Registered Offices: 80 Strand, London WC2R 0RL, England

This is an original publication of The Berkley Publishing Group.

This is a work of fiction. Names, characters, places, and incidents either are the product of the author's imagination or are used fictitiously, and any resemblance to actual persons, living or dead, business establishments, events, or locales is entirely coincidental. The publisher does not have any control over and does not assume any responsibility for author or third-party websites or their content.

ISBN-13: 978-1-61523-656-5

PRINTED IN THE UNITED STATES OF AMERICA

This book is dedicated to my grandchildren:
Bjoern, Greta, Ameline, Estella, Georgia, and Tyler,
with much love from Grammy. And, as always, to Brian.

ACKNOWLEDGMENTS

I'd like to express my gratitude to those whose expertise, patience, and generosity helped me in the writing of this book: to Erik Wesner, whose *Amish America* newsletters are enormously helpful in visualizing aspects of daily life; to Donald Kraybill and John Hostetler, whose books are the definitive works on Amish life; to Louise Stoltzfus, Lovina Eicher, and numerous others who've shared what it means to be Amish; to the unnamed Plain People, whose insights have enriched my life; and most of all to my family, for giving me a rich heritage upon which to draw.

CHAPTER ONE

*K***nowing** your proper place was a basic tenet of Amish life. Leah Beiler smiled as she watched her class of thirty-five scholars living out that belief. The number was up by three with the addition of the Glick children just today, and they were all in their assigned seats. Thirty-five heads bent over the work she'd set for her first- to eighth-graders, and not a whisper disturbed the stillness of the one-room school.

Ten years of teaching had given Leah an extra sense where her scholars were concerned. Despite the quiet, excitement rippled through the room, even though no head lifted for a furtive look at the battery clock on her desk. The prospect of a picnic lunch to welcome the newcomers had everyone, including, she had to admit, the teacher, excited. It would be a welcome break in the usual routine, with the Christmas program now in the distant past and their end-of-school-year events not yet begun.

The April weather had cooperated today, bathing Pleasant Valley, Pennsylvania, in sunshine rather than showers. Through the window, she could see the horses and buggies lined up outside that told her the scholars' mothers had arrived with food for the picnic.

She clapped her hands, amused at the alacrity with which pencils were put down. "It's time for our picnic lunch now, scholars. We'll eat first, and then there will be time to play. You may go outside."

It wasn't necessary to add that they should go in an orderly manner. Order was another precept of Amish life, ingrained since birth. Pencils were in their grooves on the desktops and books were closed before the children stood, murmuring quietly among themselves, and filed toward the door.

Leah followed her scholars between the rows of wood and wrought-iron desks, and out the door at the rear of the classroom that led onto a small porch and then to the schoolyard.

The white school building, looking like every other Amish school she'd ever seen, stood in a grove of trees, its narrow dirt lane leading out to the main road, a good half mile away. The Esch farm lay to their east and the Brand farm to the west, so that the schoolhouse seemed to nestle in their protective, encircling arms.

A trestle table had been set up under the oak tree that sheltered the yard. Her volunteer mothers and grandmothers, probably also happy with the break in routine, had spread it with a bountiful lunch—sandwich fixings of cheese, chicken, cold meat and bread, an array of salads, bowls of fruit, and jars of milk and lemonade. Trays of cupcakes and brownies were covered, reminding the children that dessert came last.

Rachel Brand, Leah's special friend since girlhood, hurried over, apron fluttering, to thrust a well-filled plate into her hands.

"Leah, I fixed a plate for you already, ja. If you waited for everyone else to be served, you might miss my macaroni salad."

"Never," she said, her pleasure at the day's treat increased by the presence of the friend who was as dear to her as a sister. "It's wonderful kind of you, Rachel, but we should be seeing to our guest of honor first."

Daniel Glick, the newcomer, stood out in the group, the only adult male in a bevy of women and children. If that bothered him, he didn't show it. He was accepting a heaping plate from Leah's mother, bending over her with courteous attention.

"Your mamm is taking good care of him," Rachel said. "And if she wasn't, someone else would jump at the chance, for sure. A widower just come from Lancaster to join our community — you know every woman in Pleasant Valley will be thinking to match him up with a daughter or sister, they will."

"They'd do better not to matchmake. Daniel Glick looks well able to decide for himself if he needs a wife."

Daniel's firm jaw and the determined set to his broad shoulders under the plain work shirt he wore suggested a man who knew what he wanted and who wouldn't be easily deflected from his course. He was probably a gut hand at avoiding any unwanted matchmaking.

Rachel, her blue eyes dancing with mischief as if they were ten again, nudged her. "You'd best tell that to your mamm, then. I expect she's already inviting him to supper so he can get to know you."

"Me?" Her voice squeaked a bit, so she was glad that she and Rachel stood a little apart from the others. "Rachel, that's foolish. Everyone has known for years that I'm a maidal."

"Years," Rachel scoffed, her rosy cheeks growing rounder with amusement.

Rachel did still look like the girl she'd once been, her kapp strings flying as they'd chased one another in a game in this same schoolyard. Leah couldn't remember a time when Rachel hadn't been part of her life. They'd shared enough joy and sorrow to bond them forever.

"I know very well how old you are, Leah Beiler," Rachel continued, "because we were born within a month of each other. And you are only an old maid if you want to be."

Leah crinkled her nose. "A maidal," she said firmly. "And I'm a schoolteacher with a love of learning besides, which frightens men off."

Rachel's smile slid away suddenly, and her smooth brow furrowed. "Leah, it would break my heart if I thought you meant to stay single all your life because of Johnny."

The name startled her, and it was all she could do to keep dismay from showing on her face. When Johnny Kile left Pleasant Valley, fence-jumping to the English world like too many young men, he'd left behind his family, including his twin sister, Rachel, who'd loved him dearly.

And he'd left Leah, the girl he'd said he'd loved. The girl he'd planned to marry that November, once the harvest season was over.

Many of those young men who left came back, penitent and ready to rejoin the community, after a brief time in the English world. But not Johnny.

She had to speak, or Rachel would think this more serious than it was. Close as they were, she didn't want Rachel to know how Johnny's loss had grieved her. It would only hurt Rachel, to no good end.

"No, of course that's not why. Johnny and I were no more than boy-and-girl sweethearts, you know that."

Rachel's hand closed over hers in a brief, warm grip. "You loved him. That's what I know."

"It was a long time ago," she said firmly, shutting away bittersweet memories. "What has brought on thoughts of him today?"

Rachel had not mentioned Johnny's name since the day she'd run to the Beiler house, tears streaming down her cheeks, to tell Leah that he had gone. It had shamed his family, as well as grieved them, that he'd left in that way, with no word for his betrothed and only a short note for them.

"No reason," Rachel said, but her gaze drifted away from Leah's.

She set down the filled plate on the nearest table so she could grasp her friend's wrist. "Rachel, tell me the truth." It was the warning tone she used with her scholars when they attempted to evade a question.

Rachel shook her head, dashing away a sudden tear. "My birthday is next week. Johnny's birthday, too, of course. It reminds me."

"And it hurts," Leah said softly. She knew about that pain.

"I'm being foolish." Rachel sniffed. "Here come your mamm and Daniel Glick to talk to you. I'd best see if any of those platters need filling." She scurried off, giving no chance for Leah to say a word of comfort, even if she could think of one.

For a moment the scene—the mothers serving food, chattering among themselves, the children eating quickly so they could scatter to swings, seesaw, and ball field—seemed to shimmer before her eyes. She was a girl again, hearing her sweetheart say he loved her.

She took a breath, clenching her hands against the dark green apron that covered her dress. She wasn't that girl in love any longer. She was a grown woman, a teacher, and she had to act like one.

And here came her mother, towing the newcomer along with her. "Leah, here is the father of your new scholars. Daniel Glick, this is my daughter Leah."

He was taller than many Amish men, that was her first thought. She had to tilt her head to look up at him. Piercing blue eyes met hers, their straight brows giving him a bit of a sober look. His beard was the same chestnut brown shade as his hair, and his mouth above the beard firm.

"Wie bist du heit. It's nice to meet you."

"Teacher Leah." He nodded in greeting, fingering the brim of his straw hat. "It's kind of you to take on three new scholars with the school year so near over."

She grasped a firm rein on her scattered thoughts. "I'm happy to have them. I look forward to getting to know Matthew and Elizabeth and Jonah."

"They are glad to be back in class again after the move." He glanced toward the table where the children sat eating, his face serious. "I would like to talk with you about their schooling. Perhaps when they finish today?"

The prompt request took her by surprise a bit. Still, since the Glick family had just moved here, their situation was different from that of her other scholars, most of whom she'd known since birth, seeing them at work frolics and worship services, watching them grow.

Daniel, being a widower, had to be both mother and father to his children, so she was glad to see he was interested in his young ones' education.

"Ser gut," she said. "I'll see you at three, then."

He gave a short nod to her, another to her mamm, and walked off toward the table where the children were having their lunch.

She watched him go, wondering a little. Still, there'd be plenty of time later to think about what changes the addition of the Glick family might make to her familiar classroom.

She turned to her mother, and her heart clenched with a familiar worry. "Mamm, why don't you let the others take care of the cleaning up and go along home after you eat? You look a little tired."

Her mother always insisted that she was well now, completely recovered from the cancer surgery that had worried them all so much a year ago, but even so, anything out of the ordinary seemed to exhaust her, though she hated to admit it.

"I'm not tired," her mother said predictably. "Well, what do you think of Daniel Glick? A strong-looking man, wouldn't you say? And the three children so bright and happy. They're a fine addition to our community. Aren't they?"

Her heart sank at the indication that her mother was, as Rachel had said, embarking on matchmaking. It was hardly surprising, since Mamm had tried her best to pair her eldest daughter up with every eligible man in their central Pennsylvania Amish community.

She had even suggested a visit to distant relatives back in Lancaster County a time or two, in hopes of finding a husband for her stubborn child.

It had taken all Leah's determination to hold out against her mother's loving wishes for her. Mamm thought Leah should forget her disappointment in Johnny and love again. But Mamm didn't know the whole story.

"They seem very nice," she said. Daniel Glick was an unknown quantity. All she could say now was that he appeared interested in his children's education. As for the children—

She had to banish a frown before Mamm saw it. Happy and healthy, Mamm had said. Certainly the children looked sturdy enough, but she was not so sure about the happy part, at least as far as the older two went. Both Matthew and Elizabeth had seemed withdrawn, resisting her efforts to get to know them this morning.

They might just be struggling to get comfortable in a new place. So why did she have this niggling feeling that something was wrong?

Jacob Esch, the eighth-grader she'd appointed to watch the clock, began to ring the bell that signaled it was time for play. She'd found that without a reminder, some of the scholars would skimp on their eating to be first on the swings.

Children ran toward the swings and seesaw, the little girls with their braids and bonnet strings flying in the wind, the boys racing one another as they always did. Some of the older ones grabbed bats and balls.

The Glick children seemed to hesitate. Then Matthew walked toward the ball field, while Elizabeth took her little brother's hand and led him to the swings.

Leah glanced toward Daniel Glick. He stood near the picnic table, arms crossed over his chest in a way that seemed to close him off from the rest of them. And the steady gaze he directed toward his children was so intent it startled her.

Leah had her work cut out for her that afternoon. She should be focused on assessing the Glick children's scholastic status in preparation for her talk with Daniel Glick later. Or else she should concentrate on the model of Pleasant Valley that her older scholars were constructing or the spelling test she'd be giving tomorrow.

Instead, her thoughts kept drifting into the past. It seemed no time at all since she'd been a scholar here, sitting at the row of desks against the right-hand wall, looking out at the blossoms on the apple tree, daydreaming.

Johnny had sat behind her, Rachel in front, making her a buffer between the twins. Johnny had tied her kapp strings together once, and spent the afternoon recess sitting on a stool in the corner as a result. She could still see him looking over his shoulder to make a face at her when the teacher's back was turned.

She pulled her rebellious thoughts into order. This was Rachel's fault, making her think of Johnny again. Making her feel that familiar sense of failure that came each time she remembered how they'd parted.

She moved to the row of first-graders, bending over to check the lined sheets on which they were practicing the letter *L*. They looked up now and then at the capital and lowercase alphabet that marched across the top of the chalkboard.

"Very nice work, Jonah." She smiled at Daniel's youngest, and the boy's chubby face crinkled in a returning smile. She'd already noticed that Jonah was the most open of the three.

"I like to make letters, Teacher Leah."

"I can see that." She patted his shoulder lightly. "Keep up the good work."

At six, Jonah's ease in English was surprising. Most of the first-graders had spoken only the Pennsylvania Dutch dialect at home before they started school, where they were expected to learn English. Jonah must have had a fine teacher at his last school to be so at ease in his second language. Or third, if one counted the High German used for worship.

Toward the back of the room, Matthew seemed contented enough, working on a model of some sort for the display. She hadn't seen him interact with any of the other children in spite of friendly overtures from several boys.

She walked back to check on the boys' progress, pausing by Matthew's desk. And blinked. What she'd taken for a model of a silo certainly wasn't, unless silos had suddenly taken on a substantial tilt.

"What are you making, Matthew?"

He squirmed a little in his seat, not looking at her. "Nothing. I mean, a silo."

She tapped the model. "I think the grain might fall out, don't you? This looks more like the Leaning Tower of Pisa."

His wide blue eyes met hers again, but this time they were lit by enthusiasm. "I'd like to see that someday. How can it lean over but not fall down? Do you know?"

She heard the wonderment in his voice. Heard it, and recognized it. She knew that yearning to see things that were far away and to understand things that seemed inexplicable. For just an instant she wanted to share the boy's curiosity.

No, of course she didn't. She'd stopped longing for the impossible years ago, when she'd put away childish dreams. She was Amish, and Amish didn't fly off to a foreign country to gape at something that had no influence on their lives.

"I don't know. But perhaps you should make a silo. I'm sure Jacob could use one for his farm."

Jacob Esch, hearing his name, looked up and nodded, and the moment passed. Matthew turned toward the other boy, and if there was disappointment in his face, she didn't see it.

She moved away. Matthew's sister, eight-year-old Elizabeth, was practicing spelling words with Rachel's oldest, Becky. She smiled a little when she made a mistake, but she shot an apprehensive glance toward Leah now and then, as if unsure of her approval.

All in all, she found the Glick children a bit of a concern, although there was nothing she could really put her finger on. As their teacher, it was her job to make them feel at home and bring out their best. Perhaps her talk with their father would help her understand them better.

Beyond the side window, the apple tree had begun to put forth its blossoms. Something fluttered inside her, like the apple blossoms trembling in the breeze. She and Johnny had stood under that tree the first time he'd told her that he loved her. And it was there that they'd said their bitter good-byes.

The automatic timer in her mind went off, and she turned to check the clock on her desk.

"It's time to clean up now. Please be sure the paste lids are on tightly." The older boys sometimes skimped on the cleanup, a little overeager to be out the door. "Who would like to wash the chalkboard today?"

Becky's hand went up immediately, and after a glance at her, Elizabeth Glick put her hand up, too.

"Ser gut. You girls may start on the boards. Please leave the spelling words."

The final routine of the day moved swiftly to its conclusion, and soon her scholars were headed toward the door in an even line, saving the running and jumping for the moment they hit the schoolyard. Leah touched Matthew Glick lightly on the arm.

"Your father is coming to talk with me, Matthew. Will you please watch your brother and sister on the playground until we finish?"

Matthew's face was very like his father's. Guarded in a way one didn't often see in an Amish child. He studied her for a moment, blue eyes serious, before he nodded. "I will."

"Ser gut." She glanced up and saw Daniel near the door, moving aside as the line of children passed him. When Matthew reached him, he extended his hand, as if to touch the boy's shoulder, but then he seemed to change his mind, standing where he was until they were all out. The door closed behind the last scholar.

"Komm in. Wilkom to our school." Leah gestured toward the rows of desks. "Matthew's desk is here, and Elizabeth's there. And Jonah is up in front, with the other first-graders."

Daniel followed her without speaking to the front of the classroom, his shoes thudding on the bare wooden floor. Not that she expected him to chatter, but a few words might ease the awkwardness.

He was a stranger, after all, and she thought again how odd

that was. Pleasant Valley's Amish community had been established in the 1970s, when the brethren had left Lancaster County for cheaper farmland in the valleys of central Pennsylvania. Since then, the population had been stable, so that she knew every member of the church district as well as she knew her own family. Daniel Glick and his children were the exception.

She pulled over the visitor's chair for him and seated herself behind her desk. "Komm, sit down. I'm glad you're willing to talk with me about the children. I want to make their move here as smooth as possible."

Daniel balanced his straw hat on his knees. He smiled, the frostiness disappearing from his blue eyes as his face relaxed. It was a very appealing smile. She'd been right—if Daniel was in search of a wife, he'd have no trouble finding one by himself.

Not her, of course. She was content with her life the way it was, and she didn't foresee any changes coming her way.

"We've been warmly welcomed here," Daniel said. "It is a change for the young ones, though."

"And for you."

He shrugged. "I don't mind a new place. I'm just glad to have a chance to buy such a fine farm." His eyes narrowed, accentuating the sun lines that fanned out from the corners. "Amish children should be raised on a farm."

"Everyone doesn't have that opportunity." Even here, farms were being lost every year to development. Most Amish parents couldn't manage to provide land for each of their children, no matter how much they wanted to. "One of my brothers has a farm machinery shop, and another is a carpenter."

Daniel's brows drew down. "My children will have that chance. I'll see to that."

It was what every Amish parent wanted, of course, but Daniel's insistence seemed a little intense, and it made her wonder what was behind it.

"They're going to be a gut addition to our class, I know. I notice that Jonah speaks English very well already—better than most of my first- and even second-graders."

For some reason that made his frown deepen. "Ja." The word was so curt that it sounded as if Jonah's skill in English was a fault.

She struggled for something else to say about his children on such short acquaintance. "Elizabeth volunteered to wash the chalkboard already, she and Becky Brand."

"She's a gut helper." He said the words absently, his gaze on the world map she'd pulled down earlier for geography. "Teacher Leah, there is something I want to say. I want to be certain my children are not learning worldly things in your classroom."

Leah stiffened. That was something the parents of her children seldom had occasion to say, knowing it was a given in an Amish school. She remembered Matthew's comments about the leaning tower. Did Daniel assume that the map meant she was encouraging the children to yearn for the outside world?

"Our course of learning is much like that of any Amish school," she said firmly, on sure ground when it came to her teaching. "I'd be happy to show you our textbooks and our course of study. Or perhaps you'd like to meet with the school board members."

He shook his head. "There's no need for that. I'll see their books soon enough when I help the young ones with their homework." He paused for a moment, as if weighing his words. "I meant no disrespect by what I said, Teacher Leah. But I care about my children's education, and it means a great deal to have them in an Amish school."

"I understand." But she didn't, not entirely. She didn't know Daniel, and she didn't know what drove him. She managed a polite smile. "Well, here is a chance to see young Jonah's primer, since he went outside without it." She picked up the ABCs book and handed it to him.

"That boy would forget his head if it weren't attached." He rose as he spoke, and his expression was indulgent at the mention of his youngest. "I'm grateful for your interest in my children, Teacher Leah. If there are any difficulties, you will let me know."

That sounded more like an order than a request, but she nodded. It seemed that, having delivered his opinion, Daniel intended to leave without further ado.

"Have there been any troubles with the children that I should know about? Any health concerns, or anything like that?"

"None." Holding his hat in one hand and the primer in the other, he turned toward the door. It gave her the feeling that if there had been any problems, she wouldn't hear about them from Daniel.

She followed him back through the row of desks and out the door to the porch. He paused on the front step, one hand on the railing, and looked back at her. "Would you want me to wait while you lock up now?"

"That's kind of you, but I have some cleaning to do before I go home." She waved to the children as they came running toward their father.

"I'll be going then." His long stride cleared the steps, but then he paused again, his eyes narrowing as he stared down the lane. "It seems you have another visitor, Teacher Leah."

Dust rose from the dirt road as a car—a bright red car—drew up to the school. The sunlight glittered on the paint and chrome, and then on the fair hair of the man who slid out and stood looking at her.

Her heart thudded to a stop. Johnny Kile had come back.

Chapter Two

Leah reached behind her, pressing her hands flat against the door frame for support. A heavy band seemed to tighten around her chest, compressing her ribs until she couldn't take a breath. Certainly she couldn't speak a single word.

But she had to. She had to breathe, had to nod, had to speak and act as if it were an everyday thing to see John Kile after all these years.

Leah managed a shallow breath, inhaling the scent of fresh-cut grass. Rachel had sent her husband over from the farm to mow yesterday, so that all would be in readiness for the picnic. Rachel couldn't have imagined that her twin brother would show up here today, not that Johnny was likely to notice the grass.

John came toward the schoolhouse porch slowly, as if unsure of his welcome now that he was here. She forced herself to raise her eyes, to look at the person he'd become in ten years away among the English.

Odd. She knew it was John. She had recognized him the

instant he stepped from the car. But the boy she'd known ten years ago had little in common with the worldly man who stood before her. The clothes, the hair, even the way he stood and the expression on his face were different. She was so used to seeing a beard on adult males that his face looked naked without it.

Then he smiled, lips quirking in the way that showed the dimple at the corner of his mouth, and he was Johnny again.

"It's been a long time, Leah. It's really good to see you."

His gaze moved from her to Daniel Glick, who stood where he'd been when he spotted the car. Daniel stared back, his face stolid, as if he waited for something. An explanation, maybe.

A natural reaction, that was certain sure. An English man coming to call at the Amish school was unusual. Daniel would stay to be sure nothing was wrong. She had no choice but to introduce them.

"Daniel Glick, this is John Kile. John is . . . an old friend." What else could she call him?

Daniel gave a short nod, not offering to shake hands. His expression didn't change, but she sensed his taut figure stiffen. Had he been in Pleasant Valley long enough to have heard of the Kiles' son, who'd broken his engagement, his baptismal vows, and his mother's heart to turn English?

They couldn't stand here staring at one another. Somehow she had to get things back to normal. Daniel shifted his gaze to her, a question in his intent face, and she managed a faint, reassuring smile.

"It was gut of you to come, Daniel. I'll see the children tomorrow."

He didn't move for a moment, and she couldn't imagine what he was thinking. It couldn't be a positive thought, she'd guess.

Finally he nodded. He turned away, walking quickly toward his buggy without a backward glance. In a moment the children had scrambled in. The buggy rolled off down the lane.

"Someone new in the community?" Johnny asked. "I don't recognize him." He stood looking up at her, one hand on the stair railing, sunlight turning his hair to flax.

"He and his family just moved here from Lancaster County." And why were they talking about Daniel when so many other things shouted to be said?

"He wasn't very friendly."

"Do you expect friendship here?" Her words sounded more in control than she felt.

His hand tightened on the railing. "Maybe not. I guess things haven't changed much, have they?"

"They don't. That's the choice we make." The choice he had rejected.

"Look, Leah, can we go inside and talk?" He planted one foot on the porch step, as if he'd come closer to her, and she felt a wave of something that might be panic.

"The porch is a fine place to talk." She kept her voice calm with an effort.

It was bad enough that Daniel had been here to witness a man who was under the meidung come to visit with her. She wouldn't compound the trouble by being inside the schoolhouse alone with someone the community had shunned.

What must Daniel be thinking about the Amish schoolteacher who apparently had a male English friend? The thought flitted through her mind, and she shooed it away. She had more serious concerns than what Daniel thought of her.

Johnny lifted his right eyebrow in a familiar movement. His

hazel eyes were unchanged, but both his brows and hair were a little darker now than they'd once been.

"It looked as if you'd invited him inside—Daniel, was that his name?"

"Daniel is the parent of three of my scholars. Naturally we talked in the schoolroom. But you have no reason to be there."

"I spent eight years there. Remember?" His smile teased, the way it had long ago.

"I remember." She had to fight against the memories, just as she'd been doing all afternoon. "But you're not the same person you were then. No one looking at you now would imagine you to be Amish."

"I'm not." He frowned. "Not anymore."

The flip answer hurt her. "Can you deny what you're born so easily?"

"Not easily." His face became set in sudden, harsh lines, and he looked years older than she knew he was. "But it can be done. You know others who've done it and been happy." His tone challenged her.

Did she? Maybe so. Once they were gone, she didn't have much opportunity to judge whether they were satisfied with their choice or not.

"If you're so happy with your decision, why are you here now?"

As soon as the question was out, her heart began to beat in hard, measured thuds, pounding against her ribcage. What if he said he was here because of her? How would she answer that?

"I'm not here to kneel in repentance and ask the church to take me back, if that's what you're thinking." His jaw hardened.

"Look, at least we can sit down and talk like civilized people, can't we?"

He even talked differently now, using phrases she'd never heard from his lips, speaking in a cadence that was so quick it could never be Amish. He clearly wouldn't go away until she'd heard him out.

"Fine." She sat down on the top step of the porch, smoothing her long skirt over her legs. "Talk, if you want."

If he wasn't here to repent, then he hadn't come with any idea of reuniting with his lost love. That should make it easier to deal with him.

She didn't want that relationship anyway, she assured herself. She'd been over her feelings for Johnny a long time now.

One thing hadn't changed about him, she noticed. He still wore that mulish expression when he was balked in what he wanted to do. He stood for a moment, frowning at her, and then he sat down next to her on the step, stretching out long, jeans-clad legs.

"So, John Kile, why are you back in Pleasant Valley, if not to rejoin the brethren?" She was satisfied that she sounded perfectly composed.

"Have you seen Rachel lately? Are you and she still close?"

He jumped from thought to thought like a June bug. That hadn't changed in his years away.

"I saw her today." She hesitated. Say the rest of it? Maybe she should. "She mentioned you, feeling a little sad because of your birthdays next week."

She certainly wouldn't mention Rachel's concern that Leah was still single because of him.

"I'm sorry." He clenched the knees of his jeans, muscles standing out on the backs of his hands. "I never meant to hurt her."

She could only gape at him. "Never meant to hurt her? Your leaving hurt everyone in the community." Especially her. "Maybe you've forgotten that in all the time you've been gone."

"No, I haven't forgotten. Anything." His voice softened. "Not you, Leah."

She laced her fingers together in her lap. It was best, safest, not to respond to that, but the words echoed in her heart. "Are you going to see Rachel?"

"I want to." He leaned toward her, his eyes darkening in intensity. "Please, you talk to her for me, Leah. Tell her I'm here, that I want to see her."

"Me?" Her throat clutched. "I can't do that."

"You two were always like sisters." His voice went low and coaxing. "She'll listen to you."

Did he have any idea how hurtful it was to remind her that she and Rachel had nearly *been* sisters? It seemed he didn't. Or if he did, he could ignore it in his need to accomplish his goal.

"She's your twin, Johnny. If you want to see her again, then—"

"I'm scared."

The words sent her gaze flying to his face. He gave her a rueful smile.

"Stupid, isn't it? But I'm afraid to walk up to my own sister."

She tried to harden her heart against that smile. Johnny wasn't her responsibility any longer. "I think you'd better. Or else just go away again."

"I can't go away. I'm going to be working here for the next six months, at least. I'm doing research at the medical clinic over in Fostertown."

She could only stare at him. "You are?"

"Hard to believe, isn't it? I just finished a degree in genetics, and I'm going to assist Dr. Brandenmyer in his work. You know about him?" He slanted a questioning look at her.

"Ja, I know."

Everyone in the community knew about the clinic and the doctor. Geneticists wanted to study the Amish because of the hereditary diseases that occurred too often in a community where most folks were descended from the same small group of ancestors.

Dr. Brandenmyer did gut work, so people said, ministering to those who were ill, in addition to conducting his research. That was not always an easy thing in a society as closed as the Amish were.

"Working with him is the opportunity of a lifetime." Johnny stared past her, as if looking at some future she couldn't see.

"Is your background why the doctor hired you? Because you were Amish once?"

Johnny frowned. "I have very good qualifications. But I suppose my heritage didn't hurt."

"And you want to get back in touch with your family for what?"

She was feeling her way. Once, she'd have said that she knew every thought that went through Johnny's mind. Now she feared that what she said to him might determine whether he saw his family or not.

Please, Father. Guide me. I don't know what is best to do or say.

"I want to see them because they're my family." His tone was sharp, but then he smiled, shaking his head. "But it's true. I need to find a way to make contact with the community again if I'm going to be much help to Dr. Brandenmyer. And it's worthwhile work—you must know that. It can save lives."

Children's lives. She thought of the children she'd known throughout the community—the ones afflicted with Crigler-Najjar syndrome, spending half their lives under the special blue lights that helped them survive to grow up. Or those with the other genetic diseases that were too common among the Amish.

She didn't want to be involved, didn't want to risk the hurt that would come with his return.

But if what Johnny talked about could help those children, wasn't it worth at least trying to smooth his path? She couldn't easily turn away from something that might help them.

Her throat tightened, and she had to push out the words. "All right. I'll talk to Rachel. I make no promises. But I'll tell her that you're back and that you want to see her."

Johnny grasped her hand in a quick, warm grip before she sensed what he was about to do. "Thank you, Leah. You're a good friend."

She pulled her hand free, denying the pleasure she felt at his touch, his words.

"I'm making no promises," she said again. She'd made promises to Johnny once, and that had come to nothing.

"Good enough." He stood, as if afraid she'd change her mind if he delayed. "I'll stop by tomorrow after school to see what she said."

"Not tomorrow." He'd turned into a typical Englischer, always in a hurry. "Maybe on Wednesday. I'll have been able to talk to Rachel by then."

He looked as if he wanted to argue, but then he nodded, his lips curving into the smile that was still familiar.

"All right. Take your time. I'll see you Wednesday."

He'd gotten what he'd come for, so he moved away quickly, sliding into the car without a backward glance toward her.

She rose, standing on the top step. Watching until the red car disappeared around the bend in the lane.

Johnny Kile was back. She didn't think she'd quite accepted it yet.

He wasn't the boy she'd loved, that was certain sure. But who he was now—she didn't quite know. Or how it would affect her, affect all of them, having him here.

Any hope Leah had of going to see Rachel that evening disappeared when she got home and discovered that her brother Levi and his family were coming for supper. Her mother was already bustling about the farmhouse kitchen, and whatever tiredness Leah had observed earlier had vanished in her excitement over having a full table for supper.

"I know the boys have big appetites, but you are making twice as much as they will eat. Why don't you just give us the leftovers from the picnic?" She'd noticed that, predictably, nearly as much food had gone home again as Mamm had brought.

Her mother shook her head, looking aghast. "I can't do that. They would think I wasn't happy to see them."

"You see Levi every day." With her oldest brother doing most of the farm chores now, that was inevitable. "And Barbara and the children at least two or three times a week."

"Not for supper," her mother said with unanswerable logic. She thrust a wooden spoon into Leah's hand. "You make the dumplings. You have a lighter hand with them than Anna does."

"Anna just doesn't want to admit how good a cook she is, for fear she'll have to do more." But she couldn't help but be pleased that her mother thought well of her cooking, even if the feeling was a bit prideful.

The Schnitz un Knepp was already steaming on the stove. Leah took the yellow mixing bowl from the shelf. She'd concentrate on getting the soft dough to just the right consistency. Maybe then she could push away thoughts of Johnny, of Rachel's reaction when she heard the news of his return, even of Daniel Glick and his children. Those worries would have to be dealt with later.

An hour later, the substantial array of food Mamm considered appropriate for a family supper was spread on the long table and the house was crowded with people—all, it seemed, talking at once. Mamm sank into her chair.

Leah, taking her place next to her, frowned slightly, her gaze on her mother's face. Even when she closed her eyes as her father began to pray, the image of her mother's face lingered.

Mamm had aged since her bout with cancer, there was no doubt about that. Her brown hair, pulled tightly back into a bun from its center part, seemed to show more gray all the time.

But it was the strained tiredness on her mother's face at the end of a long day that worried Leah. Nothing would convince Mamm that she couldn't do all the things she used to do.

When the prayer ended, Leah leaned across to murmur to her

mother under the clatter of cutlery. "Don't you get up again, Mamm. If anything needs fetched for the meal, Anna and I will take care of it." She glanced at her younger sister. "Ain't so?"

Anna's bright blue eyes registered understanding, and she nodded quickly. "Ja, that's right, Mamm. You cooked, so we'll serve and clear."

Leah smiled. The baby of the family, at eighteen Anna could be unpredictable—sweet and happy one moment, distracted and short-tempered the next. That was natural, wasn't it? When she'd been that age, she'd probably been the same.

When she'd been that age, she'd been in love with Johnny.

She shoved that thought away again, trying to focus on her sister. She couldn't help but worry sometimes that Anna's job, working at a Mennonite bakery in town, brought too many temptations into her life.

Still, Anna was gut at heart. She'd soon settle down and turn her flightiness into falling in love with a suitable young man.

"You have some new scholars at the school, Leah, ain't so?" Barbara, her brother Levi's wife, turned from spooning a dumpling into baby Sarah's mouth to look at Leah inquiringly.

"The Glick children started today," she said. "There are three of them—six, eight, and ten. The other children are making them welcome."

"It's gut for all of us to do that," her mother said. "Poor man, a widower alone with three young ones. We must do all we can for them. I've invited them to supper tomorrow night."

Leah's heart sank. Not that her mother wouldn't be welcoming even if she didn't have two unmarried daughters in the house, but still—

"A widower with young children needs a wife. Maybe a fine opportunity for our Leah, ja?" As usual, Barbara burst out with something the others might be thinking but not be ready to say.

"I'm not looking for a husband," she said, with no hope that would end the topic.

"Every woman is looking for a husband," Barbara insisted. Her face beamed with such happiness that Leah couldn't find it in her heart to be annoyed, though she did sometimes wish that Levi had found himself a wife who wasn't quite so eager to run everyone else's life. Mamm's matchmaking intentions were enough to deal with.

I shouldn't think that of Barbara. A quick prayer formed in her mind. *She is a gut soul, I know, and she makes Levi happy.*

Across the table, Anna put her fork down and leaned forward to glare at Barbara around Levi's bulk. "Every woman is not like you, Barbara."

Leah landed a gentle kick on Anna's ankle, and Anna transferred the glare to her. Anna should know by now that the best way to take their sister-in-law's pronouncements was to ignore them.

"Every woman wants a home of her own," Barbara said, her good humor unimpaired. "You'll find that out when you're a little older, Anna." She beamed around the table. "And now is a gut time to tell you that Levi and I will have an addition to the family, come December."

Under cover of the flood of congratulations from Mamm and Daad and brother Mahlon, Leah exchanged glances with Anna. Another young one coming, with Sarah not out of diapers yet and the little boys only two and four.

Children were a blessing to any Amish family, but where were

Levi and Barbara going to put them all in the small house they rented on the Evansville road? She rose, pressing her cheek against Barbara's and murmuring her good wishes.

Daad cleared his throat, and everyone turned toward the head of the table. Daad exchanged glances with Mamm, and Leah saw a faint nod.

"Your mother and I have something to tell you also." Her father's lean, weathered face was as solemn as if he were at prayer. "We feel it is time for us to move into the daadi haus and let Levi and Barbara take over the farm."

Leah felt it like a blow to the stomach. Levi taking over the farm? Was Daad really ready for that now?

But the past two years had been hard on him, too. Though he seemed as strong as ever, his beard was completely white now, and he didn't move as fast as he used to.

She'd known it would come sometime. That was the way things were done. She just hadn't thought it would be so soon.

Still, the daadi haus, connected to the farmhouse by a covered walk, had been ready for new occupants since Grossmutter died five years ago. Levi was already doing much of the farmwork, and everyone in the community knew this was his place.

But what would the change mean for her and Anna?

Mahlon took the news happily enough, as would her brother Joseph. They were already settled in jobs, Joseph with his farm machinery repair and Mahlon as a carpentry apprentice.

Joseph and his wife, Myra, were probably thinking of starting a family soon, too, and everyone knew that Mahlon was courting the youngest Miller girl, with an eye toward a wedding in November, the traditional time for Amish weddings. Their lives would not be changed by this, but Leah's and Anna's—

"What about Leah and me?" Anna's voice rose above the chatter before Leah could administer another kick. "What are we supposed to do? Do you expect us both to crowd into that small spare room in the daadi haus?"

"I'm sure we'll be fine—" Leah began, but Levi was already shaking his head at his youngest sister.

"We would not put you out of your rooms, no. You and Leah must never think that. The boys can share, and the new babe will come in with us for a while."

And she and Anna would live in a house run with relentless cheerfulness by Barbara. Barbara would change things—it was only natural that she'd want to do things her way in her own house. Leah managed to keep a smile on her face, but she feared Anna wouldn't hold on to her temper long in that situation.

"Of course if you did decide to move," Barbara added, "we would put the baby into your room."

Anna drew breath, and Leah managed to connect with her foot.

"I'm sure we can work all the details out later." She picked up the platter of smoked sausage surrounded by dried apples and dumplings, and handed it to Mahlon. "Who is ready for more? Mamm made enough to feed half the county."

Anna subsided, but the dark look she sent her sister declared that she wasn't finished with the subject.

By the time the dishes were washed, Levi and Barbara and their children had gone home. Leah hung up the tea towel and glanced around the kitchen to be sure all was as pristine as her mother expected.

The wooden cabinets had been wiped down, and the countertop and long wooden table shone. The only decoration on the wall, a calendar from the feed store in town, was a bit crooked, so she straightened it.

She frowned slightly. Her parents were in the living room, Mamm knitting and Daadi reading the latest issue of the *Budget* newspaper. Mahlon had hurried off in his courting buggy as soon as the evening chores were done, plainly headed toward the Miller farm and his sweetheart. Where was Anna?

A quick walk through the house didn't turn her up, and her bonnet and cape were missing from their usual place. Leah slung a shawl around her shoulders and stepped outside.

It was dusk, and a damp April chill permeated the air. Soon it would be May, and the lilacs and roses would perfume the night. Even now, the rhubarb in Mamm's garden had begun to unfurl its wide green leaves.

Across the fields, yellow light glowed from Daniel Glick's windows. The farmhouse had stood empty for months, and seeing lights there again felt right.

But that didn't answer the question of where her sister was. If she called out, Mamm would hear and be disturbed.

Standing there, undecided, she heard a faint jingle of metal from the stable. She clutched her shawl around her against the cool air and headed across the yard.

The stable door stood slightly ajar. She slid it open. Sure enough, Anna was there, harnessing Ben to Mamm's buggy. She swung around, startled, at the sound of the door.

"Going someplace with Mamm's horse and buggy tonight, are you?"

Leah kept her voice light, having no wish to get into a squabble. Still, she had to talk some sense into Anna over the changes that were inevitable, and this was a chance to get her sister alone.

Anna flushed guiltily. "Mamm won't mind. She lets me take it every day for work. Tonight I want to meet some of my friends."

"Amish friends or English friends?" Leah crossed the wide planks of the barn floor and stroked Ben's smooth neck. The gelding nuzzled her, as if to complain about this extra excursion in his day.

Anna shrugged impatiently. "Both, I guess. Does it matter? You and the boys did what you liked during your rumspringa, ain't so?"

Somehow she had the feeling that Anna's ideas of what to do during the traditional running-around time of Amish youth were a bit more adventurous than hers had been. But then, she'd had Johnny, with things already settled between them.

"It doesn't matter if you have English friends, I suppose." She could see that Anna was in the mood to take offense at just about anything. "I just think it's late to be setting out."

"It wouldn't be this late if Barbara hadn't insisted on going all over the house, as if she hadn't seen it before." Anger showed in Anna's quick movements as she fastened the harness and gathered the lines. "She even looked in my dower chest, as if that was any of her business."

Barbara had only too obviously been measuring the rooms for her own furniture. "I know she can be a little too enthusiastic at times, but—"

"Is that what you call it? She's a busybody, and why Levi wanted to marry her and be bossed around all of his life, I don't understand."

"None of us ever understands what makes someone fall in love." She touched Anna's shoulder, but her sister shrugged it off. "She is his wife, she makes him happy, and they are moving in. There's nothing you can do about it, so you'd best accept it with good grace."

"And if I don't want to?"

The patience she had with her sister was wearing thin. As the baby of the family, Anna had not been spoiled, exactly, but she'd certainly been treated with more indulgence than the older ones.

"You don't have a choice," she said firmly. "The decision to move into the daadi haus is Mamm and Daadi's, and they've made it. You're not going to make them unhappy over this, are you?"

Anna paused, hand on the buggy rail. "I wouldn't do that." She swung herself onto the buggy seat, the full skirt of her rose-colored dress flaring out. She picked up the lines and then paused, face sobering under the brim of her black bonnet. "Leah—do you think Mamm is really all right?"

"Of course she is." Her response came quickly, and she could only hope she sounded as sure as she'd like to feel. "Go along now and have fun with your friends." She smiled, relieved when Anna smiled back.

"All right then. I won't be late. I promise." She clucked to Ben, and the buggy moved off.

Leah stood watching the battery-operated lantern on the back of the buggy disappear down the lane. What was behind Anna's attitude?

For some reason she saw again Daniel's indulgent look at the mention of his youngest. Maybe it was human nature to be lenient with the last child.

It was too late now to go back and redo anything about Anna's rearing. Leah could only trust her sister's warm heart and common sense to get her through the changes that were coming in their lives.

And she suspected she'd need a measure of common sense and patience for herself, too.

CHAPTER THREE

Daniel and his children came for supper the next evening, as her mother had said, and Leah found herself on pins and needles throughout the meal, wondering if Daniel would mention the visit of an Englischer to the schoolhouse the previous afternoon.

He didn't. Because he knew it would make her uncomfortable? She wasn't sure, but she was grateful. Her family would know about John Kile's return soon enough, but it didn't seem right to talk to anyone else before telling Rachel.

By the time everyone went out to the backyard after the meal, her tension had eased. Daniel leaned against the corner of the porch, deep in conversation with her father about planting times in the area. His strong face was intent, and he apparently was soaking up advice.

He showed an appealing deference to the older man's opinion that she appreciated. Daadi might think he was ready to retire, but he still knew more about farming in Pleasant Valley than just about anyone.

Rachel and her family were coming for dessert, so surely she could find an opportunity to talk with Rachel about Johnny. Then perhaps she could stop feeling as if she carried the burden of his return all alone.

She'd have to be careful about the telling of it, though. Rachel's sweet face showed every emotion she felt, and this was going to be difficult news both to give and to receive.

Sunlight still slanted across the yard, making the yellow trumpets of the daffodils at the corner of the house glow as if they were made of gold. She drew in a breath, loving the mingled scents that said spring was here at last. Every season had its own beauty, but this time of rebirth and growth surely must be close to the Creator's heart.

Her brother Mahlon, still as enthusiastic as a kid about games despite his twenty-two years, had put up the croquet set, and the moment Rachel's family arrived, he recruited all the children to play.

Daniel's six-year-old, Jonah, seized a mallet. Mahlon put his big hands over Jonah's small ones to help him hit the red ball through a wicket, and Jonah laughed with pleasure.

"I see that your brother is wonderful gut with children." Daniel's voice startled her, and she swung around to find him behind her.

Had Daniel sought her out to talk about John's visit yesterday? As the parent of children in her care, he certainly had a right to be concerned about who visited the schoolhouse.

"Ja, he is. We tease him that he'd best be sure his intended wants a big family."

She'd spoken lightly, out of nervousness probably, and as she looked up at Daniel, she caught something—a tightening, maybe—in his face. The look disappeared as quickly as it had come, though, so maybe she was imagining it.

Sun lines crinkled at the corners of Daniel's deep blue eyes, as if he dismissed whatever had caused the reaction. The color of his shirt echoed that blue, making his eyes even more vivid.

"Mahlon's bride will be a fortunate woman, it seems. Is he keeping company with someone?"

"He and Esther Miller have it already settled between them, I think. At least, folks say that Esther's father is planting a long row of celery this spring."

"Gut, since they'll want plenty for the wedding feast come November." His eyebrows lifted. "And is your father planting much celery this year?"

The question's implication startled her. "I think our Anna is enjoying her rumspringa too much to settle down just yet."

He glanced toward her sister, who was chasing Jonah around the edge of the croquet lawn, heedless of the way the breeze tossed her hair loose from beneath her kapp.

"Anna is a lively girl. But she is not the only unmarried daughter of the house."

His gaze came back to her face, and the question in his blue eyes startled her. For just an instant her breath seemed to hitch before she got control of herself.

"I don't think Daad will be planting any celery for me. I have no plans to marry."

Then she realized that his intent expression and his words might well refer to John's visit to the school yesterday. He wasn't expressing interest in her. He was wondering if John was courting her. She could hardly deny it without bringing up a subject she had no wish to discuss with him.

"Your family has made us feel so welcome." He changed the subject, perhaps seeing that he'd embarrassed her by his comment. "The children were happy to eat someone else's cooking tonight. I'm not very handy in the kitchen."

He was trying to make it easier for her, but he couldn't. No one could. The timing that had brought Johnny to the schoolhouse when Daniel was there had forced Daniel into the secret, like it or not.

She took a breath, trying to find the right words to acknowledge the situation. She had a quick look around to be sure no one was within earshot.

"Daniel, about John Kile's visit to the schoolhouse yesterday—it's obvious you haven't said anything to anyone. I appreciate that."

His face sobered. "I don't know people to exchange gossip with. But I would not like to think that my children's teacher was being influenced by her English friend."

"He's not—" She stopped, trying to organize her thoughts. Naturally he'd assume John was there out of interest in her. "John Kile was Amish once."

He nodded, his gaze serious on her face. "I thought that when I saw him."

"How could you tell?" She had thought John typically English herself, with his fancy car and his blue jeans.

"Something about the way he looked at the school, maybe. As if he'd belonged there once."

"He attended school there for eight years." Sorrow swept over her, taking her by surprise. "I didn't let him go inside."

Had she been unkind? She'd thought only that she didn't want to be alone with him, not that he might have feelings about the place.

"He gave up that right when he left the church," Daniel said, his tone uncompromising. "Still, I'm sorry if his visit upset you."

It had. Rachel, not knowing that she had something huge to face, was helping Mamm put two rhubarb pies and a cake on the picnic table under the trees.

"He's Rachel's brother," she said softly, her heart aching for her friend. "Her twin. He came to me because he wants me to be—well, a go-between, I suppose. I must talk to her about whether the family is willing to see him."

"I see." His expression was veiled. "So he's just the brother of your friend."

Her chin came up at that. "Have you listened to gossip about me already, Daniel Glick? If so, you may as well hear it from me. John and I planned to marry once, but he chose to go English instead."

For a moment he didn't speak, and she had no idea what he was thinking. His face had tightened again. In disapproval? She wasn't sure of his emotion, but it was something dark.

"I see," he said at last. "No, I didn't know, but I'm sorry for your loss."

The sincerity of his tone was so intense that she couldn't doubt he meant it. His sympathy wiped away her irritation and made her ashamed that she'd spoken so abruptly.

"I'm sorry. I'm the one who should apologize." She took a deep breath, trying to ease the tightness in her throat. "It's just— People will talk about it again, once they know he's back."

"You could be careful, not give them anything new to talk about."

"Like meeting him at the schoolhouse?" Her temper, always so controlled, flared.

Daniel's strong face was impassive. "You are my children's teacher, an Amish schoolteacher, chosen for the position because of your faith and your character. What you do, who you see— that matters to all the children who are your responsibility."

Before she could say a word, he walked off toward the croquet game.

Leah stood at the end of the picnic table, setting out forks and napkins while she rehearsed all the things she should have said to Daniel. Unfortunately, he'd spoken nothing but the truth. It was too bad that he seemed to have the ability to bring out the emotions she usually kept under such careful control.

Rachel slipped an arm around her waist. "Why so deep in thought?"

Leah shook off the fear that there might have been a veiled threat in Daniel's final words. Time enough to worry about that later. Now—now she had to tell Rachel about Johnny.

"I must talk with you, Rachel." There was no easy way to break this news. She'd just have to come out with it. At least at the moment everyone else seemed occupied, either with the game or with their own talk. "I've seen Johnny."

Rachel's breath caught. "Our Johnny? Seen him? He's here in Pleasant Valley?"

"He came to the schoolhouse yesterday, wanting me to talk to you for him, to tell you why he's back."

Sudden hope blossomed on her friend's face. "He wants to

come home? To repent and be one of us again?" Her voice lifted in joy.

It hurt Leah's heart to destroy that hope, but it was best to do it quickly, since it must be done. "No. I'm sorry, Rachel."

The hope faded, and Rachel's eyes filled with tears. She turned, hiding her face from the playing children. Leah gave her time, her arm encircling her friend's waist. She longed so deeply to help her, but some pains couldn't be soothed by even the most comforting words.

Finally Rachel managed a feeble smile. "Ach, I never really thought that would happen. Johnny always wanted the outside world too strongly."

"You couldn't stop hoping he'd come back to us," Leah said softly.

Rachel shook her head. "Why is he here, then? What does he want if not to rejoin the community?"

Leah picked her words carefully, feeling a flicker of anger toward John. He should be explaining this himself instead of putting it onto her.

"He's working with that doctor who's doing the research on genetic diseases that affect the children. He said he'd be here for six months, at least."

"Six months?" Rachel bit her lip. "It will be hard, having him near that long but not one of us."

"Did you have any idea of what he was doing?"

"No." The sidelong look seemed a little guilty. "Just that he'd gone to college for some kind of science."

"You never told me that." She'd thought that she and her closest friend shared everything.

Rachel's gaze slid away from Leah's, and she fiddled with the forks much as Leah had done, as if her hands needed to be busy. "You seemed like you'd forgotten him. I didn't want to bring it all up again and make you feel bad. Did I do wrong?"

"No. It's all right." But she hadn't forgotten. She'd just learned to hide her feelings.

"What does he want from us, then?" Rachel's eyes went dark with misery, hurting Leah's heart. "Why did he come to you?"

"He wants to see you and the rest of your family. He asked me to tell you. He's coming to the schoolhouse tomorrow to hear your answer."

Her friend's eyes widened. "But I can't tell him anything, not so soon. Not until I talk to Mamm and Daadi about it. And how will I do that?"

"I know it's hard." She thanked the Lord that she'd never had to face that particular burden with her parents. "But you should tell them right away, before they hear about him being here from someone else."

"But if no one knows but you—"

"Daniel Glick saw him at the school," she said quickly, before Rachel could imagine this secret would keep. "He hasn't said anything, but anyone could see John, could start talking about his coming back. You know how fast that news would spread."

"You're right. I can't be a coward about it. I'll talk to them tonight." She shook her head, worry darkening her eyes. "I don't know what to say. I don't want to hurt them."

Leah squeezed her in a quick hug. "They haven't forgotten about him. Maybe they'll be relieved to know what he's doing. Anyway, it must be done."

"Oh, I know that. It's just so hard. I want to protect them from hurt. You'd feel the same, wouldn't you?"

Leah glanced at her mother. Mamm sat in a lawn chair, watching the children play. She was smiling, but her face seemed thin and tired.

"Ja, of course I would. I do. It's strange. All these years we've relied on our parents, and now we need to care for them. It seems we're changing places, doesn't it?"

Rachel nodded in quick understanding. "How is your mamm?"

"She says she's doing fine, but fighting the cancer has taken a lot out of her. She and my father have decided to move to the grossdaadi haus."

Rachel's face expressed all that she might be reluctant to say. "So your brother and his family will be moving into the house. What about you and Anna?"

"That's what Anna wants to know." It was a relief to pour it out to someone who would understand and keep it to herself. "Levi and Barbara say that nothing will change, that we should keep our own rooms, but she's expecting again, and—"

"And it's only a matter of time until she wants those rooms for her family." Rachel shook her head. "Even if she didn't, you know how hard it will be to live in another woman's house." Now it was Rachel's turn to give a comforting hug. "What will you do?"

"Nothing for a bit. I haven't had time to think it through. I knew it would come sometime, but I didn't think it would be so soon."

Rachel nodded, eyes clouding. "I know. It's odd, isn't it? One day life seems settled and routine, and the next it's turned upside down, as if a storm came and tipped us all on our heads."

"Ja." That was surely how she'd felt lately. She took a breath. "Well, we can get through it. Somehow."

Rachel shot her a sidelong glance. "I saw you talking to Daniel. It looked as if you were finding a lot to say to each other."

"Don't matchmake," Leah warned. Was everyone in the community trying to team her up with Daniel?

"Well, don't you dismiss the idea too quickly." Her expression was serious. "I know it's early to be thinking this, but wouldn't it be better to be living in your own house with a family to love, rather than feel like a boarder in your sister-in-law's house?"

"I don't plan to marry." And even if she did, it wouldn't be to Daniel Glick. She valued her independence too much for that. "Never mind about Daniel. What shall I tell John?"

"Say I love him. Say he must give me more time. That's all I can tell him now."

John wouldn't like that, any more than she'd like telling him, but there was nothing she could do about it.

Daniel found his gaze straying to Leah Beiler, even while he talked with her father about the best place to buy a buggy horse. Teacher Leah was an interesting mixture of gentleness and spirit. He just hoped that spirit wasn't leading her toward trouble.

Did her father know about the return of his daughter's one-time sweetheart? The older man's face was placid as he puffed on his pipe, but he suspected Elias Beiler wasn't one to show his feelings easily.

"Your young ones settling down in school all right?" Elias

nodded toward Matthew, who was helping Elizabeth knock a croquet ball through a wicket.

"They seem to be doing fine. Teacher Leah has made them feel right at home already."

A faint smile creased Elias's weathered face. "Our Leah is a gut teacher, she is. Not that I wouldn't rather see her married and with young ones of her own, but we must take what the Lord sends."

Daniel nodded. At the moment, Leah was in close conversation with Rachel, probably about the return of John Kile. Sooner, rather than later, it would be public knowledge, but despite his concerns, he was just as glad the spreading of it hadn't come from him.

"Will you be missing lots of kin back there in Lancaster County, Daniel?"

Elias only meant to express kindly interest, but even so, Daniel felt himself stiffen. Talking about his life there would lead inevitably to the reasons he'd left, and he wasn't ready to discuss that with strangers. Not yet, anyway.

"My parents hope to come for a visit later in the summer, once we're settled in. Maybe help with the harvest."

"Good to have extra hands around when the crops start to come in, especially for a man without a wife to help him."

Was that meant to be a question about his wife, or was it a hint as to whether he might be looking for a new helpmate now that he was settling in Pleasant Valley? That was how an Amish father's thoughts would go, for sure. Daniel managed a meaningless smile.

"It'll be wonderful gut to have them come for a visit. Now I'd best get Jonah. He's probably getting tired."

His younger son, who had just run across the lawn to throw himself at Teacher Leah, didn't look in the least tired, but it was a way to end a conversation that was cutting too near the bone.

He couldn't fool himself any more than he could anyone else. Most folks here had kin back in Lancaster County, and sooner or later someone would receive a letter with all the details about what had happened to his wife. To his children.

Time. That was what he wanted now, time for the children to settle down and feel at home. Then it would hurt less to have everyone know about them.

Leah smiled, bending over Jonah to say something that made him giggle, and a flicker of concern went through Daniel. Leah said she wasn't yearning for her fence-jumper fiancé, but maybe she was. He didn't want his children getting too close to a woman who could be tempted by the life outside their community.

He went quickly to them, then grabbed Jonah and tossed him in the air.

"Are you a bird then, Jonah Glick?"

"I think he's a barn swallow," Leah said, laughter filling her green eyes. Hair the color of corn silk was drawn back to the bun under her kapp, but a few tendrils had worked their way loose. They curled against the creamy skin of her cheeks.

And what was he doing noticing that about Teacher Leah? Despite his new community's obvious wish to marry him off, he was not looking for a bride. After what had happened with Ruth, he wasn't sure he'd ever take that chance again.

And if he did, it wouldn't be with a woman who seemed to be flirting with the English world in the shape of her former sweetheart.

He made Jonah swoop up and down in imitation of a barn

swallow, and then set him down and gave him a tap on the bottom. "Go and tell your brother and sister it's almost time to go home," he said.

"So soon?" Leah looked honestly regretful. "Be sure you don't leave without taking the basket of leftovers that Mamm has for you. It will save you having to cook tomorrow."

"That's kind of her. I'm grateful for your hospitality." He looked into her face, detecting a hint of strain there. "I'm sorry if Jonah interrupted your conversation with your friend."

"It's all right. We had finished what we had to say." She gave him a straightforward, serious look. "I'm sure you can guess what we were talking about."

He nodded. "How does Kile's family feel about his coming back?"

"They don't know yet, other than Rachel." Her smooth brow furrowed. "She must tell her parents before they hear from someone else."

"That would be wise."

"Many Amish have children and grandchildren who have chosen not to join the church." She seemed to look inward, as if arguing with herself. "They still find ways to have some relationship with them."

She couldn't know why the very mention of that thought made him stiffen. And he wasn't going to tell her.

"We live separate from the world. Accommodating it can only lead to trouble."

His words came out harshly, but perhaps that was just as well. Teacher Leah may as well know now where he stood on that issue, because where his children were concerned, he would not take any risks at all.

47

Chapter Four

It was perfectly normal for her to stop and see Rachel after school, Leah assured herself on Friday. So normal, in fact, that Betty turned her head toward the lane to the Brand farm even before Leah's hand tightened on the harness lines.

Her errand, however, wasn't so normal.

Surely Rachel would have talked to her parents about Johnny by now. Leah's stomach roiled at the memory of her conversation with John on Wednesday when he'd learned she had no answer for him. He'd hated being put off. And she hated being put in the middle of this tangle.

She slowed Betty to a walk as they approached the house. On either side of the lane, the Brand dairy herd munched contentedly on April-green grass, and she spotted Becky and her younger brother, five-year-old Joseph, heading for the barn.

Gut, she'd timed this visit right, then. She'd hoped to get here while Rachel's husband, Ezra, was still busy, and while the kinder were at their chores. That way she and Rachel could have a private talk.

She stopped at the back door and slid down, a prayer for guidance forming in her heart. She didn't know what to pray for in this situation, but certainly the Lord knew what was right for Rachel, for her parents, and even for Johnny.

She was fastening Betty to the hitching rail when Rachel appeared at the door, holding it open in welcome as always.

"Leah, wilkom. I hoped to see you." Her smile was warm, but those lines of strain around her eyes were not normal for easygoing Rachel.

Leah's heart sank. This situation was hurting her friend, she knew, and there was probably worse to come. No matter what Rachel's parents had decided, the way wouldn't be smooth.

"Komm, sit." Rachel led the way through the mudroom to the kitchen, warm and smelling of supper cooking already. "I have apple kuchen and coffee ready. You'll have some."

"Only if you join me." Leah sat at the well-scrubbed table, taking off her bonnet and cape, and smoothing her hair back under her kapp.

"Ja." Rachel glanced at the pot on the gas stove. "The chicken is stewing already, so I can sit for a bit."

Their conversation was natural enough, as if this were just any visit. But the cups clattered as Rachel took them from the tall pine cupboard, and the movement of her hands was stiff and clumsy.

Leah kept silent as Rachel grasped a potholder and poured the coffee. She waited while Rachel put a slice of pastry, thick with apples, on a plate in front of her.

Only when Rachel stopped her nervous fidgeting and sat down did she think it was time to speak.

"I'm sorry. This is hard for you."

Rachel nodded, her hands clasping the thick white mug that held her coffee. "Not for me only. Ezra is upset, because Johnny was his dear friend. The children, because they sense that something is wrong even though we haven't told them. And Mamm and Daadi—"

She stopped, her voice choking with tears.

"You've told them, then." However little Rachel had wanted to break the news, she couldn't risk having her parents hear of John's return from someone else.

Rachel seemed to struggle for composure. "Ja. Ezra watched the little ones so I could go over alone to talk with them." She clenched her hands together, the knuckles white. "Leah, I have never seen them look like that. It was worse, I think, than when he went away the first time."

Probably, that first time, distressed as they'd been, they'd expected Johnny to come home eventually, like so many others did. But he hadn't, and the years had slipped away, each one making it less likely he'd return.

They wouldn't have forgotten him. How could they? Her own heart ached with the thought.

But maybe they'd been able to make peace with his leaving. Now, that peace was ripped beyond repair.

"Will they— Do they want to see him?"

"Of course they want to see him!" The words burst from Rachel's lips on a sob, and she raised tear-drenched eyes to Leah's. "But they won't. They can't."

Leah clasped Rachel's hand in hers, tears filling her eyes, too.

"I know." Her throat was tight. "They feel they're doing the right thing by refusing."

"The only thing," Rachel said. "The meidung is the only thing that might make him return to the community, if that's possible."

Leah nodded in sympathy. The outside world probably thought of shunning as a punishment, but it wasn't that. It was the church's last, desperate effort to bring the stubborn rebel to his senses, and she had no doubt it hurt the family and the community more than it hurt the one who left.

She took a deep breath, knowing she had to press on with this while she could still say the words without breaking down. "If they were convinced that Johnny would never be Amish again, would they see him then?"

"I don't know." Rachel wiped tears away with her fingers. "If he came back to us penitent, ready to confess his sin and be restored to the body, it would be as if his leaving had never been. But if he's determined to live English . . ."

Her voice died out, as if she didn't have the strength to consider that possibility.

"There are those in the church who have accepted that in their children," Leah reminded her. "The Muellers and the Stoltzes both have sons who've left, but they've maintained ties with them and their families."

Everyone knew that accommodations could be made. Folks obeyed the letter of the meidung by not eating at the same table as the shunned person, not taking food from their hand, not riding in a car that person was driving. Otherwise, with good will on both sides, life could go on.

"I know they do. It's hard for them, but they've accepted that their children will never come back. I don't know if Daadi can ever accept that." She gave Leah a watery smile. "You know how he was about Johnny. His oldest son. His only son."

Unlike most Amish families, the Kiles only had two children. Something had gone wrong for Ella when the twins were born. Rachel and Johnny were all the more precious for that reason.

Rachel turned her mug, making rings on the scrubbed pine tabletop. "Daadi wouldn't admit to being proud of him, but they were so close, and Johnny so smart and hardworking. Daadi was glad to have a son to pass the farm to. After Johnny left, the heart just seemed to go out of him."

"He saw his life's work being discarded."

Leah thought fleetingly of Daniel and Matthew. There was another father determined to have a farm to pass on to his son. But Matthew—surely Daniel didn't fear that Matthew would leave the church.

"Leah, do you think—" Rachel hesitated. She was looking down at the cooling coffee in the mug, and Leah couldn't read her expression.

"Think what?" She patted Rachel's hand in encouragement.

"Do you think there's any chance Johnny could change his mind and come back to us? If there was, I would do anything to make it happen."

"I guess there's always a chance." She said the words slowly, not wanting to dash whatever hope Rachel might still cling to.

Rachel clasped Leah's hand in a tight grip. "You knew him as well as anyone. You must still be able to tell what he's thinking, no matter how much he's changed." Her voice compelled an answer. "Please, Leah. You must be honest with me."

She thought of the stranger Johnny had become, with his

clean-shaven face, his modern clothes, his fancy car. But those were externals, easily changed.

What of the man himself? Rachel was right. Once, she'd have said she knew Johnny's heart as well as she knew her own.

The passion in his voice when he'd talked of his work at the clinic, the way his eyes looked for a future she couldn't imagine. Those were the things that told who John Kile was now.

"I don't think so." Her throat tightened at the pain she must be causing. "I can't be sure, but I don't think so."

The muscles of Rachel's neck worked. She slapped her hands down on the table and pushed herself back, her face twisting.

"He should never have come back, then!" she cried, her voice harsh. "You know as well as I do, Leah. He should never have come back to Pleasant Valley at all."

Daniel stood looking across a field full of people on Saturday afternoon. The spring Mud Sale to benefit the local fire company was in full swing. True to its name, the sale took place when the ground, still wet from winter's snow followed by April showers, was rapidly turning into a sea of mud.

That didn't seem to deter any of the crowd. Amish and English alike, intent on finding a bargain, moved from used Amish buggies to lines strung with quilts to food stands offering everything from warm soft pretzels to cotton candy to funnel cakes.

He could only hope his children weren't talking Rachel Brand into buying them anything to eat. She had offered to have the younger ones walk around with her and her children, so that he could take a look at the tools that were spread out on several long trestle tables. And Matthew had gone off on his own with Jacob Esch and some other boys from his class.

Their acceptance was a sign that Matthew was settling down here, and he was relieved at that. He'd been worried about the boy, but not sure whether his worries were justified or not. Matthew had changed, and there was no way of ever getting back those lost years.

He glanced up from the harrow he was inspecting, his eye caught by someone coming from behind the small brooder coop next to the henhouse on the host farm. Even at this distance, even after meeting him only once, he had no trouble identifying the man. John Kile.

His eyebrows lifted. That was a surprise, for sure. Anyone could come to the Mud Sale. Plenty of Englischers were here, but Kile couldn't hope to pass unnoticed, not with the number of Amish in attendance. This was a public announcement of his return.

How would his family take that? They'd no doubt been through plenty of grief already. His stomach twisted. He knew that feeling only too well.

Kile moved quickly, almost like he was running away. Shoulders stiff and hands clenched, he headed for the nearest cluster of people gathered around a stand selling sausage sandwiches. He disappeared into the crowd.

Someone else came from behind the brooder coop. Black cape, black bonnet hiding her face. But as soon as she moved, Daniel knew it was Leah. Teacher Leah meeting with her old sweetheart in a not-so-secret place.

He stood, irresolute, for a moment. It was not his place to confront her. But if he had seen, others might have as well.

Even as he hesitated, she turned slightly and saw him. She

stopped, her body stiff. Then she came toward him across the stubble of grass.

He waited. If she wanted to talk to him, he wouldn't avoid it, although he didn't think she'd want to hear anything he was likely to say.

Leah stopped a few feet from him. A couple of men who'd been looking at the tools moved off, leaving them alone.

"I suppose you saw." Her mouth was firm, but her face was pale with strain.

"Ja." He hesitated. She'd be angry if he told her what he thought, but—

"I met John Kile to give him his family's answer to seeing him."

For some reason, that gave him a sense of relief. She hadn't been with Kile on her own accord, then, but had been trying to do the right thing for her friend.

"I take it the answer was no."

She nodded. "How did you know?"

"He didn't look like someone who'd just had gut news when he went off." He searched her face, understanding the strain he saw there. "It was not easy for you."

"He was very hurt."

And she'd had to be the one to deliver that hurt. Given their history, it was probably more painful for her than for him.

"I'm sorry for him," he said gravely, praying that he honestly meant it. "And for you, having to be the one to tell him. But I understand why they decided that."

Her face was still troubled. "If he had come back sorry, they'd have forgiven him in a moment. The prodigal son, home where he belongs."

"That would only be right."

But he thought of his wife and his hands tightened, pressing against his legs. If Ruth had returned, wanting to be accepted into the church again, wanting to resume their marriage, he'd have forgiven her.

But would things ever have been the same between them? He didn't think so.

Still, the relationship between a man and his wife was different from that of a parent to a child.

"They're in so much pain." She turned to start walking back toward the crowd, seeming to assume they'd walk together.

"They love him and want him back. It's hard that the only way they have to push him to return is to stay separate from him." He fell into step with her.

The brim of her bonnet moved as she nodded. "I know that's what they're thinking, and they could be right. But what if you're dealing with a person who will never come back, no matter what?"

Leah couldn't know that she was causing him pain with every word. If she knew about his wife, she would never have spoken to him about this.

But this was what he'd wanted when he'd come here, wasn't it? The chance to start fresh, where everyone didn't look at him, at his children, with pity for what had happened to them?

They'd reached a wide muddy patch, and he touched her sleeve lightly to guide her around the edge of it. "It's not so bad over here where the cars are parked."

She nodded, moving with him. It had been a long time since he'd walked anywhere, even through a muddy field, with a woman. It felt odd, but somehow natural, too.

She glanced up at him, and it seemed the strain had eased from her face a little. "Do you have no answer to the problem, then, Daniel?"

"I don't." He managed a smile. "I know that surprises you, Teacher Leah."

"It does. But you'd best be careful of expressing too much wisdom, anyway. Someone might think you'd make a gut minister."

He shook his head. "Like most, I pray the lot never falls on me. My father is the bishop of our church district back in Lancaster County, and I know how heavy a burden it can be."

Her steps slowed, and she smiled. "Now I've learned something more about you."

"Is that gut?" He could get used to that smile, to the way it made her green eyes fill with light.

"It satisfies my regrettable curiosity, I'm afraid. Yours is the first new family in our church district in quite a few years. You've given us something to talk about besides who's courting whom and whether the price of milk will go up."

That sort of curiosity was the last thing he wanted, but it was inevitable. "Both of those things are more important than anything you might learn about me."

"People are always more interesting to me than cows," she said lightly.

He found himself wondering what she had been like at eighteen, before John Kile had left her behind. More like her pert sister than he'd have originally guessed, perhaps, before grief and disappointment had taken that liveliness away.

"Not more important to a dairy farmer," he said.

They rounded a row of cars. At the end of the next row, two motorcycles were parked.

Three Amish boys surrounded one of them, gawking at the boy who'd been brave enough, or foolish enough, to climb onto the motorcycle. Daniel stopped, taking in what he saw. The boy was Matthew.

For a moment Daniel froze, feeling as if he'd taken a pitchfork in the stomach. Then he surged forward, grabbed his son, and pulled him off the contraption.

"What are you doing?" It was all he could do to keep from shaking the boy. "Is this how you behave when I let you go with your friends? Is it?"

He was vaguely aware of Leah drawing the other boys away.

"Jacob and Thomas Esch and Gabriel Stoltzfus." It was very much her teacher voice. "You go back to your parents right now, before you find yourselves in trouble."

Murmurs of agreement, and the other boys ran off, leaving them alone. Daniel looked at his son, and Matthew stared back at him.

"Well? What do you have to say for yourself, Matthew?"

His son's face was white and set. "I didn't do anything so bad. It's just a motorcycle."

"It's not for us, as you well know."

Something flashed in Matthew's eyes, an expression he'd begun to dread. One that made his son look like a stranger.

"I rode on one once, with a friend of Mamm's." He spat the words out. "She didn't think it was wrong. I didn't either. It was fun."

The pitchfork in his belly twisted. He heard the quick intake of Leah's breath. He turned to her, knowing his anger was irrational but not able to stop it.

"Ja." He snapped off the word. "You heard. My children lived in the English world for two years. Now you really know something about me."

Holding Matthew by the arm, he charged off.

"*Don't* you bother to tell me you're not interested in Daniel Glick." Barbara paused at the kitchen door on her way out on Monday afternoon, clearly determined to have the last word on the subject. "I saw you together at the Mud Sale with my own eyes already."

She waved, chuckling a little at her comment, and scurried off the porch toward the waiting buggy.

Leah counted to ten, keeping a smile pinned on her face with an effort. By the time she reached eight, Barbara was in her buggy and heading down the lane.

Leah turned to her mother, frustration building to the boiling point. If she didn't say something to someone, she'd burst with it.

"When is this matchmaking going to stop? Can't I even speak to a man without the busybodies making plans for a wedding?"

Mamm continued moving a batch of snickerdoodles from the cooling rack to a plastic container, her face placid. "Ach, Leah, you take Barbara's teasing too much to heart. She doesn't mean anything by it. Anyway, you know how she is."

"I know too well how my sister-in-law is, but she's not the only one. I heard the whispers after church yesterday."

Leah picked up a dish towel and began drying the bowls and spoons left in the sink from Mamm's baking. The whole house had smelled of cinnamon and sugar when she'd come in from school, setting her mouth watering as if she were a scholar herself, running into the kitchen ravenous.

Her mother stopped what she was doing to look at Leah. "I heard whispers, too, but they were about Johnny Kile and how he's back in Pleasant Valley. Did you know about this already, Leah?"

"I've known for a few days." Her towel slowed on the mixing bowl. "I'm sorry I didn't tell you and Daadi, but Rachel asked me not to say anything until she'd had a chance to talk with her parents about it. She's worried about how they're taking it."

Her mother nodded, but her gaze was troubled. "They are grieved, I know. But does it bother you again, knowing he's here in the valley?"

"Not as much as having half the church trying to pair me up with Daniel Glick," she said tartly. At least she thought that was true. "Whatever feelings I had for Johnny Kile were boy-and-girl notions, over a long time ago and forgotten."

"It's gut, that." Her mother put the cookie container into a basket and added several jars of rhubarb sauce. "It makes no sense to be crying over the past. Let the troubles of the day be sufficient."

"I suppose so." Mamm had a thought from Scripture for every eventuality, though Leah had never found that one especially comforting.

Her mother tucked a cloth over the basket's contents. "There. You have time before supper to take this over to the Glick place, you do."

The cookie sheet Leah was holding clattered onto the counter. "Mamm, what was I just saying? You're as bad as Barbara is, trying to match me up with Daniel just because he's a widower."

"Nonsense." Her mother bridled, but her eyes didn't meet Leah's. "I'm trying to be neighborly, that's all. I don't suppose

Daniel has time to be baking cookies for those young ones of his, running the farm all on his own the way he's doing."

"If you were just being neighborly, you could have asked Barbara to drop them off on her way home," Leah said firmly. "She'd have loved an excuse to call, and she'd probably be talking up my virtues to Daniel along with delivering the cookies."

"Barbara's not—"

"What? A maidal?" Bad enough that the rest of the valley thought that she and Daniel made a perfect match, without her mother getting into it.

"I'm just being neighborly," her mother repeated stubbornly. "But if I were trying to bring the two of you together, is that so bad?" She reached toward Leah, her eyes suddenly filling with tears. "Is it bad that I want to see my oldest daughter settled with a home and family of her own before I die?"

The words were like an arrow to Leah's heart, and her breath caught painfully. She clasped her mother's hands in hers.

"Mamm, what's wrong? Why are you talking that way? Did you get a bad report from the doctor? What did he say?"

"No, no, nothing like that." Her mother patted her cheek. "Don't fuss over me. I'm just thinking of the future."

"Why would you be thinking that way if nothing's wrong?" She should have insisted on going with her mother to that last doctor's visit. Then she'd know for certain what they faced.

"The doctor says I'm well. That the tiredness is to be expected." She sighed, putting her palm against her cheek as if to comfort herself. "I just never thought we'd be moving into the daadi haus so soon. I hoped and prayed that you and Anna would be married before that happened. Barbara's a gut woman, but—"

"Ja." They both knew how that sentence would finish. Barbara was a fine woman, but neither Leah nor Anna wanted to live with her. "Mamm, are you sure that's all? You promise?" She looked intently into her mother's lined face, trying to read the truth there.

"That's all," she said firmly. She cradled Leah's face in her hands. "You have so much love in your heart to give, daughter. I want a chance for you to give that love to a gut man and children, the Lord willing."

Leah felt the words like a physical pain. So Mamm thought she had love to give.

After the way she'd failed Johnny, she doubted it. He'd said she was a coward, and he'd been right. She didn't have what it took to love the way Mamm did.

But it would only upset her mother if she said that.

"Well." Her mother turned to the table, picking up the basket. "If you won't take this over to the Glicks, I guess I'll walk over myself with it."

Leah took the basket from her. "I'll do it." She was at least smart enough to know when she was beaten.

CHAPTER FIVE

Leah tapped at the back door of the Glick farmhouse, the basket heavy on her arm. If she'd been able to tell her mother why she really didn't want to see Daniel Glick today—

But no. She couldn't do that. The thing she'd learned at the Mud Sale was private. It had to be, until she could understand.

"Teacher Leah!" Elizabeth opened the door, drying her hands on her apron. "Please komm in."

The pleased surprise in her face gave way to a look of slight apprehension as Leah entered.

Leah knew that look. She'd encountered it enough times on the faces of her scholars when she turned up unexpectedly at their homes. Elizabeth was probably scouring her mind, trying to think of anything she might have done wrong that would have brought the teacher to see her father.

Leah hefted the basket, smiling at the child. "My mamm sent over jars of rhubarb sauce for you. And I think there are some fresh snickerdoodles in the basket, too. Do you like them?"

That was no doubt a safe question. She'd never met a child who didn't like the sweet cookies.

"Oh, ja. My grossmutter makes them sometimes for us." Elizabeth, seeming reassured, led the way into the kitchen. "That is kind of you and your mamm."

Leah set the basket down on the long wooden table. The Glick kitchen was very like their own, with its wooden cabinets, gas appliances, and plain wooden table. Very like an English kitchen, she supposed, except that everything ran on gas instead of electric.

She lifted out the jars of rhubarb, admiring their bright pink glow, and then took out the container of cookies. She'd carry the basket home and leave the containers here, knowing full well that with the way folks carted food around to each other, it wasn't worth trying to keep track of them.

"Maybe you and your brothers will have the snickerdoodles after supper."

Elizabeth nodded, eyeing the container as if judging how many cookies it might hold. "Please sit down, Teacher Leah. I was just washing up the dishes."

Her cheeks flushed a little as if she were, like any good hausfrau, embarrassed at being caught by a visitor with dishes in the sink.

"We'll finish them up together," Leah said, folding her sleeves back. "Do you like to wash or dry?"

"Wash," Elizabeth said, but her brows drew together. "You are a guest in our house. You shouldn't be doing the dishes."

"I like to dry the dishes," Leah said firmly, picking up a dish towel from the rack. "Sometimes I think the best talks I have with my sister are when we're doing the dishes together."

Giving in, Elizabeth stepped up on the small wooden stool

that stood in front of the sink. "You are wonderful lucky to have a sister. I have only brothers." She glanced through the window over the sink, as if keeping an eye out for them.

"Brothers can be fun, too." Leah started drying the plates that were already stacked in the drainer. "I have three of them, you know. Mine taught me how to ride a bicycle and catch a softball."

"They're all right," Elizabeth said a little grudgingly. "But Matthew thinks he knows everything, just because he's two years older than I am."

"My big brother always thought that, too," Leah said. "We know they don't."

She watched the child's face, intent on her washing chores. Elizabeth inspected each dish carefully before relinquishing it, as if it had to be perfect. So careful about that she was, as she seemed to be about her schoolwork, her appearance, everything.

Had that trait somehow been caused by the time she'd spent in the outside world? Two years, Daniel had said. Two years was a long time in the life of an eight-year-old. How much had Elizabeth been affected by that? How long ago had that been?

And the little one—that explained why Jonah spoke such excellent English for his age. No wonder Daniel had looked disconcerted when she'd commented on it.

So many questions burning in her mind. They weren't caused by idle curiosity. As the children's teacher, she could help them more if she knew the facts.

But she didn't imagine she'd learn much more from Daniel than she already had. He wouldn't have told her as much as he did if not for Matthew blurting out that uncomfortable truth.

The silence had stretched on too long between her and Elizabeth, and she'd be having the child worrying if she didn't say something casual.

"I enjoy having you and your brothers in my class. What do you like best in school, Elizabeth?"

"Playing with Becky," she said promptly, and then looked up at Leah, her lips forming an O of dismay. "I mean—I like reading best."

"I like reading, too." Leah tried to hide a smile. "But it's all right to enjoy making friends, especially with Becky. Her mother and I were best friends when we were young. We still are, in fact."

"Becky has a brother, too," Elizabeth said, as if that sealed the contract between them.

"Perhaps you can go to her house after school one day," Leah suggested. "I'm sure her mother would like that."

"That would be nice." Elizabeth lifted the last dish to the rack. "But I have to take care of things at home." Her small face was set with determination.

Leah's heart twisted. Elizabeth seemed too determined to take over all the household chores. Every Amish child accepted that work was a part of life, but children needed time to play as well.

She'd speak to Rachel and make sure that Elizabeth was invited to her house one day. That would be gut for both the little girls.

There was a rattle at the back door, and Leah looked that way just as Daniel stepped into the house. His gaze met hers, and his face stilled, eyes growing wary.

That wasn't surprising, was it? She undoubtedly looked the

same way, with memories of the last time they'd been together sharp in her mind.

"Teacher Leah!" Jonah squeezed around his father and ran toward her, excitement lighting his face. He was too young to think a visit from the teacher anything other than an unexpected treat.

She bent to give him a quick hug. When she looked up again, Daniel had managed to produce a polite smile that didn't reach his eyes. He had one hand on Matthew's shoulder. It looked as if without that, the boy would have run back out of the room.

"Wilkom to our home," Daniel said formally. He and Matthew came into the kitchen, and he looked an inquiry at Elizabeth.

"Teacher Leah brought us rhubarb sauce and snickerdoodles that her mamm made," she told him. "And we talked while we did the dishes."

His gaze swung back to Leah, and there was accusation in it. For an instant she could barely control her anger. How could he think that she would question a child under the guise of helping her?

"We talked about how much we like to read," she said, her voice firm. "And about her friend Becky."

He nodded, and she thought there might be an apology in his face.

"Elizabeth is our reader," he said, touching his daughter's hair lightly. "And Jonah likes to be read to, don't you?"

Jonah flashed that engaging grin. "I like animal stories best."

"This year you'll learn to read some of them for yourself," Leah told him, relieved that the conversation seemed to have moved into safe channels. "That's the best thing about first grade."

"We'll read a story together tonight after we have some of your mamm's cookies and some rhubarb sauce," Daniel said. "It was kind of her to think of us and kind of you to bring them over."

That sounded like an invitation to leave. She picked up the basket. "I'd best be on my way. I'll see you in school tomorrow."

Elizabeth looked suddenly stricken. "But I didn't serve you anything."

"I couldn't eat anything now," she said quickly. "My mamm will have supper ready when I get home."

Elizabeth's lips trembled. "But we should give you something."

She didn't know what to say. Elizabeth was so determined to be the perfect hostess that she was on the verge of tears.

"I'm sure Teacher Leah would like some of our fresh green onions to take home," Daniel said quickly, seeming to understand his small daughter. "We'll stop at the garden to pull some."

"That would be a treat," Leah said. "Ours are not ready yet."

Elizabeth's face cleared in an instant, though tears glistened on her lashes. "Be sure and tell your mamm they are from us."

"I will," she promised. She glanced from Elizabeth's tear-drenched eyes to Jonah's gap-toothed smile to the wary look on Matthew's face that was almost identical to his father's.

What happened to you out there in the English world? she asked silently. *Why were you there?*

Daniel led the way to the garden, very aware of Leah walking beside him. She hadn't bothered to put a bonnet on to walk across the field between the farmhouses, and the late afternoon sun lit her hair, turning it the warm yellow of the earliest jonquil.

The silence between them was pulling taut. The longer he waited to speak, the harder it would be.

As it was, Leah got in first. "I did not come to your home to question Elizabeth about anything."

He didn't pretend to misunderstand her. She had read him so easily. "I know. I'm sorry."

They'd reached the edge of the garden, and he stopped, staring at it absently. Too early for much to be ready to pick yet, but the lettuce he'd planted had begun to unfurl the smallest of green leaves above the soil, and the green onions were just about big enough to eat.

Leah waited. He had to say something more. He owed her that, at least.

"I wanted my children to get settled here." His voice was husky, and he had to stop and clear his throat. "What happened to us, to them—it's hard. Can't they get used to their new life before everyone knows?"

He glanced at Leah, and what he saw reassured him. Her green eyes glistened with tears.

"No one will hear about it from me," she said.

He could breathe again.

"But I could be a better teacher to them if I understood more."

He'd like to argue the point, but she was right. For some reason that annoyed him. It would be easier if he could tell himself that she was wrong.

"Look at it." The words burst out of him, and he grasped her arm to turn her, praying she saw what he did when he looked at the fertile fields stretching out all the way to the woods that covered the ridges. "I could not afford a farm like this back in Lancaster County. My father's farm goes to my oldest brother, which is only right. I came here to give my children a new start."

"I know." Warmth infused Leah's words. "I understand that need."

He took a breath. "My children were taken from me. They lived two years in the outside world. I got them back four months ago."

His throat closed. He could not say more. He prayed she could accept that.

He felt a light touch on his arm and looked down into Leah's face. A tear had escaped to trickle down her cheek.

"I am sorry for your troubles. I'll do whatever I can for the children."

The tight band that clutched his throat eased. He nodded. "Ser gut."

It was more than good, but that was all he could manage. He put his hand over hers in a mute gesture of appreciation.

Her skin was warm against his palm. That warmth seemed to travel through him, startling him so much that his breath hitched.

His gaze met Leah's. Her eyes had gone wide with a shock that matched his.

He leaned closer, drawn—

"Daadi, did you get the onions?" Elizabeth came running toward them, and her voice was a splash of cold water in his face.

He took a step back, not looking at Leah. "I'm getting them

now." He stooped to pull up an onion, not bothering to see if it was the largest one.

He had to be grateful. His daughter had called out at just the right time to keep him from doing something too foolish to be imagined.

Leah opened the stable door, stepped inside, and raised the battery lantern she carried to drive away the darkness. She gasped, and the lantern nearly fell from her hand.

"What are you doing here?"

Johnny pushed himself away from the stall he'd been leaning against. "Waiting for you."

Behind him, Betty reached over the stall door to nudge him with her head. She leaned toward Leah, whickering softly.

Johnny nodded toward the mare. "Some things never change. I figured you'd come out to give a good-night treat to your horse." He brushed at the shoulder of his leather jacket, where the mare had touched him. "What's her name?"

"Betty." Carrying the lantern with her, she went to the horse, murmuring to her as she fed her the carrot she'd brought from the house. "I've had her for nearly eight years already. She can take me back and forth to the schoolhouse without my touching the lines."

"She's in a rut," Johnny said.

"Then so am I." Her anger flashed like lightning in a summer sky.

He shrugged. "You said it, I didn't."

Her head began to throb. She'd come out to the stable to escape tension, not to find it.

Johnny had one thing right. She was predictable in this habit of hers. She made a last trip to the stable every night. Tonight it had been a reasonable excuse to leave behind the endless discussions about Mamm and Daadi's move to the daadi haus.

It was happening in less than a week now. Anna should be finding a way to accept the inevitable instead of making everyone's life miserable. And speaking of making people's life a misery to them —

"Why are you here?"

It was probably best to stay angry with Johnny, if she could. When she let herself feel sorry for him or start remembering the past, then she was likely to give in and agree to do something she didn't want to do, just out of pity.

"We have to talk." He moved next to her, stroking Betty's silky neck.

"Not here." She sent an apprehensive glance toward the stable door. "Someone could come in. Someone might have seen you."

"No one saw me." Johnny's hand stilled on the horse's neck. "I was careful, just like I always was when we used to meet here. Remember?"

There it was—the plea to her memory. She remembered. It would be far better to say that she didn't, but it would be a lie. So better to say nothing.

Still, he knew. They'd used her habit of visiting her horse every night to steal some quiet time alone together. She'd rush in, a carrot or sugar cube for the mare in her hand, and find him waiting. His arm would encircle her waist, his lips brush her cheek.

They'd been innocent times, but she'd felt guilty, nonetheless, sitting on a straw bale, leaning against Johnny's shoulder, talking about the future. But it was a future they'd never had.

"You remember," he whispered, and he was close enough that she'd feel the touch of his breath if he moved another few inches.

"It doesn't matter."

She took a step back and was reminded of Daniel, stepping carefully away from her when his daughter called him. For a moment her mind clouded with confusion. Too much was happening, too soon.

"It doesn't matter," she said again, more firmly. "I've done everything I can for you, Johnny. I cannot change your parents' minds for them."

"I can't believe they refuse to see me." He turned away with a quick, restless movement. "I'm their only son. How can they treat me this way?"

She forced her heart to harden against him. "You are the one who left."

"Now I've come back. Even the prodigal son had a warmer welcome than this."

"The prodigal son admitted his wrong and was willing even to be a servant," she reminded him.

"Is that what you expect of me?" He threw his anger at her.

"I don't expect anything," she said. "But I can see what's in front of my face."

"And what is that?" The sudden sarcasm that hardened his voice made it easier to feel that this was not the Johnny she knew.

Gut. That would make it easier to say no to whatever it was that had brought him here tonight.

"You want to keep your English life and have the advantages of being Amish, too. You can't have it both ways. You should know that by now."

Some emotion crossed his face—regret, she thought.

"Maybe so." He shook his head. "But that's not what's important right now."

Her stomach clenched. They were getting to it, then. To whatever it was he wanted from her.

"What is important, if not your family's grief?" Could he dismiss that so easily?

"I accept that I can't change them, and I'm sorry. But that doesn't alter the reason why I came back to Pleasant Valley to begin with."

"Your work at the clinic." Somehow she'd known they'd get around to it eventually.

"I need cooperation from the families of affected children. They're not going to open their doors to me." He paused, his gaze intent. "But they might to you."

The breath went out of her. She took a step back. "No. I can't."

"Of course you could." He dismissed that with an impatient gesture. "It's not difficult—it's just a matter of interviewing the parents and writing down their answers."

She fought to control her irritation. Did he really think that she'd refused because she thought herself incapable of such a simple task?

"That's not the point. I'm too busy with my teaching and with the duties I have at home as well. I can't take on another job."

"This wouldn't be a real job. Just volunteer work. You could probably get it done in a few hours a day, plus the travel time, of course."

"I don't have a few extra hours in my days."

"You could wait until after school is out to start," he countered. "As long as I know that the data will be coming in, I can get to work."

He was as impatient as always, eager to bend everyone else to suit his needs, and that enthusiasm of his had always had a way of sweeping her along with it. Not this time.

"I can't," she said firmly. "There would be too many problems with my family and the church if I were to do such a thing."

Especially with Johnny involved. There would probably be fewer objections to the clinic than to her seeing so much of him.

He brushed that away with a sweep of his hands. "You're an adult. You can make up your own mind what to do."

Her eyebrows lifted. "Have you been away so long that you've forgotten what it means to be Amish? It is not just a matter of what I might want to do. You can't judge me by English standards."

"Fair enough." He had the grace to look a bit abashed at the reminder. "I won't judge you, Leah. If you feel you need to consult the bishop about it, that's fine."

"No, it's not fine. I'm not going to work with you on this, Johnny."

He'd have to make of that what he would. She wasn't going to put herself in a situation where every day might be spent reliving the past.

He took a quick step toward her, coming into the circle of light from the lantern. His face was set, his gaze steady.

"This isn't about you and me. This is about those children. You can dismiss me if you want. But can you dismiss them so easily?"

Her heart twisted, thinking of the children she knew who suffered from the genetic diseases. Not as many here, probably, as back in Lancaster County, but even one was too many.

There were two of the Miller children, over near the crossroads, spending hours of the day and night under the special blue lamps that helped the children affected with Crigler-Najjar syndrome. Without a liver transplant, they'd never be well.

And there were the babies gone in an instant, it seemed, from a form of sudden infant death syndrome, turning a family's happiest time into one of grief.

Others, some in their own church family, suffered from diseases that seemed to have no known remedy.

No, she couldn't dismiss the children. The fact that her own siblings and their young ones had escaped the inherited diseases didn't mean her heart didn't break each time she heard of a child's suffering.

She looked at Johnny. He must still know her too well, since he'd stood quietly, letting her think. Knowing where her thoughts had gone.

"How could anything I do help those children? I'm not a scientist."

"No, but gathering the information is nearly as important as applying the science." He took a quick step toward her, his face lighting with enthusiasm. "We have the tools to start unlocking the secrets of some of those diseases. But without the cooperation of the families, even those who seem free of the illnesses, we can't use the tools we have." He held out his hand to her. "Isn't that something you'd want to do, if you could?"

She was so tempted simply to agree—to be swayed by his enthusiasm and by the ache in her heart for any hurting child. But she needed to think this through, away from John's passion about it.

"I'll think about it." She lifted the lantern so that she could see his face more clearly, see him start to speak. "No, don't try to persuade me. Just let me think it over and come to a decision. Surely you can do that."

He nodded, reluctance in the movement. "All right. But at least come to the clinic and see for yourself the work we're doing on genetic diseases. There's no reason not to do that, is there?"

"I'll think about it," she said again.

His face fell, but he nodded, maybe seeing that further argument would push her away. "I guess that's the best you can do. I'll go now. Thank you for listening, at least."

He walked to the door, his stride quick and impatient. Slipping out, he turned away from the house so that the open door would shield him from the gaze of anyone looking out the windows.

He probably thought she was a coward for refusing to jump at the chance he offered her. She stroked Betty's neck, taking comfort in the solid warmth of the animal. But then, he already knew she was a coward, didn't he?

Chapter Six

*L*eah sat at the small pine table in her bedroom, going over lesson plans. The gas lamp cast a yellow glow on the page, and she leaned back in the chair and rubbed her eyes. She'd fallen behind on schoolwork this week, and she didn't like to do that, especially with the end of the year barreling at her like a runaway wagon.

But it couldn't be helped. Mamm and Daadi were moving to the daadi haus tomorrow. Levi and Barbara were moving into the farmhouse at the same time. Her days had disappeared into a haze of trying to organize, pack, keep her mother from doing too much, and keep her sister from exploding.

She certainly hadn't had time to give more than a passing thought to Johnny's proposal. She could imagine how annoyed he'd be to know that, but he didn't have family to consider in his plans. That was sadder than he realized, to her way of thinking.

She hadn't exchanged more than a few words with Daniel, either. Her heart still ached for those children. Whatever had happened to send them away from the world they knew, it must have been traumatic.

When she tried to imagine it, she ran up against a blank wall of ignorance. If Daniel could only bring himself to confide in her about it—

She didn't think that was likely. He clearly wasn't ready to talk about his family's trials.

As for the surge of attraction that had flared so surprisingly between them—well, neither of them would want to discuss that.

She pulled the sheaf of lesson plans toward her again, but as she did so, she heard her mother calling her name up the stairs. She went quickly toward the hall. She'd expected Mamm to head straight to bed. Surely she hadn't thought of something else she wanted to do tonight.

Her mother grasped the newel post at the bottom of the stairs, sagging as if she needed its support. "Barbara is here. Will you come down and help her with these boxes?"

Leah nodded, starting down the steps. Barbara certainly had an abundance of energy. She hadn't thought to see her again before tomorrow morning, when the official moving would begin, and plenty of church members would be here then to help.

Barbara was in the kitchen, trying to maneuver an overfilled box onto the table.

"Let me take that." Leah slid the carton out of Barbara's grip. "We'll want the table clear in the morning to feed people."

"Ja, that's right." Barbara relinquished her hold. "It's kitchen things, though, so I thought best to put it in here."

"I'll stow it in the pantry. That's already cleaned out." She suited the action to the words, sliding the box out of sight into the pantry. "You look tired, Barbara. I'm sure that could have waited until tomorrow. Do you want coffee? Tea?"

Barbara slumped into a chair and fanned herself with her bonnet. Her face was flushed, her eyes bright with barely suppressed excitement. Surely she didn't anticipate the move that eagerly.

"Water would be gut," she said. "But I must tell you something."

Mamm, who had been hovering near the door, seemed to resign herself to the fact that this wasn't going to be a short visit. She took the seat across from Barbara, leaning back heavily in the chair.

Leah filled a glass with water, her movements stiff. Couldn't Barbara see that Mamm needed to go to bed?

"Can it wait until tomorrow?" she suggested. "I'm sure we're all ready for a good night's sleep."

"No, no, I must tell you, because he'll no doubt be here to help." She gulped down half the glass. "It's about your neighbor. Daniel Glick."

Leah froze. Barbara definitely had a nose for news. If something happened in the valley, she wanted to know it first. Was Daniel's secret out already?

"What about Daniel?" She kept her voice noncommittal. This might be nothing at all.

Barbara leaned forward, her eyes bright. "Miriam Miller, my neighbor, she had a letter today from her cousin back in Lancaster County. It seems that she knew all about Daniel and his family. They belonged to the same church district."

"I suppose she would know him, then." Mamm's voice was stern. "And you know that I don't hold with gossip, Barbara."

Looking a bit abashed, Barbara sat back in her chair. "Not

gossip. Truth. That's all. Just the truth about him. And I thought you ought to know, being close neighbors and Leah so interested in the children, and all. I thought to myself, 'Leah can help those children better if she knows all about it.' "

"All about what?" Best just to get it out. Then it could be dealt with.

"His wife left him." Her voice lowered, as if she didn't want anyone else to hear. "A Muller, she was, Ruth Muller before they wed. Anyway, Miriam's cousin says that it was a grief to all of them when Ruth just up and went one day, fence-jumping to the English. And taking the kinder with her."

"No." Mamm winced, as if the very thought of it caused her pain.

"She did that. Took them away, and Daniel was nearly mad with the grief of it. Two years they were gone, with him not knowing what had become of them all that time."

"What a terrible thing," Mamm murmured. "That poor man. Those poor children."

"So young to have such a thing happen to them." Barbara's eyes filled with tears. She might enjoy being the first to know, but she had a soft heart and was easily moved by a child or an animal that was hurting.

"How did he get them back?" Mamm clasped her hands in her lap, as if sending up a swift prayer for Daniel's children.

"His wife died. Killed in a car crash, she was, and drinking besides. She'd left the children all alone to fend for themselves while she went out." Barbara shook her head. "A gut thing, as it turned out, that they were not in the car with her."

"God watched over them," Leah murmured, her throat choking with tears.

Small wonder that Daniel didn't want to talk about what had happened. To go for two years not knowing where his children were—it was unthinkable.

"You can see why I thought you should be told right away." Barbara thrust herself back from the table. "He'll be here tomorrow to help, I shouldn't wonder, and folks maybe will be already talking about it. Maybe our Leah should just drop a word in his ear, let him know that folks have heard."

"I'm not sure I should—" But if she didn't tell him, who would?

"You're the teacher." Barbara patted her hand. "You'll know how to say it to him, so he won't be upset."

"It's for the best," her mother added. "The news will get around, everyone will talk about it for a day or two, and then it will be forgotten and things will get back to normal for them."

She was looking at Leah for agreement, and Leah nodded. But she wasn't so sure her mother was right.

Or at least, that Daniel would think so.

"Hold on, Daniel."

Mahlon, Leah's brother, hoisted one end of the heavy wooden cabinet they were lugging from Levi's wagon to the house. Cradling the weight against his chest, Mahlon craned his neck to see into the kitchen, and then grinned and jerked his head to the side.

"We'd best wait a bit. Barbara's changing her mind about where she wants it."

They set the load down on the grass, and Mahlon leaned

against it, pushing his straw hat back on his head. "Be glad when this movin' is done, so the women will stop buzzing around like bees."

"It's a lot of changes." Daniel propped his elbow on the cabinet. Around the corner of the farmhouse, another group of the brethren were carting furniture into the grossdaadi haus. "Two families moving in one day is enough to cause upsets."

Mahlon shrugged. "I don't see what all the fuss is about, but Mamm wants everything just so in the new place, and Barbara—" He raised his eyebrows expressively.

Daniel grinned. He liked young Mahlon, with his easygoing manner and his open, pleasant face. And it was a fine thing to feel accepted so readily by him.

Not that he wouldn't have come in any event to help his neighbors with their move. But it was the first work frolic he'd been involved in since he'd come to Pleasant Valley, and that made it a positive step toward belonging.

Some women of the church were setting up lunch tables under the trees, while others helped to unpack boxes and put things away in both houses. Men carted boxes and furniture from here to there. The children darted in and out among them, some of the older ones helping, others just getting in the way.

Matthew had been entrusted with the job of taking water to the workers, and he seemed to be taking the job seriously. Even now he came toward them, carrying a full bucket, stopping to offer Mahlon a drink first.

Such a simple thing, but it made Daniel's heart swell with pleasure. That was what he'd longed for during those years apart— just the simple tasks of Amish life, shared with his children.

Elizabeth also had a job to do. She and her friend Becky had been put in charge of some of the younger children, whom they led in a game a safe distance away from all the activity.

"A drink, Daad?" Matthew held out the dipper.

He wasn't thirsty, but he took it anyway just for the pleasure of sharing the moment with his son. "Do a gut job, now."

"I will." Matthew hurried off around the house, his face intent with responsibility.

"A fine boy, that," Mahlon said. "Not a schnickelfritz like Levi's boy."

"He gets into mischief already," he said, remembering the motorcycle. "I understand you might be setting up a family for yourself sometime soon," he said.

Mahlon flushed. "Ja, we will that." He glanced toward the kitchen, where the debate apparently still went on. "Just as well, I think, with Mamm and Daadi moving into the daadi haus. Barbara will want this place for her family, especially with another babe on the way."

"Your sisters will still be here though," Daniel pointed out.

Mahlon shrugged. "Anna's old enough to start thinking about a wedding instead of running around all the time. And Leah— well, Leah's a gut aunt."

It seemed the unspoken thought was that Barbara would be foolish to think of causing problems for Leah in the house. Still, the change couldn't make for an easy situation for Leah.

His gaze sought her out, and he realized that he'd known all along where she was, spreading a cloth over the picnic tables, even though he hadn't been consciously thinking about her.

Her situation was not easy in a lot of ways. She didn't fit in with the other unmarried girls, all younger than she, who were giggling and flirting as they went about their chores. And the young married women, who were more her age, were occupied with babies and growing families.

"She would be a gut mother herself, as well as an aunt."

The fact that he'd said the words aloud startled him. He didn't want people getting the wrong idea about him and Leah.

Mahlon looked startled as well. "Leah? She always says she's past getting married. Although I suppose—"

He stopped, apparently thinking that Daniel could be a prospective suitor. Mahlon flushed to the tips of his ears. "She's a fine person. I didn't mean—"

He stopped again, maybe because everything he tried to say seemed to lead in the wrong direction. He bent and grabbed the bottom of the cabinet.

"Let's get this inside. Maybe then Barbara will make up her mind. I'm ready for middaagesse."

It looked as if the servers were about ready for lunch, too. Women were carrying baskets to the tables, where Leah supervised setting them out.

He picked up his end of the oak cabinet. "We'd best do some carrying to earn our lunch."

Would he talk with Leah then? They hadn't spoken all week, but he felt as if that conversation in the garden had happened minutes ago.

They hoisted the cabinet into the kitchen. Faced with its size, Barbara seemed to realize there was only one proper place for it, and it was deposited there without further trouble.

"That will do it." She glanced at him. "It's kind of you to help, Daniel."

He gave the nod that was the only right response. Barbara

seemed to look at him with more interest than he'd expected. True, he was new in the district, but this wasn't the first time they'd met. He'd expect her to have gotten over her curiosity by now.

Mahlon nudged him. "Let's get some food before the others hog it all. Komm."

He'd guess that Mahlon was still filling out his long frame, but he followed him outside to the picnic tables. Leah, seeing him coming, stepped a little away from the table to meet him.

"Your brother is ready to eat," he said.

"My brother is always ready to eat." She waved her hand at Mahlon as if she shooed away a fly. "Go on, fill your plate already."

Mahlon grinned and took a ladleful of potato salad that filled half his plate.

"He's still a growing boy," Daniel suggested. "I seem to remember feeling like that."

Leah didn't smile in return. Instead she looked at him with a kind of sweet gravity. "I must tell you something, Daniel."

For a moment he could only stare at her. Then certainty pooled inside him at her expression.

"Someone has found out about what happened to us."

She nodded. "I'm sorry. One of Barbara's neighbors had a letter from a cousin in Lancaster County."

He looked for his children—Matthew and Elizabeth going about their chores, Jonah playing happily with some of the younger ones. They were fine for the moment.

"I'd hoped for a little more time."

"I know," she said softly. "But it won't matter, you'll see. The brethren will care about you and yours all the more. It will be fine."

"I hope so." His throat tightened. He didn't mind for himself. Folks could talk about him all they wanted.

But the children—how did he protect them?

Leah waved good-bye to another buggy as the Miller family left. Almost everything had been moved into the farmhouse or transferred to the daadi haus. They'd have some sorting and storing ahead of them, but at least the worst of it was finished.

She glanced around the yard. Matthew was helping his father carry a box toward the daadi haus. Her heart winced at Daniel's expression. Withdrawn, stoic—it was the face of someone prepared to endure whatever was necessary.

And Matthew looked very like him at the moment. Did that mean Matthew realized people knew about that period in his life? It was hard to tell.

She picked up a tray of dishes from the picnic table and carried them toward the kitchen. She sympathized with Daniel's feelings, but really, he had to have known that everyone would find out soon.

As Mamm had said, the brethren would be sympathetic to his troubles, wanting to help.

But they would talk. My, how they would talk. She couldn't blame Daniel for wanting to avoid that as long as possible.

She entered the kitchen to find that Barbara was busily putting dishes in the cupboard, talking all the while to Mamm. As for her mother—

One look, and Leah crossed the room quickly to put her arm around her mother's waist. "Mamm, it's time you had a rest. Barbara and I will take care of whatever else needs to be done here."

Drawn to attention by Leah's words, Barbara climbed down from the stool she'd been standing on. "Leah is right. I should have said something. You go right along to the daadi haus and rest, and I'll bring you a cup of tea as soon as the water boils." She was already putting the kettle on the stove as she spoke.

Leah smiled at her sister-in-law. Barbara might be unaware of people's feelings sometimes, but she was kind at heart despite that.

She would try harder, Leah promised silently. She would remind herself of Barbara's fine points and ignore the rest.

For once her mother didn't argue, which must be a measure of how tired she was. She went slowly out the side door that led to the daadi haus.

Leah straightened her back. She couldn't stop yet, however attractive that sounded. "I'll bring the rest of the dishes from the picnic table."

She no sooner reached the yard than Anna came toward her, half running. She grabbed Leah's arm.

"You need to come right away." The words tumbled out in an urgent undertone. "It's Elizabeth. She's in the barn, crying, and I can't get her to stop."

Leah's heart twisted. "I'll get Daniel—"

"That's what I said, but she doesn't want him." Anna's eyes were dark with concern. "When I said I must call someone, she asked for you."

She should tell Daniel, but maybe it made sense to find out

what was wrong first. She followed Anna, who was already hurrying toward the barn.

If the child had hurt herself—but surely if that was the case, she'd want her father. The fear that Daniel felt curled around her heart. Was this because people knew about Elizabeth's mother taking the children away? If so, Leah was out of her depth in dealing with it.

She caught up with Anna at the barn door. "What were you doing out here? Did you hear her?"

Anna shrugged, slid out of Leah's grasp, and sidled through the door. Leah followed. And stopped.

Elizabeth had apparently climbed into the hay mow. She curled there, hands over her face, her little body shaking with sobs. And a few feet away, looking embarrassed and uncomfortable, stood an English boy.

For a moment she could only stand there, amazed at Anna's effrontery. How could she have the boy here today, of all days, with half the church around? It was as if she wanted to get caught.

"I tried to comfort her, but she just keeps crying." He shoved his hands into the pockets of his jeans, hunching his shoulders.

"We'll take care of her," Leah said crisply. She climbed over the low barrier to the hay mow, sending Anna a glance that should have singed her. "Send him away at once," she said in Pennsylvania Dutch.

"I don't see why—" Anna began, looking mulish.

"Now," she snapped. "We'll talk about this later. There are more immediate things to deal with."

Sulky, Anna grabbed the boy's arm and shoved him toward the door, muttering something to him that Leah couldn't hear. Maybe that was just as well.

Leah sank down in the hay next to the crying child. "There, now, Elizabeth. Can you tell me what's wrong?"

She shook her head.

Leah pulled the child toward her, wrapping her arms around the small figure. "All right." She held her close. "It's going to be all right."

Some hurts went too deep for talk. She knew that for herself. Sometimes all you could do was hold someone.

Guide me now, dear Father. I don't know what to do for this suffering child. Please give me the right words to comfort her.

She held Elizabeth, rocking back and forth, crooning softly in a mix of lullabies and comforting words. She could only hope that the little girl understood enough to take comfort, at least from her presence, if not from her words.

After a while the sobs began to lessen in intensity, though the little body still shook with involuntary spasms. Elizabeth reached up to run her hand along her hair in a futile effort to right herself.

"There, now, it's all right." Leah continued in dialect instead of the English she'd have used with her in school. "Don't worry about how you look."

Elizabeth drew back a little, not meeting Leah's eyes. She sniffled, her hands twisting in her lap. "I'm sorry." She whispered the words.

"Don't be sorry." Maybe a calm, matter-of-fact approach was best. "Everyone needs to cry sometimes, and the hay mow is a good place for it. Usually it's nice and private, but today you had company, didn't you?"

"Anna came in with her friend." Elizabeth hiccoughed. "I wanted to hide, but I was crying too hard. I didn't want her to see me."

Leah stroked Elizabeth's hair, smoothing the tumbled strands. "Anna won't say anything to anyone. Besides, she's done her share of crying out here from time to time."

"She comes here to cry?" Elizabeth looked up at her, eyes round.

"She used to." Today she'd come with something different in mind, and that was still to be dealt with. "Or she'd climb up in the willow tree when she wanted to be by herself. Once she went too high and couldn't get down, and Levi had to bring the ladder to fetch her."

That brought the faint smile to the child's face Leah had been hoping for.

She used her handkerchief to wipe the last traces of tears from Elizabeth's cheeks. "Were you upset because people found out about when you . . ."

She hesitated. What was the right phrase? She wasn't sure.

"They were talking about my mamma." Elizabeth burst out with it before Leah could come up with the proper words. "I don't want them to."

Leah's throat tightened. "I'm sorry, Elizabeth. Sometimes people talk, but they're not really being mean. They're just not thinking about the fact that you might be missing her."

"I don't miss her." The child's hands clenched. "I don't. I don't want to talk about her ever again!"

The vehemence in the child's voice took Leah aback.

"It's all right. You don't have to."

Was this grief or anger? She wasn't sure, and not knowing the circumstances made it impossible for her to respond the right way. If Daniel had seen fit to open up a little more, maybe she'd be better able to deal with this.

Elizabeth was looking at her with a doubting expression, and all she could do was try to reassure her.

"Really. You don't have to talk about her at all if you don't want to."

Elizabeth stared at her for another moment. Then her face seemed to relax, and she sighed. "Ser gut," she murmured.

Was it good? She didn't think so, but she didn't have the right to interfere.

The barn door creaked open. Daniel loomed for a moment on the threshold, probably to let his eyes grow accustomed to the dim light. Then he strode toward them, scooped his daughter up in his arms, and turned away.

Leah scrambled out of the hay, shaking her skirt. "Daniel—"

He glanced at her, his face shuttered tight against her. "I'll take care of my daughter," he said, and walked out.

CHAPTER SEVEN

Leah tapped lightly on Anna's bedroom door. At a murmur from within, she opened it. Barbara and Levi were on the back porch, watching the children play as twilight drew in. This was probably the one chance she'd have to talk to Anna without anyone hearing.

She closed the door and leaned on it. Anna was rebraiding her hair, meaning that she intended to go out again. A small navy duffel bag lay on the bed, zipped closed.

If Leah looked, which she wouldn't, she'd probably find it contained English clothes. Many, if not most, Amish teens tried out modern clothing at one time or another during their rumspringa.

If only that was all Anna was doing. It was one thing to have English friends. It was another to be meeting a strange boy in the barn. She murmured a silent prayer for guidance.

"Well?" Anna, apparently tired of waiting, swung toward her. "Say what you've been waiting the whole day to say already."

Leah sank down on the bed. She wanted to have this conversation without blaming or scolding, but how could she?

"What were you thinking, Anna? Why did you invite that boy here today, of all days? With all that had to be done and with half the church here—well, it was foolhardy, at best."

"I didn't invite him today." The defiance in Anna's face faded, and she shifted her gaze away from her sister. "I'm not that dumb. He just showed up. And don't call him 'that boy.' His name is Jarrod Wells."

"All right." At least her little sister had more sense than she'd been fearing. "Why did Jarrod Wells come today, then, if you didn't ask him?"

Anna shrugged. "I don't know. He just wanted to talk, that's all."

"Talk?"

"Ja, talk," Anna flared. "I have a right to my own friends, don't I? You and the boys had your rumspringa, and I'm having mine. Don't tell me you didn't do things you wouldn't want Mammi and Daadi to know about."

"I suppose I did." But those things had been pretty tame, it seemed, by Anna's standards.

She suddenly felt the more than ten years' difference in their ages. Those years separated them as if they stood on opposite banks of a river.

She had been nearly twelve when Anna—the much longed-for baby sister after the boys—was born. Leah had been her second mother, so happy to take care of her and play with her. She'd thought they would always be as close as they had been then.

"Anna, please." She tried to put all those years of love into the words. "You must know I don't want to be the interfering older sister, out to ruin your fun."

"Then leave me alone. Trust me." Anna grasped the footboard of the bed, leaning forward with urgency in her voice, every line of her body proclaiming how passionate she was about this.

When Anna wanted, she wanted with her whole heart. Her emotions were always on the surface, ready to burst out in an instant. Maybe that was what frightened Leah so about her sister's choices.

She put her hand over Anna's. "I just want you to be safe."

"I'm careful."

"Is it careful to be meeting that . . . Jarrod in the barn? How many times has he met you there?"

Anna jerked her hand free. "All right, so I met him there a few times. Don't tell me you never smooched with Johnny in the stable when you were young, because I wouldn't believe it."

That hurt, but she wouldn't let it show in her face. "That was different."

"Different why?" Anna demanded. "Because Johnny was Amish? Because you were going to marry him? But Johnny's not Amish anymore, and you didn't get married."

The pain sharpened, all the worse because the hurtful words came from her precious little sister. She wrapped her fingers around the bedpost, trying to focus on the present.

"Are you in love with Jarrod?"

Please, she murmured silently. *Please.*

Anna shrugged. "I don't know. I might be."

"Anna, stop and think what you're saying. You can't fall in love with him. He's—"

"Englischer. Auslander." She threw up her hands in an extravagant gesture. "Listen to yourself, Leah. You talk as if a person can control who they fall in love with. Love isn't like that."

Leah's fingers tightened; her stomach twisted. She had to find the words that would turn her sister from her headstrong course.

"What is love like, then?"

Anna looked startled at the question. "Love is—well, it's overwhelming. It takes you over and makes you willing to do anything, anything for the person you love."

"What about the other people you love? The people who love you and want what's best for you? What about your duty to them?"

"You don't understand." Anna swung away from her. "Honestly, Leah, sometimes I think you don't have any feelings at all. You can't talk about duty when you're in love. If you were really in love, that wouldn't matter at all."

No feelings. That was what Johnny had said to her, too, long ago, when she'd sent him away. But if she had no feelings, what was this pain in her chest, so sharp it took an effort to breathe?

But she would breathe. And she would control her emotions, because that was what she did. It was for the best.

"Anna, I just want you to be careful. And I want Mamm not to have to worry about you. Is that so much to ask?"

Anna's lips tightened. She grabbed the bag and headed for the door.

But when she reached it, she stopped, hand on the latch. She didn't look back at Leah.

"I'll be careful, all right?" Her voice was impatient. "I promise I'll be careful."

She opened the door and was gone.

. . .

"Come in, come in." John Kile stood in the center hallway of the medical clinic a few days later, holding the door open for Leah. "Let me show you around our facility."

She stepped inside a little gingerly, not sure what awaited her. She'd hired a driver to bring her, because the clinic was too far to go with horse and buggy after school and still get home by dark. Her driver, Ben Morgan, would be waiting for her when she finished.

It wasn't that the idea of the clinic was foreign to her. She'd certainly spent a great deal of time in medical facilities last year when Mamm had been ill.

But this was different, both because Johnny was here and because of what he wanted from her.

The decision to come, even to look around, hadn't been easy. She'd struggled with it for over a week, praying endlessly, staring at the ceiling when she should have been sleeping.

Finally she'd realized why it was so hard. Because of Johnny. Because Johnny was the one who'd asked her.

If anyone else had approached her, her thoughts would have been for the children and how she could help them. Chastened, she'd made her decision.

"You can hang your bonnet there." Johnny nodded to a row of wooden pegs on the wall of the hallway. His blue eyes were alive with excitement, and he was as eager as a child with a new scooter.

She took her time removing her bonnet and straightening her head covering, trying to get accustomed to the place.

On the outside, the clinic had clearly been designed to make

Amish visitors feel welcome. Although new, it was built in a style reminiscent of a sturdy Pennsylvania Dutch barn. A row of hitching posts lined one side of the parking lot under a row of shade trees.

"This is the clinic area." Obviously impatient, Johnny seized her elbow and steered her through the archway into a waiting room lined with chairs.

Leah had to pause and blink. In contrast to the mellow exterior, this room fairly shouted at her. The walls were covered with bright wallpaper in an abstract design, the plastic chairs bore brightly colored pads, and posters were plastered on the walls over the chairs.

"Great, isn't it?" Johnny gestured. "We even have a play area for the children."

The play corner was filled with bright plastic toys, some of them representing objects Leah couldn't identify, but she nodded and smiled.

He ushered her over to the counter that lined one end of the room. "I'd like to introduce our receptionist, the person who keeps us all on track. Leah, this is Julia Alcott. Julia, Leah Beiler."

Johnny gave Julia his most charming smile, and in that moment Leah realized that underneath his outward assurance, he was nervous. With all his education, did he still question his acceptance here?

Julia nodded, her eyes cool. She was probably in her midthirties, although Leah found it difficult to judge the ages of non-Amish women, and the beige suit she wore made her look more like one of the professionals than a receptionist.

Before Leah could decide what, if anything, to say, a door behind the counter opened. The man who loped through was tall and thin, with keen gray eyes behind his glasses and an eager, youthful smile. He came quickly through the break in the counter and extended his hand to her.

"Welcome, welcome. I'm Alex Brandenmyer. You must be the friend of John's who's going to help us. I'm pleased to meet you."

"Leah Beiler," Johnny said, and his voice had an undertone of increased nervousness.

It was little wonder. Leah shot a look at Johnny. She had said she'd consider this job, and the doctor acted as if her acceptance was an accomplished fact. Either Johnny was overly optimistic about persuading her to do this, or else he felt he knew her so well that there was no question of her cooperation.

With no help for it, Leah shook the man's hand, feeling awkward. "I'm not completely sure that I will be able to help you."

His eyebrows lifted at that, and he gave Johnny a questioning glance. "Well, we'll just have to convince you that we need you, won't we? Tell me, what do you think of our waiting room? We want it to be comfortable and welcoming for our Amish clients."

"It's . . . It's very nice." She found it anything but comfortable, but she couldn't say that.

"That isn't really what you think, is it?" He smiled, but his gaze was keen and assessing. "Tell me. I'd like to hear your opinion."

He was quick to size people up. A good quality in a doctor, she supposed, but she found it a bit uncomfortable when it was turned on her.

"Well, I . . ." She glanced at Johnny, hoping he could get her out of this awkward situation, but he was gazing attentively at his mentor. "It's very . . . busy. If your visitors are already nervous about being here, they might find it a little overwhelming."

"Good point. See, you've helped us already."

The doctor beamed, apparently pleased, but Julia looked annoyed. Had the woman picked out the colors and patterns? Leah hadn't meant to offend anyone, but he'd forced her to give her opinion.

"This is the clinic area, as you can see."

Dr. Brandenmyer seemed determined to take over the tour. She'd find it less intimidating to be shown around by Johnny, but he faded back in the presence of Dr. Brandenmyer.

"We see patients daily, but over here on the other side of the hallway is where the real work is done."

He moved quickly, towing her along as he crossed the hallway and opened the door. A completely different atmosphere permeated this side of the entry area. A hallway stretched the depth of the building, with rooms and cubicles off it to the left.

Dr. Brandenmyer gestured as he walked, giving her the impression that he liked to do more than one thing at a time. "Here we have an exam room with an area for drawing blood. Next we have the laboratory to analyze that blood." He nodded to a young man in a blue lab coat wearing goggles.

"The Amish provide a unique opportunity to study genetic diseases, you know." He paused. "Genetic diseases are those that are carried in the genes, passed on from parent to child."

He apparently assumed that she had no understanding of the problems at all.

"Like the Crigler-Najjar syndrome and the maple syrup urine disease," she suggested.

"Yes, exactly." He looked at her approvingly, as if she were a brighter pupil than he'd anticipated. "You see, most Pennsylvania Amish are descended from the same small group of ancestors. That means that genetic diseases can be more prevalent. If we're able to trace the family trees of those who are affected, we can come that much closer to identifying the causes."

"And finding a cure?" Her heart clenched at the thought of the families who would be touched by such a thing.

"We're a long way from that right now," he admitted. "But everything we learn moves us forward. Early testing and intervention can help many of the affected children live a much more normal life."

He stopped at the entrance to a room that seemed completely filled with computers. Johnny brushed past her and crossed to a woman who swung away from one of the screens as they came in.

"Leah, this is Stacie Corson." He rested his hand lightly on the back of her chair.

The slight, dark-haired young woman shot Johnny an intense glance before nodding at Leah.

"This is where Stacie and I analyze the data," he said, gazing around at the computers the way her father might look at a field overflowing with ripe corn. "But we need more information to work on."

"That's where you come in," Dr. Brandenmyer said. "You see, the information you bring us will be keyed into the computer." He moved to one of the machines, patting it lovingly. "This is the most advanced equipment on the market today." He bent over to tap something, so that a complex chart appeared on the screen. "You see, this is a sample of the—"

"It's not necessary to give Leah a crash course in computers." The woman who spoke had been sitting behind one of the machines in the corner of the room, and Leah hadn't noticed her until that moment.

But she was relieved at the interruption. Very relieved. Her head had begun to ache with the strain of trying to follow Dr. Brandenmyer's explanations. She'd been keeping up all right, she thought, until they'd reached the computer room, but here she was totally out of her depth.

"Lydia, I didn't see you back there. This is Leah Beiler, the young woman John told us about. Leah, this is Lydia Weaver."

"Leah is the teacher, I know," Lydia said, coming toward them. Her smile was piercingly sweet, lighting her plain face with an inward beauty. She wore a simple dark dress with low-heeled shoes, her graying hair short and swept back from a face that was frankly middle-aged and didn't attempt to hide that fact.

"Goodness, look at the time," Dr. Brandenmyer exclaimed. "It's a good thing you stopped me, Lydia. I must go. I have a conference call with those researchers in Luzerne in a few minutes. John, you'd better come with me. Stacie can show Leah the charts and explain about the interviews."

In an instant they were both gone. Stacie didn't look especially happy at being left behind. She shoved her chair, and it rolled to the next desk so quickly that Leah had to step out of the way.

"It's very simple, really," she said, sounding doubtful that Leah could manage no matter how simple. "We'd expect you to visit families who have an instance of genetically linked illness and persuade them to cooperate. There's a family-tree form to fill out." She shoved a paper into Leah's hands. "And an interview form." She passed her another one. "We encourage all the members of the family to come in for DNA testing. You know what that is, don't you?"

Leah's hands tightened on the forms that had been thrust into her hands. This woman didn't like her, and she wasn't sure why. Because she was Amish? Plenty of Englischers were prejudiced against the Amish, but this would be a funny place to work if you felt that way.

Or did this have something to do with Johnny?

"I said do you know about DNA testing?"

"Yes."

Leah clipped off the word and put the papers down on the desk carefully because she wanted to throw them. If Johnny thought she'd be convinced to help them by making her the object of condescension and rudeness, he was mistaken.

"I'm sure there's time for all of these explanations once Leah has had a chance to think about this," Lydia interrupted smoothly. "I always have a cup of tea about this time." She touched Leah's arm lightly. "Please, come and join me."

Leah would rather leave, but she would not return rudeness for rudeness by saying so. "That is very kind of you."

With the sense that the woman had unexpectedly come to her rescue, Leah went with her.

Lydia led the way into yet another office, but this one was totally different. There was not a computer in sight. The room was simplicity itself, with off-white walls and matching fabric shades on the windows, drawn up to give a view across green pasture. In the distance, an old orchard spread along the hillside, its apple trees gnarled and bent, but still bearing blossoms.

There were blossoms inside, as well, with pots of African violets filling the windowsills. Though there was a desk in the far corner near crowded bookshelves, the focus of the room seemed to be two comfortable-looking padded rockers on an oval hooked rug.

"I like your office." At an inviting gesture from Lydia, Leah sank into one of the rockers. Its bentwood back fit her perfectly.

"My aim was to make it look as little like an office as possible."

Lydia turned on what seemed to be an electric kettle and put two mugs on a tray. Her movements were slow and smooth. Calming.

Leah leaned her head back, feeling the last of her stress drain away. "You succeeded. It's peaceful here." She hesitated. "You rescued me. That was kind of you."

Lydia opened a tin and began arranging cookies on a plate. "You looked as if you needed it. I'm afraid this place can be overwhelming."

"Ja." The word was heartfelt.

"I've noticed that scientists become so focused on their own subject that they're totally unaware of other people's reactions." The kettle was boiling already, and she poured hot water into the cups. "You can be staring at them with a totally blank expression, and they'll just keep talking."

That surprised Leah into a laugh. "I'm afraid blank is a wonderful gut description of how I felt when they started talking about the computers."

"I'm a little familiar with computers, but I confess, the complex programs John and Stacie work with are beyond me."

Lydia carried the tray to the small, round table that stood between the rockers and put a steaming mug down next to Leah.

Once Leah had taken the tea and an obviously homemade oatmeal cookie, Lydia served herself and sank back in the other rocker.

"That's better. I always want a break in the late afternoon."

"This is pleasant." Leah looked at the woman, curious. "You talk about the scientists as if they're different from you, but you work here, don't you?"

"Yes, but I'm a psychologist, not a genetics researcher. I help the families and the children cope with the difficulties of their situation."

"It is very hard," Leah agreed. "I know of several children who ought to be in my school, but their condition doesn't permit. I try to do what I can, taking them books and learning activities, but it's not enough."

Lydia nodded in understanding. "Whatever we do never seems enough, does it? Still, no matter what their condition, the children are a blessing. And those we lose—well, they're safe in the hands of Jesus."

Leah studied the woman, caught by the turn of phrase, the way she dressed, even the way she sat. "Lydia, are you . . ."

She stopped, realizing that the question she wanted to ask might be considered rude.

"Am I Plain?" Lydia finished the question for her, smiling. "I was raised Amish, yes." She shrugged. "But I wanted more education, more choices about the life I would have. So I chose not to join the church."

"Are you—" Questions flooded her mind. "Do you have a relationship with your family?"

"Oh, yes. It took some time, but we're close now. They live in Indiana, so I don't see them as often as I'd like, but we write often, and my nieces and nephews visit in the summer."

"That's gut."

At least, she supposed it was. So far, Johnny didn't have that chance, but perhaps it would come, given a little patience. Unfortunately, patience had never been one of his strong points.

"You're happy?"

Lydia considered the question. "Not entirely, I suppose. Sometimes I long to be an Amish woman again, sitting in my own kitchen with my children around me. But none of us gets everything we want, Amish or English. I am content. And I'm very satisfied to be part of the work we're doing here."

"I know that it is important work." Leah stared down at the dark brew in her cup, a little troubled. "But I'm not sure it is right for me."

For a long moment Lydia didn't speak. Then she nodded. "I understand. It would be difficult for you in any event, but having John here makes it worse."

She wanted to deny it, but Lydia saw too much. Or maybe Johnny had been talking about her. That thought was distasteful.

Lydia's chair rocked as she patted Leah's hand. "Think about it. Pray about it. See what God's answer is. That's all we can ask of you."

Leah managed a smile, grateful that Lydia, at least, didn't intend to pressure her. "All right. That I will do."

CHAPTER EIGHT

*H*e shouldn't be letting his mind stray to Teacher Leah when he was worshipping, Daniel reminded himself. He would not glance toward the other side of the aisle to where the women sat, even though he knew perfectly well that she was on the fifth bench back, sitting on the end of the row next to her mother.

His interest was only drawn in that direction because Elizabeth had asked to sit with Teacher Leah, he reasoned. Instead of staying with her father and the boys, she wanted to be on the women's side of the barn for the worship service, like a grown-up woman.

The Miller family's large barn had been cleaned and scrubbed until it shone, so that it would be ready to host the service today. The backless benches, which would have arrived by wagon sometime during the week, were arranged in rows so straight that someone might have measured the distance between each of them. When they'd entered, black copies of the Ausbund, the songbook, lay on each bench, ready for the singing.

With the number of families in the district and the every-other-Sunday schedule for worship, Daniel would estimate each family's turn probably came around only once a year. Twenty-six families was considered ideal for a district back home for that reason, but often the number went up or down a few. If it went up too many, or the homes were too far apart for everyone to make the drive easily by horse and buggy, the district would have to be split into two congregations.

He'd not be added into the schedule here in Pleasant Valley until next year, but when the time came, he'd have to use the barn, just as the Millers did. Some of the brethren had homes large enough to hold worship in, but that seemed to be more common back in Lancaster County, where houses were built with that in mind.

The three-hour service was drawing to a close, as one of their three ministers concluded his sermon. Jonah sagged against Daniel, and he put his arm around the boy. Little ones couldn't help but grow sleepy during the long service with its slow hymns. Jonah would liven up plenty when it came time to eat.

He felt his gaze stray toward Leah again, and he pulled it back. He hadn't seen her to speak to in more than a week. He'd best be honest with himself about it. The reason he felt so compelled to see her now was plain and simple—guilt.

He'd misjudged her when he'd found her with Elizabeth that day of the moving. He'd thought she'd overstepped her boundaries, prying into his grief by talking to his daughter instead of calling him and leaving it to him to deal with.

It had been a few days later when he'd brought up the subject with Elizabeth, hoping she was ready to talk about it, and learned that Elizabeth, upset at hearing folk talk, had asked for Leah. Not him. That bitter pill still choked in his throat when he thought of it.

Gracious Lord, guide me to deal with these children You've given me. I hoped everything would be fine once I had them back with me, but it's been hard. Each day I question whether I'm doing the right thing.

They are my responsibility, Lord, given by You into my care. Guide my words and my choices.

That couldn't be the extent of his prayer, and he knew it. He'd wronged Leah in his thoughts and in his attitude, and that must be confessed.

Forgive me, Dear Father, for my hasty thoughts and attitudes where Teacher Leah is concerned. I was wrong. Forgive me.

He stared down at his hand, clenched on the black fabric of the broadfall trousers of his best suit. That wasn't enough. His confession wouldn't be complete until he'd mended matters with Leah herself.

He stood with the others for the final prayer, lifting Jonah in his arms as Bishop Mose spoke the words. Maybe he'd be able to speak with Leah during the visiting that went on before the brethren sat down for lunch. He had to mend things with her.

"Komm." He grasped the boys' hands, and the community surged out of the barn into the sunshine.

Jonah tugged at his hand. "My friends from school are here, Daadi. Can I go and see them?"

"Ja, both of you can go. Just mind you komm schnell when the lunch is served."

Elizabeth, he noted, had already gone over to the picnic tables, probably offering to help. She was very much the little mammi already.

He glanced around. Women were intent on helping with the lunch, while men gathered to catch up on the week's events. He spotted Leah, carrying a large jar of what looked like lemonade from her buggy. This might be his best chance for a private talk, although he hadn't figured out the right words yet.

He walked toward her, hoping it didn't look to the others as if he were seeking her out.

"May I carry that for you?" He reached for the jar as he spoke.

Leah looked up at him, green eyes wide and unguarded for an instant. Then her gaze slipped away from his. "I can manage."

She wasn't going to make this easy, but that was only fair.

"I know that you can carry it, but helping gives me an opportunity to speak with you."

Again that startled look, but she surrendered the jar without further argument. They moved together toward the tables.

"Is there a problem with the children?"

That would always be her first concern, of course. She only thought of him, if she thought of him at all, as the father of his children.

"The children are well. I am not. I must apologize to you."

"You mean about what happened with Elizabeth last Saturday." She stopped under the shade of an overhanging willow tree, and he stopped with her.

"I was rude to you when you were trying to help. That wasn't fair."

"It's all right." Her quick forgiveness shamed him. "You were concerned about your daughter. You felt you should have been told about her immediately. That's natural."

"She told me she asked your sister to find you. And not to tell me." He tried to keep the hurt out of his voice but probably didn't succeed very well.

Leah's eyes darkened with concern. "Anna didn't know what else to do. Elizabeth was so upset that she felt it best to do as she wanted."

"Elizabeth asked for you. Not me." The words came out flatly. He hadn't intended to say that, but Leah's obvious caring made it easier than he'd expected to bring up the thing that still pained him.

Leah looked up at him, her gaze filled with sympathy. The leaves of the willow, moving in the breeze, dappled her face.

"I understand that bothers you, Daniel, but I'm sure Elizabeth was trying to protect you. She knew you would be worried if you realized how upset she'd become. She didn't want to hurt you."

"I hope that's all it was." His throat tightened, and the worries he had for his children rushed in upon him. "Those years we were apart— I don't know what they've done to my relationship with my children."

He was sorry he'd spoken the instant the words were out of his mouth. It sounded as if he was inviting Leah to help him, and he didn't want that. He was the father. He had to figure this out for himself.

"You love them," she said quietly. "That's the most important thing."

"Ja." He grappled for steadier ground. "We will be all right. We just need time."

"Time to adjust." She seemed to agree, but her eyes were troubled. "Elizabeth and Matthew struggle more than Jonah, because they're older. Elizabeth is trying so hard to be perfect that it concerns me."

He took a step back. "She's a helpful and conscientious child. That's a gut thing."

"Sometimes it's too much of a gut thing." She softened the words with a smile.

Still, they annoyed him. He had not asked for advice. Leah, however well-intentioned, was not a parent.

"You are kind to be concerned about my children. But I think you have enough worries of your own about your sister."

Her chin came up at that. "Elizabeth told you about Anna's friend."

"Ja, she did." He paused, struggling to be fair. "She said that he was kind to her. But he was English."

"Anna did not invite him to meet her in the barn, if that's what you're thinking." She paused, probably trying to get her irritation under control. "But you're right. We do each have our own problems to deal with."

Taking the jar of lemonade, she walked quickly over to the picnic tables, her back very straight.

Leah reached the picnic table and set down the lemonade. As was traditional, the host family had prepared a cold lunch. There were trays of bologna and Swiss cheese already on the table, and Naomi Miller came out the back door of the farmhouse, carrying baskets of whole wheat and white bread.

"Naomi, I don't know how you found the time to bake two kinds of bread."

Naomi Miller was busier than most young mothers, since two

of her three preschool-aged children were among those in the valley suffering from the Crigler-Najjar illness.

"Ach, what I would do without my mother-in-law, I don't know," Naomi said, putting the tray on the table. "Her baking is wonderful gut, it is." Her eyes twinkled. "And your Mahlon will soon be as fortunate as I am, I think."

"Shh," Leah whispered, smiling. "Mahlon thinks no one has figured it out yet. As if no one notices him and Esther looking at each other all the time."

"Or the amount of celery my husband's daad has planted this year." She turned to go back to the house, probably for more food.

Leah caught her arm. "Since you and I are almost family, let me help bring things out."

"That is kind of you, Leah." One of her young ones rushed up to grasp her skirt just then, and she nodded. "Everything is on the kitchen table."

Leah went quickly into the house. She would have offered to help in any event, but she was just as happy to be safely away from the group for a moment. That exchange with Daniel had shaken her more than she wanted to admit.

He knew about Anna and the Englischer. Well, that in itself was not so bad. As Anna herself had said, it was her rumspringa. Such goings-on were tolerated, if not welcomed, by the community. Parents turned their eyes away and prayed for the best.

The danger lay in what Anna made of the situation. *I might be in love,* she'd said. It was tempting to believe that her younger sister wasn't old enough to know what love was, but she'd been Anna's age when she'd fallen in love with Johnny.

And look how that had turned out. She certainly couldn't hold herself up as any sort of example.

Sometimes I think you don't have any feelings at all.

Anna's words echoed relentlessly in her heart. The very fact that she couldn't forget them told her that she feared they were true. Certainly Johnny would have agreed with that, once at least.

And now? Well, now he simply didn't care.

Forcing herself to move, she picked up a tray and began filling it with the dishes on the table. Naomi, and perhaps her mother-in-law, had gone all out. There were sweet pickles and dill pickles, red beets, even peanut butter and strawberry jelly for the children. Additional plates were filled with sweets: pumpkin, chocolate chip, and sugar cookies.

She gripped the tray, but for a moment didn't move. Whether others would accept Anna's flirtation or not, Daniel was the worst person to trust with it.

She could understand why he felt as he did. With just the little she knew about his wife's jumping the fence to the outside world and taking the children with her, the reason for his feelings was clear. She could sympathize with his pain.

But she wished he didn't know about Anna.

She started out the door with the filled tray and nearly bumped into Elizabeth, coming in.

The child looked up at her, small face intent. "Naomi said that I could help carry things out."

"That's kind of you, Elizabeth, but wouldn't you rather play with the other scholars? I can take everything out."

"But I said I would help." Elizabeth's lower lip trembled. "I must do as I said."

"Ser gut," Leah said quickly. "You can take the plates of cookies that are on the table."

Elizabeth nodded and hurried to the table. Leah watched as she picked up the first plate carefully, holding it with both hands.

Dear Father, help me to understand this child. There is something not right about her frantic need to be good. Help me to see.

And if she did see, would Daniel listen to her? The way things were going, she doubted it.

She shoved through the screen door, holding it open against her hip while Elizabeth came out. They carried their burdens to the picnic tables, where people already clustered, plates at the ready.

Naomi seized the tray, putting its contents quickly on the table, the bishop lifted his voice in prayer, and the fellowship meal began.

In spite of her concerns about Daniel and his children and her worries about Anna, Leah began to relax. This time—this bonding with her community—was surely one of the great strengths of Amish life. Sharing worship and a common meal, they did what the earliest followers of Jesus did, and it built the ties between them more surely with every bite, every joke, every shared story.

By the time folks were settling into groups with their coffee and cookies, the peace of the day had calmed Leah. She sat down next to Naomi, who had her five-year-old son on her lap. Leah reached over to stroke light brown hair out of the boy's eyes.

"Eli, will you be coming to school in the fall?"

Eli burrowed his face in his mother's shoulder.

"Ach, now, answer Teacher Leah," Naomi chided.

The boy stole a glance at her face. "Ja, Teacher Leah," he whispered.

She smiled. "I will be glad to have you in my class, I will."

"You will be teaching in the fall, then?" Naomi asked.

Leah blinked. "Ja, of course I will, for sure. Why not?"

Naomi's gaze slid away from hers. "No reason. I just thought— folks were saying—maybe you'd be doing somethin' else in the fall."

For a moment her mind spun. And then it settled on the right answer. Daniel. Folks were saying she would wed Daniel.

She managed to smile. Managed to force her tone to be light. "I see the matchmakers are busy as always. I hate to disappoint them, but I have no plans to do anything but continue to teach."

Naomi's gaze met hers, and for a moment it seemed the young mother could see into her heart. "Sometimes it surprises us what God has for us."

A thin wail sounded from the second-floor window of the house. "It sounds as if young Jacob is awake." Leah was relieved at the interruption.

Naomi moved, starting to put Eli down, but Leah stopped her with a hand on her arm.

"Let me get him, please? I haven't seen him in weeks, it seems."

Naomi hesitated a moment, and then she nodded. "His clothes are hanging on the rack by the crib."

"I'll take care of him." She hurried toward the house. Escaping again? She'd hate to think that.

The wail grew louder as she mounted the enclosed staircase. Little Jacob was growing impatient. "I'm coming, Jacob."

The bedroom at the top of the stairs was typical of a small child's room in most Amish houses, with one dramatic exception. Over Jacob's crib hung a metal rack filled with blue lights, sending an eerie blue glow through the room. Run by a generator, the lights were the only thing that kept Jacob and his sister, who was two years older, alive.

Crossing to the crib, she switched off the lights and lifted them out of the way. Jacob, clad only in his diaper, reached chubby arms to her, and she picked him up, holding him close.

Jacob looked like any other fourteen-month-old, except for the golden color of his skin and the yellow whites of his eyes, caused by the jaundice that built up in his little body. Without spending twelve hours a day under the lights, Jacob would die.

Bouncing him a little, she carried him to the changing pad on top of the wooden dresser. "There we go, little man. We'll get you all dressed and take you down to your mammi."

Jacob stared at her intently for a moment and then gave her a grin. She tickled him, and he chortled, clapping his hands.

Her heart turned over, and she knew that she had one answer, at least, to the difficulties that surrounded her. She might not know what to do about Daniel and his children, or about Anna, but if it meant helping Jacob and those like him, she would ask Bishop Mose for permission to volunteer at the clinic.

"I'm wonderful glad to have a chance to talk to you." Rachel sat down beside Leah in the back row of schoolroom desks. "We've been too busy to visit lately, we have."

At the front of the room, the teacher's helper who came in to assist Leah several days a week was beginning to rehearse the scholars for their end-of-year program.

"Of course," she murmured, her mind only partially on Rachel. "I can't believe school will be out so soon. The years go faster all the time."

"That's because we're older all the time," Rachel said. She nodded toward Leah's seventeen-year-old helper. "How is Mary Yoder shaping up? Will you make a teacher of her?"

"I will if she keeps at it and doesn't let herself stray off after a job in town, as so many girls want to do."

Rachel's gaze sought out her own Becky, whispering with the other eight- and nine-year-olds as they practiced their parts. "That's a worry, for sure."

Already Rachel feared the world would lure her child away. *Be ye separate. In the world, not of the world.*

Those were the teachings they lived by, ingrained from birth, but still, the world called too loudly for some.

Like Rachel's twin. Leah glanced at her friend's face. Was she remembering Johnny?

"I hear that you are going to volunteer at the clinic where Johnny is." Rachel said the words softly, her face averted.

Leah hesitated, not sure of Rachel's reaction. When they were girls, they'd told each other everything, but now— Well, life was like that, wasn't it? They couldn't stay girls forever, and they wouldn't want to.

"I am. Once school is out, I'll start calling on folks, getting information about those who have the inherited illnesses."

Rachel looked at her then, her gaze troubled. "Are you sure that's wise?"

How could I be sure? No, she wouldn't say that. It would be giving in to her own doubts and fears.

"I've talked with Bishop Mose about it. He's approved." She stopped, not willing to repeat to Rachel the gist of Bishop Mose's concerns about her being near Johnny again.

"Have you seen him? Johnny, I mean?" Rachel lowered her voice, though none of the children could hear their conversation.

"Ja." She hesitated. "Are you upset with me for doing this?"

"No, no." Rachel put her hand over Leah's. "Not upset. Just worried."

"Don't be," she said, her tone firm. "There's nothing between John and me now, and that's as it should be."

"That's gut, much as I hate to say it." She paused, and her eyes grew wistful. "How is he?"

Leah's heart twisted. "He seems successful. Driven to succeed in his work, I'd say."

"But something about him worries you," Rachel said. "Don't deny it. I know you too well."

Leah spread her hands, palms up. "I'm not sure. The others seem to respect him, but he still is nervous, as if he's not quite sure of himself among them."

"Because he was Amish?"

"I don't know." She struggled with feelings she didn't fully understand. "Sometimes I catch flashes of the old Johnny, and I understand him. But then he becomes someone so different."

Rachel nodded. "If I could see for myself—"

"You could, if you wanted." Leah's hand closed over hers.

Rachel shook her head. "Not now. Maybe later." She focused

on Leah's face, her blue eyes piercing. "Just tell me one thing for sure. Are you going to help there because of Johnny?"

In that, at least, she knew her own heart. "No. I'm going because of the children. Little Jacob and Naomi Grace Miller, and all the rest. And those yet to be born."

Her heart clutched. Mahlon was marrying into the Miller family. She wouldn't want him to give up his Esther, but she feared for the children they would have.

"Gut." Rachel patted her hand. "That's gut."

Mary came halfway down the aisle toward them and stopped, obviously not wanting to interrupt. Leah smiled at her.

"What is it, Mary?"

"The middle-grade scholars are ready to practice for us."

"Ser gut. We'll come a little closer." She rose and moved toward the front of the classroom, Rachel following her.

This end-of-year program was one she'd written her first year of teaching—so long ago she hoped no one would remember it. Although if any of her scholars from that year came to the program, which they probably would, they might still be able to recite the poetry by heart.

She settled herself to listen attentively, smiling and nodding encouragingly at each child as he or she spoke. Mary, who was prompting as needed, looked a bit worried. She'd have to assure her that mistakes were normal at this stage. Experience had taught Leah that just when you thought the program would be a complete disaster, it all came together.

Elizabeth stepped forward, her hands linked on her apron, her gaze on the ceiling, as if she looked for inspiration there. "I am but a little scholar," she began. "Still I've learned to—" She stopped, her hands tightening as she sought for the elusive words.

"—listen well," Mary whispered loudly.

Elizabeth didn't seem to hear. Her eyes grew panic-stricken.

"It's all right," Leah began.

But it was too late. Elizabeth burst into tears and ran from the room.

CHAPTER NINE

Matthew!" Daniel, on his knees in the vegetable garden, pushed himself to his feet, scanning the area between garden and barn for his son. "Matthew, wo bist du? Where are you?"

No answer. He glanced at the tomato plants, ready to be put into the ground now that the threat of frost was past. He'd hoped he and Matthew could get the job done quickly once the children got home from school.

He could have done it himself, but he'd wanted to share it with his son. He longed to have the pleasure of working beside him, planting something that would help to feed the family.

But Matthew, while never openly rebellious, had found many ways of avoiding chores lately. He'd been sent to the barn on a simple enough errand to bring back an extra trowel. He'd had time enough to do that a dozen times by now.

Daniel looked again at the two dozen tomato plants he'd decided would be enough for them. They'd begin to wilt in another few minutes. Blowing out an irritated breath, he headed for the barn.

Matthew seemed to get more distracted every day. Before Ruth left, Daniel had thought that he and Matthew were as close as a father and son could possibly be. He'd never expected that could change.

Now, he wasn't so sure. He didn't know his oldest son any longer, and that cut him to the heart.

The barn door stood open a few feet, where Matthew had gone in. Daniel gave it an impatient shove and stepped inside.

At the sound, Matthew popped up from the hay mow, eyes round with surprise. He made a quick movement with his hand, as if shoving something out of sight.

Daniel crossed to him, his jaw tightening.

"I'm sorry, Daadi. I—I guess I forgot to bring the trowel." He scrambled out of the hay mow. "I'll get it right now."

Daniel brushed past him, heading for the spot where the boy had been sitting.

"Daadi, let's go plant the tomatoes." Matthew's voice held an edge of nerves, a sure sign that he was trying to hide something.

Leaning on the low wall of the hay mow, Daniel bent over, probing into the hay with his hand. In an instant his fingers met something hard and rectangular.

He pulled it out and stood staring, hardly believing his eyes. It was some sort of game, with blinking lights and figures moving on a tiny screen.

He swung around, holding it up in front of his son. "What is this thing?"

Matthew stared back, sullen and defiant. "It's called an electronic game."

"Where did you get it?" His head started to throb. He had no desire to interrogate his son, but the boy wasn't being open with him.

Matthew didn't answer. He just stared, and Daniel couldn't tell what was going on behind that blank expression.

"Matthew?"

Matthew's jaw clenched, too. Daniel felt as if he looked into a mirror. Then Matthew's gaze slid away. He focused on the wide planks of the barn floor.

"It's mine." He muttered the words.

"Yours? How can it be yours?" How could an Amish child come by something like this?

"Mammi gave it to me." The words burst out of him. "It's mine."

Daniel froze. He tried to swallow, but his throat seemed paralyzed.

Help me. Show me what to say. If I say the wrong thing, I could drive a wedge between us we might never get rid of.

He took a long, slow breath. "I thought I had seen everything you brought from your mamm's house. I have not seen this."

Matthew's face seemed to ease a fraction at his father's calm tone. "I hid it."

"Why did you do that?" He'd tried hard to be gentle and understanding in the aftermath of Ruth's death. Had he failed so badly?

"It is English, so I knew you wouldn't want me to have it."

He didn't. That was his first instinctive reaction. And then he realized that he was asking himself what Leah would advise. Leah, with her quick intelligence and her knowledge of children, would know what to do.

But Leah wasn't here. And his children were not her concern.

"Matthew—"

"Mamm would let me have it," Matthew blurted out. "She would."

For just an instant he saw Ruth's face, lit with love when she looked at their son for the first time. His heart twisted. If only they could wipe out all the pain since that moment.

But there was no going back. He could only move ahead, trying to do what God willed.

He looked at the game—so small it nestled in the palm of his hand. Its light blinked at him.

He took a deep breath, praying he was making the right choice, and held it out to his son.

"I can keep it?" Matthew stared at him, disbelief in his eyes.

"You can keep it because your mammi gave it to you. But I don't want Elizabeth or Jonah to see it. Do you understand?"

"Ja. They won't. I'll keep it where they won't see it."

"And it's not to interfere with chores."

"It won't, Daadi. I promise." Matthew scampered to the hay loft and quickly rehid his device. "I'll get the trowel right away."

Matthew would come with him and plant tomatoes. But would he be thinking of planting and growing? Or would his mind be on that remnant of his English world?

"*Don't* walk in the living room," Barbara said the minute Leah came in the back door from school. "The floor is still wet." She stood at the kitchen sink, wringing out a cloth, her sleeves pushed back.

Leah nodded. The quilt frolic Barbara was hosting would be tomorrow, which meant that the house must be spotless. Leah pushed aside her plan to go over the materials from the clinic this afternoon.

"Mamm will enjoy the quilting, for sure." She hung her bonnet on the peg in the back hall. Her mother's quilts were works of art, with love in every stitch. "What are you working on tomorrow?"

"That tumbling blocks quilt. It'll go to one of the wedding couples in November." Her eyes twinkled. "Maybe Esther and Mahlon, if they get around to announcing in time."

Leah smiled back at her sister-in-law. "I think they will, if Mahlon has anything to say about it."

"Before you know it, it will be time to start a baby quilt," Barbara said. She hung the cleaning rags on the wooden rack to dry.

"I guess so." She thought again of Naomi's children under their blue lights. Would Esther and Mahlon have healthy babies? "I'll put my school things upstairs and come down to help you."

Barbara nodded. "Ser gut. Oh, and if you have any nice tea towels in your dower chest, maybe we could use them tomorrow. I tried to look, but the chest is locked, it is."

Leah's hands tightened on the case that held her school materials, and she forced the grip to ease before she spoke. Barbara had been in her room, trying to open her dower chest.

Rachel's words about living in another woman's house surfaced in her mind. Rachel had been right, but how many choices did she have?

"Leah?" Barbara questioned.

"I'm not sure what I have. Is there something wrong with yours?"

"Ach, they're worn through with using. Would be nice to have something pretty out when the sisters are here tomorrow."

Given the number of times Leah had told her family that she didn't intend to wed, Barbara's request was only natural. She didn't like it, but surely a few dish towels weren't worth starting a family argument over.

"I'll look and see what I have," she said, and made her escape to her room.

Once upstairs, with the bedroom door closed behind her, she massaged her temples. Barbara meant well, she reminded herself. And this was her house now.

Still, some rebellious part of her wanted to lock the door, something she'd never done before in her life.

She put her school materials on the table under the window and turned to look at the dower chest that stood against the wall opposite her bed. Daadi had made it for her sixteenth birthday, and even though she'd known that would be her gift, she'd been overwhelmed by it.

She bent, stroking the warm grain of the wood. Daad had saved the pieces from the walnut tree near the spring after it came down in a storm. She and her brothers had played under that tree from her earliest memories, and touching it was like touching a piece of her life.

The key was in the top drawer of her dresser. She took it out, sat down on the rag rug, unlocked the chest, and lifted the lid.

She had put a clean sheet over the contents to protect them. Touching the fabric, she remembered the day she'd done that. It had been nearly a month after Johnny left the valley.

To her shame, it had taken her that long to face that he wasn't coming back. The life they'd planned together would never be. She had to stop looking for him to return, put on a calm face, and never let anyone know how much it hurt.

She grasped the sheet and pulled it off in one quick movement. All this time, and still she didn't want to face it.

There was a light knock at the door, and then it opened a few inches. She stiffened. If it was Barbara, come to press her about the dish towels, she might not be able to hang on to her temper.

"Leah? May I come in?" It was her mother.

"Of course." She started to get up, but her mother had already entered, waving her back to her place.

"Sit, sit." Mamm sank into the rocking chair. "Go on with what you were doing."

Leah's fingers clenched on the edge of the chest. "Barbara wanted to borrow some tea towels for tomorrow. I was just going to look for them."

"I know." Mamm's voice was soft. "You don't have to do that. I'll settle it with Barbara."

She shook her head. "No, it means nothing. It's time I sorted these things out." She lifted out the quilt that lay on top.

Mamma reached out to touch it. "That is the log cabin quilt that you and your grossmutter made together."

"She did most of it." Leah unfolded it, and the colorful geometric pattern spread between her and her mother. "I'll never be the quilter she was. Or that you are as well. Look at those tiny stitches."

"She loved making it with you, for sure. It's something to treasure."

Leah stared at the quilt. Once, she'd expected that it would cover her marriage bed. Now . . . Well, how foolish was it to keep it hidden away instead of using it?

"I should have it out, where I can see it every day and remember her."

"Ja, that would be gut." Mamm's tone was careful.

Leah managed a smile. "I'm all right about it, Mamm. Really I am. I should have gotten these things out and made use of them a long time ago."

"They were put away for your wedding. They come with memories."

They were tangible reminders of the life she'd expected to have with Johnny. She'd been so happy with each thing she'd added, thinking about how she would use it in their new home. She lifted out a stack of tea towels.

"Life doesn't always happen the way we think it will. It's foolish to live in the past."

Mamm's face was troubled. "Does it still grieve you, thinking about Johnny? His coming back to the valley makes it harder, ain't so?"

Did it? She wasn't sure how to find an honest answer to that question. She looked into her mother's worn face, trying to find the right words.

"It's made me think about those times, for sure. I'm sorry for the way it ended."

"Do you still love him?"

Did she? "I love the boy he was. I can't stop doing that. But the man he is now—I don't even know him. So how could I love him?"

Mamm leaned forward to touch her cheek lightly. "The heart

has reasons of its own. I just don't want you to be hurting any more because of him already."

"I know, Mamm." She covered her mother's hand with hers, taking comfort from the gentle touch. "I'm not."

"And I don't want you to give up thoughts of marriage because of what happened with him." Mamm sounded as stern as she ever could. "That wasn't your doing, it was his."

Leah pushed down the doubts that assailed her at that. "I know you want me to be happy, Mammi. But I don't think marriage is for me. I am happy with my teaching."

"You spill out so much love on other people's children. Don't you want to have your own to love?"

There was an odd little pain in her heart at that. "I'm contented," she said firmly, remembering Lydia saying those words. "As much as most, married or single, I think." She scrambled to her feet. "Now, let's get these dish towels down to Barbara before she comes up looking for them."

Six thirty in the morning that Saturday, and already the buggies were pulling in at the Stoltzfus farm. Leah watched the line of buggies ahead of her in the lane, letting Betty take her time. Aaron Stoltzfus's barn had been destroyed by fire in a spring thunderstorm, and this was the day appointed for the barn raising.

In a few moments she was pulling into a grassy area, one of a veritable fleet of buggies parked in a neat row. No sooner had she stopped than several boys ran up to tend to the horses—their first job of the day. She greeted them before turning to her mother.

"Here we are, Mamm." She considered asking her mother not to overdo, but that would be futile. And really, Mamm looked bright-eyed and excited about the prospect of spending the whole day with the church family, doing a gut work.

Mamm was already sliding from the buggy, not waiting for help. "Hand me one of the baskets down, and I'll take it."

Obediently, Leah lifted the smallest of the baskets and gave it to her. "I'll bring the rest," she said firmly. "One of the boys will help me."

Mamm trotted off toward the kitchen, and Leah unloaded the rest of the food and joined the chattering crowd of women and children moving along the lane. Daad, Levi, and Mahlon had come even earlier than they had, eager to get a start on the day's work. Barbara would be along later, in their family buggy, wanting to let the little ones have their sleep.

Crews had come already to clear away the rubble, prepare the site, and lay the foundation. Today, with the entire church involved, the barn would be built.

Englischers sometimes wondered at the Amish reluctance to buy insurance on their property, probably seeing it as foolhardy. To the Plain People, that would be like trusting in the insurance instead of in God.

And if lightning did happen to strike, well, that was God's will, and the whole community would join in rebuilding. Perhaps that was part of His plan, too, teaching them to rely on one another, building community at the same time that they raised the barn.

She followed the crowd into the kitchen, joining the group that would produce enough food to satisfy more than a hundred hungry folks come noon. The necessary chores, familiar to everyone, were quickly parceled out, just as they were outside among the men.

Leah found herself paired with Rachel and Naomi to slice bread and make sandwiches. The three of them were soon deep in conversation as they sliced and spread and piled meat and cheese high.

By ten, the food was ready as ready could be, and Leah's head had started to ache with the constant chatter and clatter of pans.

"I'm going to help take drinks out to the men." She spread a linen tea towel over a tray of sandwiches. "Want to come?"

"I'd best check on my young ones." Rachel wiped her hands on a towel.

"Ja, me also," Naomi said. For a moment her eyes clouded, and Leah suspected she was mentally counting the hours until she'd have to get the children home and under the lights again. "Gut to see you both. We don't get to visit often enough." She gave them a quick hug and scurried off.

Rachel stood motionless for a moment, watching her. "I wonder sometimes," she said softly, for only Leah to hear. "I wonder if I would cope with such grace as Naomi does."

"You would," Leah murmured. "You do."

Rachel looked startled for a moment, and then she nodded. "Ja. But having a brother go English is not as bad as if the grief were for my husband or my child. I think of her often."

Leah nodded. She knew that Rachel really meant she prayed for Naomi, just as she did.

When Leah emerged from the house carrying a pitcher and paper cups, she had to blink at the scene that met her gaze. The ribs of the new barn rose toward the sky, the uprights pale and new-looking. They swarmed with men, busy as so many worker bees.

In their black pants, colored shirts, and straw hats, they might have looked alike to someone else, but she picked out individual people easily. There was Daad, consulting with Ammon Esh, who had overseen every barn raising in the valley since before she could remember.

Mahlon was up in the rafters, where he loved to be. Her breath caught as he walked along a beam as easily as strolling down the road. He'd always had a head for heights. He was the one called on when the kitten got too far up the tree or a kite was stuck in the branches.

Levi, hammer in hand, pounded away steadily and methodically, as he did everything.

Her brother Joseph wasn't hard to find, since he was running the gas-powered winch that carried materials up to the top. Joseph's talent with machinery was put to good use today.

Daniel worked not far from him, frowning a little as he framed in a door. She looked for Matthew and found him with the crew of young boys who were fetching and carrying for the men. They learned as they watched, handed nails, and held boards. In a few years they'd be taking their places in the work crew.

Was Elizabeth here today? She hadn't seen her yet. The child worried her, especially after the incident at the rehearsal. She'd smoothed it over with Elizabeth, encouraging her to try again. Still, it worried her. Maybe she should have talked with Daniel about it, but she didn't want to make too much of it.

She waved at Naomi, who had joined the cluster of younger children, and carried her pitcher and paper cups toward the barn.

She'd start with Joseph, since she hadn't seen him in more than a week.

"Leah." His face lit when he saw her. "I wondered when you were going to remember your thirsty brother."

She gave him a quick hug. "Thirsty, indeed," she teased. "Looks to me as if you have it easy here in the shade with your machine."

He grinned. "Daad always says, use your head and you won't have to use your feet. Have you seen Myra yet?"

"Not to talk to so far, but I'll catch up with her soon."

There was a movement beside her, and she turned to find Matthew, staring at Joseph's contraption with fascination.

"Matthew." She touched his shoulder. "Joseph, this is our new neighbor, Matthew Glick. Matthew, my brother Joseph."

Joseph nodded to the boy with his usual friendly smile. Matthew seemed almost too engrossed in the machinery to pay proper heed to the introductions.

"Did you make that?" he asked.

"I did. Are you interested in machinery?" Without waiting for the obvious answer, Joseph began describing how the winch worked, how he'd built it, and why it was an improvement over the last one.

Knowing that once Joseph had started on his precious machinery he'd go on for ages, Leah left his cup of water for him and started working her way along the perimeter of the barn.

In a few minutes she'd come to Daniel. "Water, Daniel?"

He put down his tools and took the cup she held out. He drained it quickly, the strong muscles of his neck working.

"Gut." He handed her back the cup and wiped his forehead

with the back of his arm, resettling his hat. "Though it might feel better to pour it over my head."

"I can give you another for that," she offered.

He shook his head, smiling, but then he seemed to sober as he glanced toward his son. "Is that another of your brothers?"

"Joseph. He's between me and Mahlon in age. He has the farm machinery shop."

Daniel's face tightened with a concern she didn't understand. "I hope Matthew isn't being a pest."

"Not at all. Joseph loves to find someone as interested in machinery as he is."

"Matthew is that." For some reason, that seemed to deepen his frown. Was he imagining his son deserting the farm to run a shop, like Joseph?

"A farmer has to know how to take care of his equipment as well as his animals," she said.

"Ja." He picked up his hammer and turned back to the door frame.

Well, that was that. Her conversations with Daniel always seemed to end in frustration, if not outright annoyance. And yet she couldn't help being drawn to him, which made no sense at all.

By the time she returned from the barn, tables were being set up under the trees. She joined her sister-in-law Myra in covering them with tablecloths.

"I saw you talking with Daniel Glick," Myra said as the table-cloth billowed between them. "Nice to have a new neighbor who is so helpful. And single and good-looking, too."

Leah pulled her end of the cloth down sharply. Apparently the matchmaking had reached further than she'd thought.

"He's very nice," she said flatly. "And how are you? It's hard to believe, it is, that you and Joseph have been wed six months already. It seems yesterday that you were getting back from your wedding trip."

"It seems that way to me, too," Myra said, a flush coming up in her fair skin. "Being married is wonderful gut, Leah."

The implication that she should try it wasn't lost on Leah. She'd expected shy, sweet Myra, who always seemed a bit in awe of her schoolteacher sister-in-law, to refrain from joining the matchmaking.

"When you find the right person it is," Leah said firmly. "You and Joseph are so gut together that it makes work light."

"We are that." The flush deepened, but at least she was distracted from marrying off Leah. "I'm not telling anyone else yet, but I wanted to tell you. I think, I pray, I might be pregnant."

Leah went quickly to put her arms around Myra. "That would make us all so happy."

"Don't tell," Myra cautioned. "I want to wait until I'm sure. But keeping it in today just seemed too hard—I had to tell someone or I'd burst."

"I won't say anything," Leah assured her. She hugged her again.

Surely that wasn't a tinge of envy she felt, was it? That would be wrong, and foolish besides.

"I just—" Myra hesitated, then seemed to gather up her courage to go on. "You are always so kind, Leah. You make me feel welcome in the family. I wish for you the happiness I feel, and Daniel seems so right for you. Especially since—"

She stopped, but Leah thought she could fill in the rest of that

sentence. Especially since Johnny Kile had come back to the valley, making everyone fear that he might lure her away.

"I'm happy as I am," she said, turning away. "Now I think it's
time to start getting the food ready to come out."

But she couldn't ignore the feeling, as she walked toward the
kitchen, that gazes followed her, then turned to Daniel as folks
wondered and speculated and wanted to make something happen
that wouldn't be.

She loved her community—loved the closeness, the mutual
support, the love of God and each other that made them strong—
but at moments like this, she almost wished they didn't care so
much.

Chapter Ten

"*Da Herr sei mit du*. God be with you." Verena Stoltzfus stood in the kitchen doorway, waving good-bye to another buggy-load of folks headed for home. She turned back to Leah, who was up to her elbows in hot, soapy water at the sink.

"Leah, it's kind of you to stay, but are you sure you don't want to go along home already?"

"I'm fine, Verena. Barbara and Mamm took the children home, so I'm free to stay as long as you need help." She waved a soapy hand.

Verena heaved what might have been a sigh of relief. "I'll go and bring the rest of the crockery in from the table, then."

The screen door banged behind her, and the farmhouse kitchen filled with quiet after the hustle and bustle of the afternoon. The day was winding down, though she could still hear the occasional shout of a child from the kickball game in the backyard.

She looked out the window over the sink. A fine new barn stood where there'd once been nothing but charred timbers. It was complete down to the coat of red paint that was probably still wet in places. Even as she watched, the oldest Stoltzfus boy led the cows in for the evening milking.

Many of the women had left, ready to get their children settled for the night. Some of the men lingered, though, a cluster of them standing looking at their handiwork, or maybe rehashing the building of it, others sitting on the grass, gossiping.

She concentrated on washing the large platter with its design of hearts and birds. By her count, five people had commented to her today on what a fine man Daniel Glick was. Three others, bolder, had come right out and said she'd be a gut mother to his kinder.

It had been a long afternoon.

The door swung open with a rattle of dishes on a tray. She glanced over, prepared to see Verena. She didn't. It was Daniel.

He stopped, probably startled by the glare she sent his way, and then he crossed the room and set the tray carefully on the table.

"Verena sent me in for a basket of leftovers she'd fixed for the family."

She felt sure that wasn't Verena's only reason. She nodded toward the basket, waiting on the dry sink. "It's there."

Daniel made no move to pick it up. Instead, he walked over to stand next to her. "Have I done something to offend you, Teacher Leah?"

It wasn't fair to take her frustrations out on Daniel. "No. But I see that they're still at it."

His eyebrows lifted. "At what?"

"Matchmaking." She snapped out the word. "Don't tell me you haven't noticed."

He braced his hands on the counter next to her, his expression more amused than offended. "No, I can't say I have."

"Didn't you wonder why Verena sent you into the kitchen for the basket, instead of carrying it out to you, which would be much more natural?" She blew out an exasperated breath. "She wants to get us alone together, and she decided this would do it."

There was definitely a twinkle in his blue eyes now. "So we are. It's not such a bad thing, is it, to talk with me for a moment?"

She set the platter down carefully. "I seem to remember that our conversations often end up in disagreement."

"That's one way to get to know someone."

He was close to her, so close that the sleeve of his blue work shirt brushed her arm. He smelled of soap and good, honest work, and his hands were strong where they pressed against the counter.

She drew her hands from the soapy water and dried them, using the movement to put a few more inches between them. "It's gut to know our neighbors," she said. "It's the idea that other people are trying to push us together that bothers me."

He turned so that he was facing her more fully, the deep blue of his gaze searching her face. "I can see that it does, but why? It amuses them, but it doesn't affect us."

"I don't like folks talking about me, wondering if I'm thinking of . . ." She stopped, not liking where that sentence was going.

His brow furrowed a little. "Perhaps their thoughts are running that way because John Kile has come back to the valley, not because of me."

She wanted to deny it, but that would be foolish when they both knew it to be true. "No one needs to worry about that.

What was between John and me was over a long time ago. It's just a memory."

"Memories can be powerful things." He said that as if he spoke from personal experience, and she wondered again about his wife.

"I am not affected by having John here."

"Yet you're volunteering at the clinic where he's working."

"I see him sometimes. But only in a working way, not even as friends." She hesitated, wondering why she was saying this to Daniel, of all people, a virtual stranger.

Maybe that was why. He didn't speak, and the moment stretched out.

Finally she let out her breath, trying to ease the tension that gripped her shoulders. "I don't even know him any longer. I have no intention of marrying, and if I did, it wouldn't be to him."

Daniel's gaze searched her face again, seeming to penetrate to her very soul, and she read nothing but kindness there. "This determination of yours not to wed—is it caused by John Kile's leaving?"

"Not by his leaving. By what it told me about myself."

She wanted the words back, but it was too late. They hung there in the air between them—the thing she hated to admit, even to herself.

She couldn't look at his face, so she focused on his hands instead, tightening on the edge of the counter. It was a long moment until he spoke.

"Leah." He touched her hand, a featherlight touch that was gone in an instant but that brought her startled gaze to his face. "I haven't known you for very long. But I can't imagine that whatever happened between you could possibly cause anyone to think ill of you. Or would cause you to think ill of yourself."

Her throat tightened at his perception, and it was a moment before she could speak. Maybe that was just as well. It was past time to get the conversation off her personal business.

"You are very kind, Daniel. Denke." She cleared her throat, trying to get control of her voice, which had gone suddenly soft. "Enough about my maidal state. You and your children are at least half the reason for this spate of matchmaking, you know."

He nodded, as if recognizing the barrier she'd chosen to put up. "True enough. A widower with young children is assumed to be in need of a wife."

There was something behind the light words, but she wasn't sure what it was. "You don't feel that way?"

He didn't move, and at first she thought he would ignore the question. But then he spoke.

"For a long time, I thought that I wouldn't marry again. Now—well, maybe the brethren are right that my children need a mother."

He frowned, and shutters seemed to close over the blue eyes that had been so warm and caring a moment ago.

"But if I wed again, there's one thing I'm sure of. The marriage will be based on common sense and shared needs. Not on love."

Daniel leaned against the smooth warmth of the cow's side, hands moving automatically in the milking rhythm. He'd been doing this since he was younger than Matthew, and sometimes he thought he could do it in his sleep. But he always found it comforting.

He glanced over toward his son, milking at the next stanchion. He couldn't see the boy's face—only his legs, spread out on the milking stool, and the movement of his hands.

"Gut job," he said. He glanced at the barn cats, lined up at each animal in anticipation. He aimed a squirt at the nearest cat, and she caught it deftly. "Give the cats a drink now already."

"I always miss," Matthew said, but then he aimed and squirted. The cat, surprised, took some of the milk on its face, but it quickly cleaned it off with a long pink tongue.

"Your aim is getting better." Daniel glanced down at the milk foaming into the bucket. "Next year we can add to our herd. Elizabeth will be big enough to help then."

"We'll need a bigger tank, ja," Matthew said.

It was satisfying, talking about the future of the farm with his son. It was something he'd once thought was robbed of him forever.

"We've been working on our program for the end-of-school picnic. Will you be there, Daadi?"

His heart seemed to clench that his boy had to even ask the question. "Certain sure," he said quickly. "I wouldn't miss it for anything."

That was one of the remnants of their time apart—that hesitation Matthew had to take it for granted that his father would be there. Daniel couldn't wonder at that, though every day he prayed it would soon be a thing of the past.

A year ago, he hadn't known what his children had done at the end of the school year. He hadn't known where they were or what they were feeling. Were they well? Did they cry for him? Had they forgotten him? The questions had haunted him for so long. But no more.

"What are you doing for the program?"

Matthew, his bucket full, carried it carefully to the cooler. "It's a surprise." He grinned as he passed, the expression so like the boy he'd been before Ruth took them away that it nearly brought tears to Daniel's eyes. "It's going to be outside, so folks can sit at the picnic tables, and Teacher Leah's brother came today to help."

"Ja? Levi came?" This natural conversation was so much better than the long weeks when every word from Matthew was strained and stilted.

"Joseph. The one that has the farm machine shop." His bucket empty, he came back. He paused, his eyes lighting up. "He helped us make a platform, and we used pulleys to put up real curtains that pull apart. He let me help with that, too, and showed me how the pulleys work."

Daniel swallowed his concerns about Matthew's fascination with all things mechanical. Nothing wrong with that, but he feared that interest would lead him past the things that were approved for Amish life and further, into things of the outside world.

He had taken too long to respond, and Matthew would be thinking that he disapproved. "It's gut of him to show you that. Useful, it will be, when we start bringing the hay in." He nodded toward the large pulleys, high above them, that would help with that work.

"Ja." Matthew studied them. "Maybe—"

But the door slid open then, and Jonah ran in, distracting Matthew from whatever idea he had.

"I finished my chores, Daadi. Can I help with the milking? I'm big enough."

Matthew suppressed a laugh.

"Well, let's see." Daniel took Jonah's small hands in his. "Maybe these hands are big enough to get some milk out. What do you think, Matthew?"

"Enough for the cat, maybe," Matthew said, beginning to clean up.

"I can fill a bucket," Jonah declared. "I can."

"Ah, but Daisy doesn't have a bucket left in her, I'm afraid. Here, you can help me get the last bit."

Guiding the boy's hands as they finished, he felt a sense of satisfaction move through him again. This was what he'd been missing. What the children had missed, too. Now that they were together again, everything would be well.

The contentment stayed with him as they started back toward the house. Sunlight slanted across the fields, and the boys romped ahead, playing tag. It had been right, moving to the valley. The children were happier. He had a gut farm. Next year they'd add to their dairy herd, and they'd make a fine living here.

But for now, he'd do well to think about what he was going to fix for supper. He'd never been much of a cook, but a man without a wife had to learn.

That reminded him of the conversation with Leah on Saturday at the barn raising. Strange, that they'd been so open with each other, but maybe it was good, too. They'd be easier with each other now.

"Daadi, Teacher Leah is coming!" Jonah cried, and set off at a run.

He looked toward the Beiler farm, shielding his eyes against the setting sun with his hand. Sure enough, Leah Beiler came toward them across the field, a basket on her arm.

He went quickly to the outside pump, folding back his sleeves. By the time she drew near, he'd done a quick washup.

"Teacher Leah. This is a nice surprise."

"It's even nicer than you know," she said, smiling. She lifted the towel that covered the basket's contents. "Mamm was making chicken potpie today for the family, and she made extra for you."

"It smells wonderful gut," he said, speaking no more than the truth. "It's kind of her to think of us." He lifted an eyebrow and said softly, "Matchmaking?"

"Probably." Leah's smile lit her eyes. "I've decided to ignore it."

"That's gut." It was better between them, now that they had this matchmaking business out in the open already. "I—"

A crash and a cry from the house cut off his words.

"Elizabeth!" He spun and ran toward the kitchen, vaguely aware of Leah following him, of the quick murmur of prayer from her. Elizabeth—

His heart twisted, and he bolted through the mudroom and into the kitchen.

"Was ist letz? What happened?"

Elizabeth had stumbled back against the table, her face white. She held her right hand outstretched, gripping the wrist with her left hand. Then he saw the skillet, tipped from the stove, sausage spilling onto the floor.

"She's burned." He lifted her in his arms, his mind racing. "The doctor—"

"Here." Leah brushed past him, shoving the basket onto the countertop and turning on the water full force in the sink. She grabbed a bowl and shoved it under the spigot. "Bring her here. We want to get the hand cooled off as quick as we can."

Leah had such an air of calm command that it didn't occur to him to argue. He carried his sobbing child to the sink, and Leah grasped the reddened hand and thrust it into the water.

"There, now, there." She held it firmly, in spite of Elizabeth's instinctive withdrawal. "Just leave it there, Elizabeth. The water will make it feel better. I promise it will."

"Maybe some butter," he said, with distant memories of his mother's remedies.

"That just seals in the heat. We need to get the heat out, and then it will stop hurting so."

Sure enough, Elizabeth's sobs lessened, and she leaned her head against his shoulder. The two boys pressed close, their eyes round, and Jonah's lower lip trembled.

Leah glanced at them. "Elizabeth is going to be fine," she said, still in that calm manner that he realized was her teacher attitude. "Matthew, do you think you can bring me some ice from the refrigerator?"

"Ja, Teacher Leah." Matthew hurried across the kitchen.

Jonah tugged at her skirt. "I want to help Elizabeth, too."

"Fine. You can get me some dish towels. Do you know where they are?"

Jonah nodded, scurrying to pull out the drawer that held dish towels, spilling several on the floor in his haste.

"Should I hitch up the buggy?" Daniel asked in a quiet undertone.

Leah turned the small hand, still in the water, studying it carefully. "I don't think so. I don't see any signs of blistering. Let's just keep cooling it down."

Matthew returned with the ice cubes, and she directed him to drop them into the bowl, giving him a quick smile of approval. Elizabeth whimpered a little, the sound tearing at Daniel's heart. Leah turned to her, patting her cheek.

"You're tired of leaning over to keep your hand in the water, I know," she said. "But it's making you better. I see you were cooking sausage."

"I was making supper for Daadi and the boys," she said. Her voice trembled. "But it's all spoiled."

"Elizabeth, I told you I would fix supper after the milking." He didn't want to scold her, but she shouldn't have attempted to manage that on her own.

"Well, the dog will have a fine meal instead. He'll be wanting to come inside," Leah said. "Luckily my mamm made a lot of extra chicken potpie today, so your daadi and the boys won't go hungry. Do you like chicken potpie?"

"Mmm-hmm." Elizabeth nodded.

"Maybe you can come over one day when she's making it and help her," Leah said. "Now, let's get you a little more comfortable."

She eased the hand out of the water. Elizabeth caught her breath when the air hit the burn, but Leah was there instantly with a cold compress, wrapping it gently.

"You can sit on Daadi's lap at the table." Leah deftly transferred the bowl of ice water and the extra towel to the table. "I'll clean up the sausage."

"You sit," Daniel said, urging her toward the chair. "I'll do better cleaning up, I think."

She didn't dispute it but sat down, taking Elizabeth on her lap, guarding her hand from any contact. His daughter leaned against her trustingly.

He turned away, bending to pick up the pan and sausages, glad to hide his face for a moment. His fear had subsided, but its remnants lingered, tight in his stomach, stinging his eyes. He hadn't been here, and Elizabeth had been hurt.

He dumped the pan and its contents into the sink. Matthew began picking out the sausage, putting it into the pail of scraps for the dog.

Daniel glanced toward the table. Elizabeth, calm now, leaned against Leah's shoulder, her gaze intent on Leah's face as Leah told her a story. Jonah leaned against her knee to listen as well.

His heart clenched. He'd admitted his children needed a mother. He was looking at the woman who would be perfect—for them and for him, if not for that dangerous link she kept to the outside world.

It had been natural enough to stay for supper with Daniel and the children, Leah told herself as she dried the last dish. She glanced out the window. The boys were practicing baseball in the backyard while Elizabeth watched from the porch, seeming to enjoy her invalid status at the moment.

Natural enough to stay, she repeated to herself, but now it was time to go home, before she gave folks even more to talk about than they had already. She was hanging the towel on the rack when Daniel came in the back door.

"Leah, you did not need to wash the dishes. I said that I would do them later."

He bent to stow the pail he carried under the sink. His hair was thick, growing vigorously from the whorl on the top of his head, and the brown had lightened where the sun hit it.

"It made no trouble," she said. She'd best be going home, if she was noticing things like that about her neighbor. "I'm just happy that Elizabeth is all right."

He straightened. "You don't think I need to have a doctor look at it?"

"Well, I'm not a doctor, for sure. But my brothers managed to hurt themselves on a regular basis, and Anna wasn't far behind, so I've seen my share of burns. I think it will be fine, as long as you keep it clean and put the burn ointment on it often."

"That much I can do." His voice roughened. "Even if I did let her get hurt."

Her heart twisted, but she kept her voice firm, even tart. "That's nonsense, Daniel, and you know it. Children hurt themselves."

"Not like that." His face tightened with pain. "You told me that she was trying too hard to be perfect, and I didn't listen to you. And this is the result."

"I certainly wasn't imagining anything like this. I just thought that it worried her too much when she didn't do things perfectly."

"She shouldn't have tried to fix supper." He glared at the gas stove, as if it were to blame. "I should have come in from the barn more quickly or taken her out with me and the boys."

"It's natural to blame yourself when a child in your care is injured." She knew that well enough as a teacher. "But you couldn't have predicted that would happen. As for her attempts to be perfect—" She hesitated, but it had to be said. "Have you thought that maybe she is trying to take her mother's place?"

He stared at her, eyes wide and appalled. "No." He tried to push the thought away with his hands. "No. I never wanted, never expected—" He stopped, seeming to catch his breath. "I've never wanted Elizabeth to do more than the chores that would be normal for a child her age."

"I'm sure that's true. I didn't mean that it was coming from you. But often a girl models herself on her mother, and she may be sensing the lack—"

She stopped, because he was shaking his head. Because he disagreed with her? Or because he feared what she said was true?

"Have you talked to her much about her mother?" she asked gently.

Anger flared in his eyes at that. "No. Do you think I wanted to remind them of that time when we were apart? I want them to forget that. To forget that they ever lived in the English world."

"They can't forget their mother." Didn't he see how wrong that would be?

His face twisted. "How do I separate it? How do I divide what I feel about what Ruth did—" He stopped. Shook his head. "You don't understand. She took my children away. For two years I didn't see them. I didn't know where they were. I didn't even know if they were alive or dead."

His voice broke. Hurting for him, she put her hand on his arm, feeling the muscles so tight it seemed they'd never release.

"I'm sorry. That's the worst thing I can imagine."

To be without your children was dreadful enough. Not to even know if they were alive—the utter desolation of it swept her soul.

"Ja." He took a strangled breath. "I didn't go to the law. That's not the Amish way. But now I wonder if I did right. Ruth—" He

shook his head. "When she said she'd marry me, I was the luck-
iest man in the world, I thought. She was so bright, so lively, so
happy that she made everyone else smile, just to be near her. Half
the Amish boys in the county wanted to marry her, but she
picked me."

Did he even realize he was telling her this? Or was he just talking out of a soul-deep need to say it out loud to someone? It
didn't matter. If all she could do was listen, she'd listen.

"Something went wrong," she said softly.

"Ja." His voice was rough. "When the babies were born, she
seemed so happy, but afterward—she couldn't settle down to
being a wife and mother. She always wanted more. Not more
things, you understand. Just—" He shrugged, as if he couldn't
find the words for it. "She was restless, always. As if looking for
something and not knowing what it was."

He stopped. Blaming himself for that, the way he'd blamed
himself for Elizabeth's accident?

"She started working at a quilt shop that her cousin ran. Lots
of English shopped there, some of them taking lessons in quilting. She started wanting to be like them—to wear pretty clothes,
have everyone looking at her the way they did when she was a
girl." He spread his hands. "I tried to understand, tried to pay
more attention to her, tried to make her happy. What did she
want?" He sounded baffled.

She hurt for him, sympathized with him. But somewhere in
her heart, she had sympathy for Ruth as well. She'd known what
it was like to long for more.

Not pretty clothes, like Ruth. But more learning, more knowledge, more experiences than she could ever have in Pleasant
Valley.

"I don't know," she said softly. "Maybe she didn't know, either."

"She took my children." The pain in his voice was as fresh as if it had happened yesterday. "Two years, and every minute of it I was asking God to keep them safe and bring them back to me."

"He answered your prayer."

"Ja. But Ruth—" His lips twisted. "The state police troopers came to tell me. How she'd been out with a man. Drinking, both of them, and she was driving. She ran the car into a tree. The police went to the place where she'd been living—a couple of rooms, it was. They found the children there alone. Nothing to eat, no one to watch them."

She made a small sound of pain and distress.

He looked at her. "Ja. I forgive her, because God commands it. I try to forget, and that's what I want my children to do. That's what they must do." He sounded desperate.

He had trusted her with this, and she had to do the best for him she could. That meant she had to say something he wouldn't want to hear.

"I understand why you feel you can't talk to the children about it," she said carefully. "But I think Elizabeth needs to talk to someone. Some adult who can help her sort it all out, help her find out why she's trying so hard to be grown-up before her time." She hesitated. "There is a woman at the clinic, a psychologist. I think she could help Elizabeth—"

"No." It came swift and hard. "I will not turn to the English to help my daughter. She cannot help a child adjust to being Amish."

It was on the tip of her tongue to say that Lydia had once been

Amish, but that would hardly recommend her to Daniel under the circumstances.

"Elizabeth needs help," she said. "Perhaps maybe more than you can give her. There's no shame in seeking out a specialist when you need one."

His hands shot out to grasp hers in a firm, warm grip. She couldn't turn away from the intensity in his eyes. "We are an Amish community. You are the teacher, with more knowledge and experience than most. You are our specialist. You can help her."

All her instincts told her to refuse. Told her that deeper involvement with Daniel and his family could only lead to difficulty later.

But her heart was thudding to the beat of the pulse she felt in his hands, and his need struck at her core. She couldn't say no. She was afraid to say yes.

She took a breath. "All right," she said, feeling as if she took a step from which there was no going back. "I'll try."

CHAPTER ELEVEN

She was being confronted with one thing after another that she didn't feel capable of handling. Leah gripped the set of interview papers in her hands as her taxi driver, Ben Morgan, the elderly Englischer who enjoyed driving the Amish for a small fee, stopped in front of the clinic.

It was the last week of school, and she should be dealing with a hundred last-minute details for the picnic and program. But Johnny had recommended she do a trial interview and bring the forms in to discuss with him before she started working on the project in earnest once school was out, so here she was.

Thanking Ben, who had brought a book and announced his plan to park in the shade and wait for her, she headed for the door, her mind going faster than the car had.

She was avoiding thinking about the most serious problem facing her, she knew. Elizabeth Glick. How had she let Daniel persuade her to attempt to counsel Elizabeth? A wave of panic went through her. She wasn't equipped to do that. What if she tried and made things worse?

Father, was I becoming too confident, too prideful in my own abilities? Have You sent me these things to show me that it is You, and You only, who is capable? Guide me, Lord, and show me the path You would have me follow. Amen.

Taking a deep breath, she opened the door to the clinic.

Two Amish families waited in the reception area, and she stopped to greet them. It gave her a breathing space before she realized that she was stalling, putting off the moment when she'd see Johnny again.

With a final smile for the children, she removed her bonnet, hanging it on a peg in the hallway, and entered the door to the research side of the building. A young man with long hair tied back at the nape of his neck glanced at her, dark eyes curious, before turning back to something he was doing with vials of blood.

He didn't challenge her, so she walked down the hallway. Perhaps she should have asked Johnny exactly where she was to meet him. The place still felt alien to her, with its whirring noises and the equipment whose function she couldn't even guess.

The young woman she'd met on her first visit—Stacie, her name was—walked swiftly out of the computer room and came to a dead stop when she saw Leah. "Oh. It's you."

"Yes." There seemed no other answer to that question. Who else would she be? "I am supposed to meet John Kile this afternoon. Can you tell me where he is?"

"He's not here. He asked me to go over the interview form with you and make sure you know how to do it properly."

Her tone said that she doubted that was even possible, and her demeanor was so unwelcoming that Leah wanted to flee.

"I can come again when John is here—" she began, but Stacie cut her off with a decisive shake of her head.

"Dr. Brandenmyer has him assigned to a much more important project." Stacie held out her hand. "Let me see them. I'll have to take time from my work to catch your mistakes, I suppose."

Leah had been treated more rudely than that at other times, she supposed. Most Amish had. But she wasn't sure it had ever bothered her quite so much. When a tourist stuck a camera in your face, it was rude, but it was also not aimed at you, specifically. Any Amish person would do.

Stacie's attitude was personal, and she had no idea how to handle it.

Submit. The word echoed in her mind. That was the Christian response, the Amish response.

She nodded, not speaking, and followed Stacie to a desk. Stacie flung herself into the chair behind the desk, fanning the interview sheets out in front of her. Leah perched on the edge of the chair opposite her, folded her hands in her lap, and waited.

Frowning, Stacie stuck a pencil into her mass of dark hair and stared at the papers. Leah forced down her resentment that the woman obviously expected to find something wrong. Of course there would be something. That was why she was here—to be corrected, so that she would do it right in the future.

Still, she'd rather have met with John. Only because he'd have done this in a friendly manner, she assured herself. Not because she wanted to see him again.

But it was better this way. The Ordnung—the rules by which

the congregation lived, discussed and prayerfully accepted by the people—would find her meeting with an English woman on a matter of business perfectly acceptable. Meeting with a person who was under the bann was considerably trickier.

That could be done, of course. She knew families who lived that way, setting a separate table for those under the meidung, so that they didn't actually break bread together. Would the Kile family come to that, eventually? She couldn't guess.

Stacie came to the end of the form and tapped it with her pencil. "Not bad," she said, her tone grudging. "Going back several generations is helpful, but only if it's accurate. How can you be sure some of these are facts, not just family stories?"

Family stories *were* facts, but it was hardly worth arguing the point.

"The information came from the genealogical records in the family Bible," she said. "Amish families usually keep very complete records. However, if you don't wish me to provide that—"

Stacie shook her head quickly. "No, don't stop. It's great as long as you make accurate notes. I don't suppose you could get a photocopy of the Bible page and bring it in, so we wouldn't have to rely on your accuracy."

Leah tried counting to ten. Supposedly that helped one control an unruly temper. "I don't believe the families would like to have the Bibles taken out of the house to be copied."

"This will have to do, then." Stacie shuffled the papers together and put a paper clip on them. "If you could type instead of print them, it'd be easier to read, but I guess you Amish don't use newfangled inventions like typewriters, do you?"

Leah wanted to ask the woman why, if she looked down on the Amish so much, she was involved in research here. She didn't.

She kept her voice colorless. "We do use typewriters in business, but I don't have access to one, and I'm sure I can print them more quickly."

"And Leah always had the neatest printing in the whole class," said a voice behind her.

"Johnny." She couldn't stem her pleasure at the sight of his warm smile as he came in, dropping a case of some sort on the nearest desk. It was a joy to see any friendly face after Stacie's open antagonism. "I thought you weren't here today."

"Just got back." He moved toward her with such enthusiasm she thought for a moment that he intended to hug her, but then he seemed to recall himself and touched her shoulder lightly instead.

"You brought back all the information?" Stacie interrupted.

"The files are on my computer," Johnny said, turning his attention to her, and then embarked upon a discussion that was so technical that, to Leah, they might as well have been speaking in Russian.

Today he wore what she supposed was a business shirt, with a collar that buttoned down and a tie. How long, she wondered, had it taken him to learn how to tie one of those? How long to feel comfortable with a belt instead of suspenders?

Johnny swung back to her so quickly that perhaps he'd felt her looking at him. "If you're finished, let's go have a cup of coffee or a sandwich. We have a lot of catching up to do."

He smiled at her, and she was transported into the past, becoming again the young girl whose pulse had fluttered when he'd held out his hand to her at a danze with just that smile.

And that was why it was so dangerous. She wasn't that girl now, and Johnny wasn't that boy.

"I don't think—"

His mood changed, lightning fast as always. "You're not going to let some ridiculous rules stand in the way of talking to an old friend, are you?"

He should know her well enough to know that he was making her uncomfortable.

"I can't."

"Leah promised to have tea with me today." Lydia Weaver emerged from behind one of the shoulder-high partitions in the room. She smiled at Leah. "If you're ready, I have the water hot."

"That is kind of you," Leah said quickly. She walked away from Johnny without looking back.

You have rescued me again," Leah said as soon as the door of Lydia's office closed behind them. "But it is not necessary to give me tea."

"It is a pleasure to give you tea," Lydia replied, nodding toward the rocking chair Leah had taken the last time and busying herself with the tea things. "And I don't think you needed rescuing. It was obvious from your face that you would say no to John's invitation, not because of the Ordnung but because that was what your conscience told you to do."

Leah sat, the rocker giving instant comfort. "I don't want to be unkind to him, but as much as I like seeing him again, I'm not sure it's wise to spend time alone with him."

"John Kile is a gifted researcher, but he doesn't understand people well, including himself. He wants two contradictory things at the same time." Lydia set the cup of tea on the table next to Leah.

Leah appreciated the gesture. Lydia was, without making an issue of it, allowing Leah not to have to take the cup from her hand, which was the letter of the law in most communities in regard to eating and drinking with those under the meidung.

Johnny, on the other hand, had been only too ready to make an issue of it.

Lydia sat down opposite her, holding her own cup. She seemed very willing to let the silence stretch out comfortably between them.

Leah sipped the hot, fragrant brew. Her thoughts drifted to the past, measuring the Johnny she knew against Lydia's words.

"You're right," she said finally. "When he was a child, if he had to choose between a jumble cookie and a snickerdoodle, he'd end up with none if he couldn't have both."

Sharing a laugh with Lydia dissipated the last of her tension, but it still left a question in Leah's mind.

"Tell me, if you will. Is Stacie like that with everyone or just with me?"

"Especially with you." Lydia smiled. "Although, like many researchers, she is impatient of anything that gets in the way of her work, including good manners."

"But why? She doesn't even know me."

Lydia's pale eyebrows quirked. "I think you know the answer to that, don't you? She's interested in John."

"Well, but—" Leah paused, trying to assimilate that. She would want for John to find someone to love, wouldn't she? "I'm not a threat to a relationship she might have with Johnny."

"Aren't you?"

"You mean she knows that we once planned to marry, and she's jealous? But I can't compare to her."

"You're his first love," Lydia said. "She's afraid that knowing you again will make him realize that you are what he wants."

She wanted to deny it, to say it couldn't be. In a way, this was the opposite of her experience. Those who loved her were pushing her toward Daniel because they feared she would be lured to the English world by her first love. Meanwhile, the person who loved John feared that Leah would draw him back to the Amish world.

She shook her head finally. "He would never return. She doesn't have to worry about that. But if she cares about him, why is she so derisive of the life that he came from? She has so many misconceptions about the Amish that it's hard to understand why she's here."

Lydia shrugged. "As for that, I think the research is all that matters to her. The Amish are only of interest because their custom of marrying within the church provides such a classic genetic workshop."

"You could clear up some of her false ideas," Leah suggested.

"I could." Lydia looked down at her cup. "Not doing so is one of the accommodations I make to get along in the English world."

Leah didn't know how to respond to that. It seemed that jumping the fence was not so simple as shedding one life and picking up another.

They were quiet again for a few minutes. Leah let her gaze drift over the wall of books behind Lydia's desk. How much pleasure must it be to have a room like this, with more books than you could have time to read?

"May I . . ." She hesitated. Daniel would not allow her to bring Elizabeth to see Lydia. But there was no reason why she couldn't use the woman as a resource if Lydia were willing. "May I ask you—consult you—about something?"

"Of course."

"I've been asked to help a family." She chose her words carefully. "The three children were taken away from their Amish home by their mother. They lived in the English world for two years before she died in an accident, and then they came back to their father."

There, that was a neat, anonymous recounting of the facts. Lydia wasn't from the community, so she was unlikely to know about Daniel and his family.

"They're having problems adjusting?" Lydia looked interested. Probably something like this didn't come her way very often.

"The middle child, the only girl, is eight, one of my scholars. She is so determined to be perfect at everything she does that she becomes overly upset when she can't." She censored herself, not feeling she should trust Lydia with the story of Elizabeth's injury. "She wants to take on duties that a woman would do, instead of a child's chores."

"Does the father push her to do that?"

"No. Just the opposite, in fact. He's very concerned about her." She hesitated. Her opinions weren't facts, but perhaps it would help Lydia to know them. "I wondered if she's trying to emulate her mother, but her father doesn't agree. He has difficulty talking with them about their time in the outside world."

Lydia nodded slowly, as if she sifted the facts through her mind. "Would he allow me to see his daughter?"

"I suggested that already. He refused. He feels that I am the one to help her." She opened her hand, as if exposing her inadequacy. "I know how ill equipped I am to do any such thing. But if I don't help, there will be no one."

"I don't think I can counsel at secondhand," Lydia said.

Leah's heart sank. She hadn't realized until that moment how much she'd hoped for from Lydia.

"But what do your own instincts tell you the child needs?"

"To talk to an adult who cares about her," Leah said promptly. "Probably not her father, since he finds it so hard. Someone who will listen and reassure her."

Lydia smiled. "You're a good teacher, I'm sure. Your instincts are sound." She stood, going to the bookshelves. "I may not be able to counsel her, but I can lend you some materials that might give you guidance."

"That would be so appreciated." Leah stood, accepting the books as Lydia pulled them from the shelves and handed them to her.

Lydia's hand rested for a moment on the stack of books. "Just—be careful. What you are doing is risky, both for the child and for you."

"For me?"

Lydia studied her face intently. "It is difficult enough in a counseling situation to stay detached from the client's problems. In your case, I think that will be nearly impossible. You'll risk caring too much."

Lydia's words gripped her heart. She'd failed Johnny when it came to caring enough. She couldn't fail a child who depended on her.

"I can only do my best and trust God with it," she said.

"Da Herr sei mit du," Lydia said softly, like a benediction. "The Lord be with you."

Leah pressed her hand. She'd reached the door when Lydia spoke again.

"One thing you should be aware of. In the situation you describe, chances are good the little girl isn't the only one affected. The whole family may need help in working through their feelings about the mother." She paused. "Especially the father."

Daniel. Daniel might need help. But he wouldn't allow her anywhere near his feelings about his dead wife, would he?

The makeshift curtains, probably sheets from someone's bed, pulled together for the final time, and the audience, gathered on benches under the trees in the schoolyard, burst into applause. Daniel clapped as heartily as the rest.

Every parent was nervous when his or her child performed, of course, but he might have been more jittery than most. This was his children's first end-of-school program in Pleasant Valley, and it was more than a marking of the end of classes for him. It was another sign of their belonging here.

The scholars marched out, beaming broadly now that the difficult part was over, and the audience clapped again, the clapping growing deafening when Teacher Leah appeared. The community must realize how fortunate they were to have such a dedicated, skillful teacher.

Lest he be caught staring at Teacher Leah, he sought out his own young ones. He'd held his breath while Elizabeth said her part, fearful of what might happen if she faltered. She'd held her friend Becky's hand and been letter-perfect.

The curtains, operated with care by Matthew and another boy, had opened and closed on cue, something that clearly mattered to Matthew far more than the piece he'd gotten through.

As for Jonah—well, Jonah forgot his poem before he reached the end and turned to the assistant teacher to be prompted with such an engaging grin that everyone had chuckled.

Women started uncovering the dishes that marched down the centers of the rows of tables, while the men moved benches and tried to stay out of their way. A buzz of conversation and laughter filled the air.

On an afternoon like this, with the sun shining, the church family around him, and all going well, he wondered why he'd told Leah all that he had. More, why he'd asked for her help.

They were going to be all right. Surely that incident with Elizabeth had been a onetime thing. He'd talked to her, getting her to promise that she'd never again try anything so foolish.

Still, he had to admit that it might be gut for Elizabeth to spend time with a woman she admired as she did Teacher Leah. He disliked Leah's continued association with her former sweetheart, but he couldn't doubt that she had the interest of the children at heart.

Elias Beiler, Leah's father, came over to him, a broad smile on his face. "They've done well, those young ones of our Leah's, haven't they?"

"They have indeed. I was just thinking that the community is fortunate in our teacher."

Since Leah's father was looking at her, it seemed natural that Daniel look as well. The excitement of the day had brought a flush to Leah's cheeks, and her green eyes sparkled with pleasure.

"I understand we're to have your little Elizabeth around a bit this summer," Elias said.

Daniel nodded. "I hope she won't be in the way of things your wife is doing."

Leah and her mother had hatched a plan whereby they would teach Elizabeth quilting over the summer. He didn't doubt that the teaching would branch into some cooking and baking and other things that girls her age were normally learning from their own mothers.

"Not a bit of it," Elias said quickly. "My Mattie loves showing young ones how to do things, and your Elizabeth is a sweet, quiet child, not like those schnickelfritzes of our Levi."

Since the two young boys in question were wrestling in the grass at the moment, the comment seemed apt, but Elias looked at them with an indulgent eye.

"Elizabeth will enjoy it, I know. My mamm and daad hope to come for a long visit, but with my sister about to give birth, they won't get away for another month or two, at least."

"Well, they'll be most welcome any time."

Another man wandered over with a comment about the corn crop, and the conversation turned more general. Daniel listened attentively, figuring that Elias, like his own father, had no doubt forgotten more about farming than he'd learn in a lifetime.

His gaze wandered over the crowd while they talked. Elizabeth and Becky were helping Rachel, Becky's mamm, spread things on the table for lunch. It looked as if they'd all be called to the food shortly. Bishop Mose Yoder, white-bearded and saintly, stood at the head of one of the tables, surveying the food he'd be called upon to bless.

Fortunate, Daniel thought again. The Lord had blessed the families that settled in Pleasant Valley. He had been right to bring the children here. With no reminders of Ruth, it was easier to forget.

Jonah raced by, and Daniel reached out to collar his youngest. "We'll be eating soon. You'd best wash your hands. Where is your brother?"

"I dunno, Daadi." Released, Jonah ran off in the general direction of the outside pump.

Scanning the hosts of children, Daniel failed to come up with Matthew. But Leah moved toward him, her smile a little tentative. Perhaps she worried that her knowing so much about his past would make the situation uncomfortable between them.

"A grand program, Teacher Leah."

Her smile eased. "The scholars did well, I thought."

"Speaking of scholars, do you know where Matthew is? We're about ready to eat."

She glanced around. "He and Thomas were taking the curtains down. They're probably packing up in the schoolroom."

With a nod, he retreated toward the schoolhouse. The trouble with talking to Leah was that he always wanted to prolong the conversation. But when he did, it seemed they got into things he'd rather not discuss. Or into a disagreement.

The door stood open. He stepped inside. Sure enough, the two boys were there, but they didn't seem to be putting things away. Ropes, pulleys, and curtains lay on the floor between them, and they faced each other like two roosters squaring off over who was to rule the henhouse.

"I tell you I did." Matthew's voice was shrill. "I flew on an airplane and I rode on a motorcycle, and lots of other stuff, too."

"I don't believe it." The other boy's jaw came out. "You're making it all up, Matthew Glick. When did you do all those things, tell me that?"

"When I was English." Matthew practically shouted the words. "When I was English."

It was like an axe handle to the belly. Daniel grabbed the door, just to keep standing upright as the wave of fury hit him.

Ruth. This was Ruth's fault. His children would never really be his again because of her betrayal.

He knew, in that moment, that he'd been lying to himself. Lying to Leah, too, for that matter. Because he hadn't forgiven Ruth. She was six months dead, and he hadn't forgiven her at all.

Chapter Twelve

*L*eah closed the kitchen door behind her, shutting out the sound of her two nephews squabbling over a toy train, and crossed the covered walkway that led to the daadi haus. Mamm had seemed unusually quiet at supper, and since Daadi had gone out, she'd best check on her.

She tapped gently as she opened the door. "Mamm?"

How many times over the years had she come this way to see Grossmutter? She'd invariably found her grandmother in the rocking chair by the window, fingers busy with a quilt for someone's new baby or a hooked rug to cover a bedroom floor on cold mornings.

Now it was Mamm who looked up with a smile from that same rocker. Instead of a quilt patch, her lap was covered with the massive family Bible.

"Leah. Am I needed for something?" She started to close the Bible.

"Nothing at all." Leah went quickly to pull a chair over next to her. "I thought you might like a little visit is all. But if you're busy reading—"

"Not reading," Mamm said, patting the Bible, which Leah saw was opened to the family tree that covered several pages in the front of the book. "Just remembering. Come sit with me if you have time."

Leah sat, guilt crowding in on her. She was busy, but she could have found the time to sit quietly with Mamm more often.

She leaned on the arm of her mother's chair to scan the fine, faded printing on the genealogy chart. Since her work with the clinic, she'd never look at a family tree in the same way again.

"What are you remembering, Mamm?" She looked more closely, realizing it was the Lapp family Bible—her mother's family. "I didn't realize you had this one. I thought Uncle Jacob and Aunt Emma kept it." The Bible, like the farm, usually went to the oldest son of the family.

"Ja, they do, but Em wanted me to fill in names and dates for Levi and Barbara's children." Mamm's finger traced a line. "Look, there is me and all my brothers and sisters. Twelve of us, there were. Such a noise when we sat down to supper that you couldn't hear yourself think."

"I can imagine." She squinted to read the faded ink in the failing light. "Was that Uncle Mose who came after Jacob?"

"Elizabeth," Mamm corrected, her fingers seeming to caress the page. "Elizabeth came next, you remember. Only eight when she died."

Again her newly acquired information surfaced. "Was she ill, Mamm? What did she die of?"

"She fell." Tears glistened in her mother's eyes. "Such a daring girl she was. Like our Anna. Always had to try and climb the highest or run the fastest."

"I'm sorry. You were close."

"Only thirteen months apart." Mamm wiped away a tear that had spilled onto her cheek. "Ach, it's foolish to cry. She has been safe in God's hands these many years, but still, sometimes in my mind I see her scrambling up that tree."

Leah clasped the hand that had always been so strong, so comforting. Frailer now, but still, the comfort was there. "I wish I could have known her."

Her mother seemed to look into the past. "I wonder, sometimes. What would she have been like as a woman? How many babies would she have had?" She smiled a little. "Brothers are fine, in their way, but sisters are closer, I think. Ain't so?"

"I guess so." Were she and Anna close? Once she'd thought so, but that had changed in recent years. It was as if the gap between their ages had suddenly started to matter more, instead of less.

"Uncle Jofie, now, he and his twin sister were close as could be, but maybe that came of bein' twins. You remember him, don't you?"

Since Uncle Jofie, for whom her brother Joseph was named, had died before she was born, she didn't. "I remember you talking about him."

"You remember him," Mamm repeated. "Hair the color of ripe horse-chestnuts he had. You remember."

"Uncle Jofie died before I was born." She forced her voice to gentleness, trying to deny the panic that rose in her. Did Mamm really not realize—

"Ach, how foolish." Her mother shook her head. "Of course you don't remember Jofie. How silly I am. Seems like my memory gets mixed up sometimes, ever since I had that chemo."

"That must be it," Leah said soothingly. "Mammi, you're— If something is wrong, you'd tell me, wouldn't you?"

Her mother's gaze focused on her face. "Now I've scared you, making you think I'm getting sick again, when I'm fine. Just a touch forgetful now and again, is all."

Reassured, Leah smiled at her. "You seemed—well, a little tired and a bit confused."

"I'm fine." Her mother's voice seemed to gain strength on the words. "But you know, having the cancer showed me how true it is that our time is in His hands. God could call us at any moment."

"You beat the cancer." Leah infused confidence into the words. "You're going to be with us for many more years."

"If God wills." Her mother stroked the page. "There's comfort here, Leah, in looking at those I loved who are gone ahead of me. Here or in Heaven, I know I am surrounded by the family's love."

"I hadn't thought of it that way," Leah admitted.

She touched the page, running her fingers along the generations. Her family. Spread out through time and space, those were her kin.

The names of the women drifted through her mind like dandelion puffs carried on the breeze. They were women who had held their faith strong, who had passed it on to their children and their children's children. Women who mourned for those who died young and those who left, who rejoiced and welcomed those who came back.

Love welled in Leah's heart. She was connected to all of them.

She ran her finger down the page until she found her name. She was connected to all of them, but nothing led from her name. It sat there alone.

"We were more fortunate than some," her mother said. "Not many of our family jumped the fence to the outside world."

It almost sounded as if there were a question in that.

"That's right, Mammi. Not many from our family."

Her mother looked at her, and Leah had the feeling that she saw right into her heart.

"You are worrying about Anna. About what she's getting up to in her rumspringa."

"N-no." How had her mother guessed that? "I mean, not exactly. Our Anna is a smart girl."

"Smart, ja. But maybe not so much common sense as you had at her age."

"She'll be fine." *Please, God.*

"Everyone feels the pull of the world at one time or another," her mother said gently. "For Anna now it is pretty clothes and parties. For others—" Her mother hesitated. "For others it might be something different."

Something different. For an instant Leah was back in Lydia's office again. She knew what she'd really wanted, looking at all those books. She'd thought what a pleasure it would be to have Lydia's life, to be an educated woman with a serious job to do.

Mamm was right. The world tempted different people in different ways.

"Remember this, Leah." Mamm clasped her hand firmly, leaning toward her. "No matter what my children do, I will never stop loving them. Never."

A chill went down Leah's back. Were Mamm's words for Anna? Or for her?

Leah walked into the clinic for her reporting session with Stacie, a determined smile pinned to her face. She would not allow the woman to irritate her this time. As for Lydia's idea of what was behind it—well, she wasn't going to think about that at all.

But when she reached the desk, it wasn't Stacie who waited for her. It was John.

He rose, giving her that sweet smile that made him look like the boy he'd been once. If Lydia was right about Stacie's feelings, it would be that smile that had snared her heart.

"I'm looking for Stacie." She gestured with the sheaf of papers in her hand. "I have my latest interviews."

"Great." John took them from her. "But as you can see, Stacie is occupied." He waved a hand down the long row of computers. Stacie sat at the far end, frowning at the screen in front of her. At his movement, she transferred the frown to them.

"I can wait—" Leah began.

He shook his head, sitting down and riffling through the papers. "Not necessary. I've switched places with her for today. I'll go through the reports with you." That smile again. "Though if I know you, Teacher Leah, everything will be perfect."

Teacher Leah. Had he ever called her that before?

She could continue to argue, but he was looking at her in a faintly challenging manner, and the lift of his eyebrow seemed to dare her.

She sat down, and he turned to the forms.

Well, fine. She realized that her hands were clenched in her lap, and she smoothed the fingers out. This was business, and she would handle it that way. Meeting with Johnny would not be a difficulty either for the Ordnung or for her conscience.

She turned slightly, not wanting to stare at him while he read her carefully written reports. But doing so brought her around so that Stacie was in her line of sight. The woman's head came up again, and she stared at Leah.

Taking a deep breath, she ordered herself not to fidget. She was not a nervous scholar, turning in sloppy homework. She was a conscientious volunteer, and the interviews had been conducted to the best of her ability. If John found something to criticize, she would learn from that and do better the next time.

The desk was a pale gray metal, and when John moved slightly, his knee bumped it, making a small thumping sound. Behind him, a coffeemaker burbled on a countertop.

Two long-haired young men passed them, arguing loudly about something to do with the computers, she thought. The terms were so unfamiliar that she couldn't be sure.

John glanced up, frowning in annoyance, as they seemed to settle in front of the coffeemaker to continue their conversation.

He gathered up the papers.

"I can't hear myself think in here." He beckoned to Leah. "We'll move this to the conference room." He turned and walked away, leaving Leah to follow.

Conscious of the men's gazes on her, Leah went after him down the hall, around a corner, and through a glass-paneled door. A rectangular table with chairs around it filled most of the room.

John jerked out a chair and slumped into it, spreading the

papers out with an intentness that made her uneasy. Was something wrong with her work?

She slid into the chair that stood at right angles to his and waited. At least here she was away from Stacie's gaze. She was used to the stares of the curious when she was out among the English, but she wasn't used to having someone look at her with such open dislike.

On the other hand, here she was alone with Johnny. Business, she reminded herself. He seemed perfectly able to keep this on a businesslike basis, and she could, too.

Finally he pressed his hands against the sheets. "Who told you to do a family tree?" He shot the question at her.

"Well, I . . . I think Stacie said something about how seeing the family Bibles would be useful, but I told her I didn't believe people would be willing to lend them out. I thought perhaps a transcription of the tree would work, but if not—"

"If not?" That smile lit his face again, this time tinged with something like triumph. "Leah, this is fantastic. It's exactly what we need."

A footstep sounded in the hallway outside, and Dr. Brandenmyer poked his head in the doorway. "Do I hear the noise of a scientific triumph in here?"

Johnny waved the paper. "Leah has brought us a complete family tree for the Miller family, going all the way back to the early 1700s. It gives us exactly when the genetic illnesses began showing up."

"I copied it just as it was worded in the original." Her hands twisted in her lap again, and she forced them to be still. "I hope—"

"Excellent, excellent." Dr. Brandenmyer studied the sheets and then beamed at her. "We've never had such a detailed source before, not even from the families seeking treatment here. You've done a superb job, Ms. Beiler. Superb."

She could feel the heat rushing to her face. It wasn't the Amish way to lavish praise, and to accept it was prideful. She lowered her gaze.

"The Miller family has a very complete family tree in their Bible, and because we are nearly related, they were willing to let me copy it. I can't hope to obtain such results every time."

"If you bring in something half as good, we'll be pleased." Dr. Brandenmyer reached out, as if he intended to pat her shoulder, and then drew his hand back. "Excellent," he said again. "Well, I'll leave you to it. Get those results into the computer as soon as possible, John. Well done."

"I will, sir." Johnny straightened in his chair, looking almost as if he would like to salute, as the older man walked away with that long, loping stride.

Once he was gone, Johnny turned to her, his expression exultant. "I knew I was right to bring you in on this, Leah. You have access the rest of us couldn't possibly get."

Her hands gripped each other. "Don't count on that much information every time. Please. I can't promise to do that with every family."

"It's fine," he said quickly. Maybe he thought he was putting too much pressure on her. "I don't mean to make you uncomfortable, Leah."

"Praise is what makes me uncomfortable, as you well know." She felt a trace of annoyance with him. She couldn't expect the English to understand, but Johnny certainly should.

"Oh, yes." His mouth tightened. "I remember. Accepting a compliment would be prideful. Lacking in proper Amish humility."

She would not apologize for her beliefs. "The instruction to have a humble and contrite heart is not only for the Amish."

He lifted his hands in a gesture of surrender. "I'm sorry. I guess I still have trouble with that one. What's so bad about accepting that people think you did a good job?"

For a moment she couldn't speak. John did sound like an Englischer now. He'd been raised on the same Scriptures she had.

Blessed are the meek. Do not think yourself better than anyone else, but humble yourselves in obedience to God.

Apparently he had forgotten.

"I don't want to argue with you about it." She started to rise. "If that's all—"

"Leah, don't. Please don't leave. I didn't mean to offend you." He rubbed the back of his neck with his palm, as if trying to wipe away tension.

"Is it hard?" She asked the question abruptly, thinking about his obvious eagerness to please Dr. Brandenmyer. "Feeling you belong in this world now?"

A muscle jerked at the corner of his mouth. "Sometimes not at all. Sometimes every minute of the day."

"I'm sorry." She was. Not trying to convince him he'd been wrong in his choice. Just sorry it was hard for him.

He shrugged. "It was worth it."

Did he really feel that? Apparently so.

He stared down at the chart of the Miller family. Finally he cleared his throat.

"I remember Naomi. So she married Nathan Miller. Everybody thought they'd make a match of it."

"Ja." Everyone had thought that. Just as they'd thought she and Johnny would.

He smiled suddenly. "Remember when Nathan and I took our daads' buggies out on that dirt road behind the Esch farm and tried to have a harness race?"

"I remember that Naomi and I told you not to. And that you both ate your meals standing up for a few days."

"Don't give me that." His eyes laughed at her. "I distinctly remember Naomi jumping up and down waving her bonnet, and you yelling at me to go."

She couldn't prevent the chuckle that escaped her. "We did not."

But she remembered that day so clearly—the dust hanging in the air like fog, the buggy wheels flashing, the boys standing up in the buggies like chariot racers.

Johnny laughed, a delighted chuckle that was so familiar it plucked her heartstrings. "You're a liar, Leah Beiler." He closed his hand over hers. "You were just as ready to get into that mischief as I was, but you got off easier." His fingers tightened, and his gaze was warm on her face. "Admit it."

For an instant they were Leah and Johnny again—young and in love. A flush mounted her face.

They weren't, and she couldn't let herself think that way.

She pulled her hand away. "We did plenty of foolish things when we were young. It was a long time ago."

"Afraid, Leah?" His voice mocked her. "Afraid holding hands for a minute with a fence-jumper will ruin your reputation as the perfect Amish schoolteacher?"

She clasped her hands in her lap and took refuge for the tumult of feelings in anger. "At least I can accept who I am."

Anger, quick as summer lightning, sparked in his face. "What's that supposed to mean?"

"It means that if you were as confident you made the right choice as you claim you are, you'd correct your friend Stacie's misconceptions about what it means to be Amish."

His chair scraped as he stood, planting his hands on the table. "And are you so convinced you've made the right choice? Maybe that's what you tell yourself, Leah, but don't expect me to buy it. I know you—I know how much you've always wanted to learn and know and experience the world you can only dream about."

Would his words hurt so much if they weren't true? "I know my place," she said, fighting to keep her voice even. "I have my family, my faith, the children I teach. That is what matters to me."

"Is it? You give kids an eighth-grade education that doesn't prepare them for the real world and think you're doing a good job. Well, you're not."

She looked at him steadily. Johnny said he knew her. Maybe he did and maybe he didn't, but she knew him. That moment when he'd admitted his struggle had shown her too much, and she could sense the pain beneath his words.

"I'm not preparing them for the English world," she reminded him. "I'm preparing them to be Amish men and women. But I don't think you're talking about my scholars, anyway. I think you're talking about yourself."

Her hands were shaking, and she had to concentrate in order to pick up the folder with the unused forms.

"I think I'd best meet with Stacie in the future," she said, and walked quickly from the office.

. . .

A car approached the buggy from behind, going fast, if the sound it made was any indication. Hands firm on the lines, Leah kept Betty moving at a steady pace. She darted a glance to the side of the road—hardly any berm and then a drop-off to a deep ditch.

A horn blared. Leah's nerves tightened but Betty, bless her, merely flicked an ear. And then the car whizzed past the buggy, so close that she could have reached out and touched it, cutting in again sharply in front of the horse.

The horn blared again, a harsh, derisive sound. Leah stared after it as her pulse steadied. Bright red it was, filled with teenagers, it looked like, and one—

Her fingers tensed on the lines. That sheet of pale blond hair flying in the wind as the girl turned to look back at her looked familiar. Too familiar.

Anna. But it couldn't be, could it? Anna was supposed to be working at the bakery this afternoon. She couldn't be riding around out on the Hedgeville Road in the farthest reaches of the district. The only reason Leah had come so far up the valley was to do an interview with another family.

It had been a branch of the Stoltzfus family, this one with four affected children. The mother had been willing to talk, but unfortunately hadn't known much about the ramifications of her husband's family.

The grossmutter knew it all, she'd said, but she was on a visit to a married daughter over near Mifflinburg. Teacher Leah was welcome to come back another time and talk with her.

Leah glanced down at the black case that sat beside her feet.

That would mean another long buggy ride, eating up time that could have accommodated visits to two or three closer families. She would not have anything near as satisfying to report this week as her triumph with the Miller genealogy.

She backed away from that word, frowning. *Triumph.* What a decidedly un-Amish concept that was. If God led her to learn anything that helped the children, His was the glory, not hers.

There was more traffic on the road as she approached Hedgeville, and she had to concentrate on that, putting aside for a moment thoughts of the work. And especially worries about the girl in the red car who could not possibly have been Anna.

Hedgeville sported a small area of strip development on its outskirts—an auto parts store, a donut shop, a fast-food place. She frowned. A red car, surely the same one, was parked at the fast-food restaurant.

Without giving herself a chance to think too much, she turned Betty into the parking lot. It was hot, and she had a long way home yet. A cold drink would taste good.

As was usual in Pleasant Valley, the restaurant provided a hitching rail at the back of the parking lot, under the shade of the trees that lined it, for their horse-and-buggy customers. She drew up to the rail and Betty halted. Before she could get down, someone was there, beside the buggy, blocking her way.

Anna. But not the Anna she knew. This Anna had a wave of straight, silky hair falling nearly to the waist of her tight jeans. Her gray T-shirt bore the logo of a local college. Only the sneakers on her feet were familiar.

"You recognized me."

"Barely." A flicker of anger went through Leah. "You might have told your friend not to blare the horn at a buggy horse."

Anna dismissed that with a flick of her fingers. "Betty's too stolid to let that bother her."

"Every buggy horse in the valley is not so well-trained as Betty. Driving like that could cause an accident."

"The way the English see it, roads are for cars. It's the horses and buggies that cause the accidents."

"And is that what you believe, Anna?" Leah studied her sister's face, trying to find some indication of the Anna she knew.

Anna shrugged, her gaze evading Leah's. "No. I mean, I guess I can see their point. It wasn't my doing. I was just a passenger."

"And why were you a passenger at all? You're supposed to be at work this afternoon, aren't you?"

Another shrug. "We weren't busy this afternoon. Mrs. Schatz said I could go home early. My friends offered me a ride."

So she could racket around the county with a boy who drove too fast, wearing English clothes, pretending she was one of them. "This isn't the way home."

"We stopped for something to eat." The flippant tone grated on Leah's nerves. "There's nothing wrong with that. What are you doing out this way, anyway?"

"I had a family to interview." Worry for her little sister replaced the annoyance she felt. "Why don't you get your things and come along with me now?"

"I'm not ready to leave yet. Don't worry about me. I'll be back in time for supper."

"Not worrying is easier said than done." She wanted to reach out, to touch that silky hair she'd brushed and braided so often for her little sister, but she was afraid Anna would pull away. What had happened to them, that there was such distance between them now?

She moved, intending to get down. Anna's hand shot out to grab the buggy, blocking her way.

"You're not coming in, are you?"

She froze. "I thought I'd get something cold to drink. Are you ashamed of me, Anna?"

Anna's face turned sulky. "Well, you're ashamed of me, dressed this way, aren't you?"

"Not ashamed. Never ashamed." Now she did reach out and touch her sister's hair lightly. "Just worried that you are flirting too much with the English world. I love you, Anna. I don't want you to be hurt."

"I can take care of myself."

"I know you think that, but—"

"I can." Now Anna did jerk away from her. "And you're a fine one to talk about that to me when you're doing the same thing."

Leah's heart seemed to turn cold in her chest. "What are you talking about?"

"You. Johnny Kile." Anna took a step back, throwing the words at her. "All that work you're doing at the clinic." She shot an angry glance toward the black case. "Everyone knows you're only doing it to get close to Johnny Kile again. So maybe you'd better save your lectures for yourself."

Chapter Thirteen

"*Let's* pick out the colors you want to use for your doll quilt," Leah said, spreading out the contents of her mother's scrap basket on the table in the living room at the daadi haus.

Elizabeth looked at them doubtfully and shrugged. "I don't know. Whatever you think is best."

Elizabeth's impassive little face didn't give Leah any clues to her feelings. Did she want to learn how to quilt, or was she going along only because her daadi wanted her to?

Leah moved scraps of colors around, hoping for an inspiration. She had suggested teaching the child to quilt, thinking that it would lead to conversations while they worked together. Most Amish girls of eight were already fairly accomplished with a needle, but then, most had a mammi or grossmutter to guide them.

She glanced at Elizabeth's solemn little face. Did she feel that something was missing in her life, without a mother to teach her the skills of Amish life?

Or was she longing to go back to the English world her mother had taken her to? If that was the case, it would devastate Daniel, who was trying so hard to restore his relationship with his children after their time apart.

"These might be pretty together." She moved a dark blue piece next to a coral rose.

"That's a nice color." One small finger touched the rose fabric. "Do you have a dress made of that?"

"No, that piece is left from a dress my sister Anna made."

Leah kept her voice calm, but her mind winced away from thoughts of her sister. She and Anna had been painfully polite to each other in public since the incident at the fast-food restaurant. In private, they had been silent, living in the same house without speaking.

The hurt would go away in time. They'd be normal to each other again. Just not right now.

"This is a doll quilt that I made when I was about your age."

Leah unfolded the small, faded one-patch quilt. With its simple arrangement of seven squares across and seven squares down, it would be the simplest design to start with.

"I remember I thought the yellow and the green would look fine together, but once it was done, I wasn't so sure." She'd sat in this room with Grossmutter, trying so hard to make her stitches as smooth and tiny as her grandmother's had been.

"I think it's pretty."

That was the first positive thing Elizabeth had said, and it pleased Leah, even if the child was just being polite.

"Your quilt will be really pretty, too, I know. And I'll make one along with you. I think I'd like this light blue piece for one of my colors." She took a good-sized piece of fabric, hoping that would encourage Elizabeth to do the same.

Elizabeth looked at her, forehead wrinkling in a frown. "Do you have a doll bed?"

"Well, not anymore. I gave it to my little sister when she started playing with dolls. But I'll make a quilt anyway, and I can put it away to give when I need a gift for someone."

Elizabeth picked at the piece of rose fabric. "I don't have a doll bed, either." Her mouth seemed to tighten on the words, and Leah had a sense of some emotion quickly suppressed.

"You have a doll, don't you?" She couldn't imagine any Amish girl without at least one of the faceless cloth dolls that were so much a part of childhood.

Elizabeth nodded. "But she has to sleep on my bed, because she doesn't have one of her own."

Again Leah sensed that tension. She longed to find out what the significance was of a doll bed, but if she probed, Elizabeth would retreat, and they'd be left in silence again.

Best to let it go for the moment. Perhaps Daniel would be able to shed some light.

"I'm sure your doll will like to have her own quilt, even if she's sleeping on your bed." She was going to have to move things along, or she had the sense that Elizabeth would sit looking at the fabric pieces until it was time for Daniel to come for her. "Let's decide what colors we want." She pointed to her old doll quilt. "How many colors would we need to make a quilt like this?"

Elizabeth studied the design, obviously counting to herself. "Seven." Her fingers lingered on the rose fabric. "May I use this one? And the light green?"

"Ser gut." Leah's heart warmed at the show of interest. "Choose five more, now, and then we can start cutting them out."

Nodding, Elizabeth began moving fabric pieces around, face intent as she considered each one.

Somehow Leah had attracted the child's attention. That was the first hurdle, and she'd have to be content with that for today.

She watched Elizabeth's face, longing to do more. The trauma of what had happened to Elizabeth had made her put up barriers against showing what she truly felt. Leah, of all people, knew about that. She had guarded her own feelings just as carefully after Johnny left.

The thought hit her, taking her breath away for a moment. She hoped to help Elizabeth surmount her fears, but how could she do that when she hadn't succeeded with her own?

And if she did, through God's grace, manage to help Elizabeth, who would help her?

Matthew and Jonah darted ahead of Daniel as he headed across the field to the Beiler farm to collect Elizabeth. Matthew seemed more settled in recent days, for which Daniel was truly thankful.

As for Jonah—he had to smile as his youngest grabbed Matthew's hat and took off, Matthew in hot pursuit. Nothing ever seemed to dampen Jonah's spirits. He had the gift of taking things as they came, unlike the other two.

Still, even Elizabeth had been better lately, making him wonder if this business of having Leah work with her was necessary. Maybe all his daughter needed was time to adjust to her life here.

"Daadi!" Matthew, having retrieved his hat, came racing back to him. "Mahlon and Joseph are working on something at the barn. Can we go see?"

"Go, but mind you stay out of their way."

Matthew ran off again, Jonah chugging along behind him like a little shadow. The Beiler brothers would make time for them, he knew, and maybe that was the answer with Elizabeth as well. Whether or not she really needed the counseling, as Leah thought, it would be good for her to be around a family like the Beilers.

When he reached the back porch, Leah and Elizabeth were just coming out. As usual, Elizabeth's face didn't give anything away.

"How was the quilting?" He hated that his voice sounded too hearty, as if he still couldn't be at ease with his own child.

"It went very well," Leah said, resting her hand lightly on Elizabeth's shoulder. "Elizabeth has a natural talent for needlework, I think."

Elizabeth darted a glance at her, as if checking to be sure Leah really meant it. Apparently she was satisfied with whatever she saw on Teacher Leah's face, because a smile played on her lips.

"I'm making a one-patch quilt for my doll," she announced. "Can I go tell Matthew about it?"

Leah nodded slightly over the child's head. She wanted to talk with him privately, then. Apprehension tightened his stomach.

"Your brothers are out at the barn. Go and find them, but don't get in the way."

"There's no need to worry about that." Leah sat down on the porch swing as Elizabeth crossed toward the barn. "Mahlon and

Joseph are working on some project, but they always have time for company."

He sat down next to her. "What's wrong?" He said the words bluntly, not willing to wait for her to lead up to whatever troubled her.

"Nothing." She reached out toward him, a tentative little gesture. "I'm sorry if I gave you that impression."

"There is something, Teacher Leah, or you would not be so cautious. Just tell me."

She looked troubled. "Daniel, it's important that Elizabeth not feel I'm reporting to you on what happens between us."

Irritation flickered. "I'm her father. I have a right to know what concerns her."

"Please understand." Leah's voice went soft with caring. "I won't keep anything important from you, but Elizabeth must know that she can trust me, or she won't open up at all. You can see that, can't you?"

He pushed past his annoyance, past his instinctive response that he was the only one responsible for his daughter's happiness. If Leah could help Elizabeth, he must swallow his pride and let her.

"Ja," he said. "I see. I'll be careful."

"Ser gut." She glanced toward the barn, as if checking to be sure that Elizabeth was well out of earshot. "When we were planning the doll quilts we're making, Elizabeth said that she doesn't have a doll cradle. It seemed to upset her a little, so I wanted to ask if it means something I should be aware of."

For a moment he looked at her blankly. The doll cradle—

"I made one for her," he said slowly. "For her third birthday, that was. It was one of the things Ruth took with her when she went away." He could feel the tension tightening inside him like a spring.

"Do you know what happened to it?" Leah's voice was carefully neutral.

"When I went to pick them up, I stopped at the place where they'd been living." He had to force himself to remember that, hating the fact that his children had lived in a place with dirty dishes in the sink and clothes strewn on the floor. "I wanted to pack up their things, but the cradle wasn't there." His voice roughened. "There was nothing left to remind them that they'd been Amish. Ruth must have gotten rid of all of it."

"I'm sorry." Leah's green eyes went dark with sympathy.

His hands had curled into fists on his knees. He forced them to relax, one finger at a time.

The anger is still here, Father. How am I ever to be rid of it? Please, take it away.

Leah put her hand over his, her touch startling him. "It's so hard, I know. But they were things. Things don't make us Amish." She paused, as if groping for words. "It is Gelassenheit that defines who we are. If they've forgotten, your children will learn it again, now that they're safe with you."

Gelassenheit. It meant humility, but it was so much more, encompassing all that was simple and humble and good about their way of life.

He took a deep breath. "I pray you are right," he said. "Certainly I can make a new doll cradle for Elizabeth."

"Her birthday is later in the summer, isn't it?" Leah drew her hand away, flushing a little. "We'll try to finish the quilt by then, too, so that she can have both the cradle and the quilt together. And my mamm has already started making a doll for her."

"That is kind of her. And you."

"It's a pleasure for both of us. We're glad to have Elizabeth in our lives."

The warmth in Leah's voice touched the sore place in his heart, soothing it. He glanced at her, liking the delicate line of her profile, the warmth and caring that flowed from her so effortlessly.

His family kept telling him that he should marry again, that his children needed a mother and he needed a wife. If he intended to do that, wasn't Teacher Leah the logical person to ask?

She had been kind to them from the moment they'd arrived, had gone out of her way to help his children. And he was attracted to her—he couldn't deny that.

But balanced against that was her work at the clinic, bringing her again and again into contact with her onetime intended. He knew, better than most, the trouble that could come from flirtation with the outside world.

And even if he did decide to risk it, the truth was that despite her kindness, despite the attraction that he thought was mutual, he had no idea how Leah would react if he courted her.

Leah got up, setting the porch swing moving slightly. She was getting too close to Daniel, and that was a problem. She neither wanted nor was ready for any further changes in her life. She was dealing with enough already.

"Shall we go out to the barn and see what they're up to?"

Daniel nodded, standing and falling into step with her. The silence between them bothered her, filled as it was with the things unsaid.

"It's hard to tell what Joseph and Mahlon might be doing," she said to fill the gap. "When the two of them get together, they turn back into young ones again, ready for all kinds of foolishness."

"They've always been close?"

She nodded. "They're near each other in age and sandwiched between the girls, so maybe that accounts for it."

"My brother Caleb and I were like that." His smile flickered, reminiscent. "Mamm declared we gave her more gray hairs than the rest of the family put together."

"She probably enjoyed it, even if she didn't want you to know."

He glanced toward the barn, as if looking for his own young ones. "Maybe so. I'd like to see Matthew and Jonah be closer."

"When they've grown a bit, the age difference between them won't mean as much," she suggested.

He nodded, frowning a little. In this, as in everything connected with his children, Daniel wanted so much to have everything be right. He was a good man, trying hard to be both mother and father to his family.

She admired that, as she should, but that didn't mean she ought to be drawn any deeper into a relationship that might not be what either of them wanted for their lives.

Daniel slid the barn door back. Joseph and Mahlon were bent over a piece of machinery, and Matthew knelt next to them, obviously intrigued. Elizabeth and Jonah were in the hay mow, engrossed in some game of their own that seemed to involve Elizabeth putting strands of hay into her little brother's hair.

"Don't tell me you're still trying to get that corn binder working. Last year it broke down so often that Daadi said it was simpler to do it by hand."

Joseph, a streak of grease on his forehead, grinned at her. "That's why we're working on it early this year. Come time to harvest the corn, we'll have this running like a top."

"That's what you said last year," she reminded him.

"This year we have Matthew helping us," Mahlon said, reaching out to tousle the boy's hair. "He's a natural with machines already."

"That he is," Joseph said. "I could use a bright boy like this as an apprentice in a few years."

A slight movement drew Leah's gaze to Daniel. His hands pressed tightly against the sides of his trousers, and his mouth was a firm, straight line.

"We'd best be getting along home now." He softened the words with a smile, but she thought it took an effort.

Matthew scowled. "But I want to see the corn binder work. Please, Daadi, can't I stay until they get it working?"

"No." The word was sharp and uncompromising, sounding loud in the quiet barn.

Mahlon and Joseph exchanged glances, and then Mahlon gave Matthew a friendly cuff on the shoulder. "Knowin' my brother, that could be a long wait. You come again another time, all right?"

Matthew's lower lip came out, but he bobbed his head and got to his feet. Elizabeth and Jonah slid over the low wall of the hay mow, and in a moment the Glick family had gone.

Leah stood still, fingers clenched. *It's not your place to interfere. You're not going to get any more involved, remember?*

But it was no good. She crossed the barn floor quickly and hurried after them.

The children were already running ahead. Since Daniel seemed to have no intention of stopping when he saw her coming, she fell into step with him.

"What is it?" A plain, frank question seemed to be the only thing that worked with Daniel. "Why did you pull the children away like that?"

"It's time we were getting to the chores." But his gaze evaded hers.

"Do you object to using the corn binder? It's been approved by the bishop long since, and most farmers in the valley use them. As long as they're pulled by horses—"

"It's not the corn binder," he snapped.

"Then what?"

He stopped, swinging to face her. "I don't like Matthew's interest in things mechanical, that's all. He won't be looking for any apprenticeship, either, because he's got a gut farm waiting for him."

"Joseph didn't mean anything but to encourage the boy."

"I don't want him encouraged."

She struggled to understand. "Surely it's right for a farmer to understand the machinery he uses. Levi always says he'd be lost if he didn't have Joseph to keep things running."

Daniel's jaw tightened. "If it was only farm machinery—" He stopped, as if thinking that he didn't need to explain himself to her.

But she thought she understood. "You're afraid Matthew's interest in how things work draws him closer to the English world."

He wore the expression of a man goaded too far. "I know. I

know it will. I've seen it already. 'When I was English,' that's what my son said to me. 'When I was English.'"

Her heart twisted. She reached toward him. "Daniel—"

He shook his head, clearly fighting to regain his composure. "I'm grateful for your help with Elizabeth, Teacher Leah. But this I have to take care of on my own."

Chapter Fourteen

Leah, it's been too long since you stopped to visit me like this." Rachel chided Leah gently as she poured glasses of lemonade and arranged cookies on a plate. "You've been even busier since school let out, it seems like."

Leah felt a combination of pleasure that she'd stopped at Rachel's place on her rounds today and guilt that she hadn't done it sooner. This was just like the situation with Mamm. She shouldn't let her new responsibilities affect her old relationships.

It was gut to be in Rachel's kitchen again, able to talk with her about anything. The two older children were outside, but little Mary played with blocks in the corner.

"I'm sorry I haven't come before this." She took a sip of the lemonade, tart on her tongue, and accepted a crisp, cinnamon-topped snickerdoodle. "It does seem that I have a lot to do lately."

"I've heard." Rachel's lips twitched, as if she tried without success to hold back a smile. "It seems like you've been spending a lot of time with Daniel Glick and his young ones this summer."

So that was the way the talk was going. She might have known her actions wouldn't have gone unnoticed in a community as tightly knit as theirs was.

"Rachel . . ." she began, then realized that she was gripping the edge of Rachel's pine kitchen table so tightly her fingers hurt. She relaxed her grip and deliberately took another sip of the lemonade.

"I have been seeing a lot of Elizabeth Glick lately." She hesitated. Daniel had talked about his wife in confidence, and she couldn't repeat his words, even though it would probably silence the gossip about the two of them. "She wants to learn to quilt, and since she doesn't have a mother or other female relative here to help her, I've been trying. And Mamm is working with her, too." She smiled, thinking of her mother with the solemn little girl. "Mamm's enjoying it as much as Elizabeth, for sure."

"That poor little girl." Rachel's quick sympathy overflowed. "I should have been thinking of that, too. I'll have her over to do some things with my Becky this summer. The two of them are sweet together."

"That would be wonderful gut. Anything we can do to fill the gaps in those children's lives, we should do."

"And in Daniel's life, too." Rachel's smile said that she might have been distracted for a moment, but she wasn't giving up on her matchmaking. "He's a gut man, for sure. I bet he appreciates what you're doing for his child."

Clearly Rachel wouldn't be diverted from her conviction that Leah and Daniel were meant to be together. Leah bit back her frustration. Denying it would only subject her to more teasing. Maybe it was best to ignore the topic entirely.

"I'd like to do more, but I've been traveling from one end of the church district to the other several days a week, interviewing families with sick children."

"For the clinic. I know." Rachel's blue eyes seemed to darken with concern. She pressed her lips together, as if to keep back words she wanted to speak.

Leah hesitated for a moment. She leaned across the table to put her hand over Rachel's. "Go on. Say whatever it is that's put those worry lines between your brows. We've been too close for too long to hold back now, that's certain sure."

Rachel clasped Leah's hand warmly. "I just— I don't know what to say. I want to warn you about gettin' too close with Johnny again, while a little piece of me hopes that loving you might be the thing that will bring him home."

Leah's throat tightened with pity. "Rachel, I'm sorry. But I'm afraid there's nothing that will bring John back to the church. I hoped you'd accepted that."

Rachel sighed, shaking her head a little and blinking back tears. "It's not so easy. Hope keeps slipping back in. And when you started working at the clinic, well, I thought maybe Johnny was the reason."

"He's the one who asked me. But I didn't agree because of him. I'm doing this for the children. If anything I do keeps a child from suffering, that's worth it."

Rachel wiped away tears with her fingers, much as she'd done when they were girls. "God gave you a heart for children, that's for sure, Leah Beiler. I just wish you had some of your own to love."

Little Mary chose that moment to knock her block tower down, sending blocks skidding across the floor and surprising Leah into a chuckle. "There's one of your little blessings in action."

"Ach, Mary, don't do that. Someone might trip on them."

But Mary had lost interest in building, it appeared. She trotted across to Leah and dumped a handful of blocks into her lap.

"How kind of you, Mary. Can I play with these?" Any interruption that got them safely off the subject of her childlessness was a good one.

Mary stared at her with round blue eyes, her fine blond hair curling loose from her braids. Then, suddenly, she smiled, dimple showing, and held out her arms to Leah.

"Up," she demanded.

"There now, little girl, you're a sweet child." Leah picked her up, holding her close.

Mary looked so like Johnny that it shocked her that she'd never noticed it before. Not surprising, since Mary's mamm and the uncle she might never know were twins.

If Leah and Johnny had had a babe, this was what he or she might have looked like. She brushed a kiss against the soft cheek, a peculiar ache spreading in her chest. She'd have said she'd accepted never having children of her own, but in this moment, she wasn't so sure.

"She looks like Johnny, doesn't she?" Rachel seemed to understand Leah's thoughts. Her voice was soft, and her eyes glistened with tears.

"Ja." Her own voice was thick all of a sudden. She shouldn't ask the question that pressed against her lips—she shouldn't, but she had to.

"Rachel, if I could arrange it, would you see him? It hurts so much to think of the two of you apart."

Something that might have been hope dawned in Rachel's eyes. "Do you think— Should I? I wouldn't want the folks to know, but oh, how I'd love to see him again."

"You could talk to him." At least, she could if Johnny put his pride aside and agreed. "Surely there's someplace the two of you could meet and talk. Maybe that would even ease the way for your parents to accept seeing him eventually."

"I don't know about that." Rachel clasped her hands, hope and doubt warring in her expression. "But I would do it, if you can set it up. Will you talk to Johnny about it, Leah? Will you?"

Doing so would mean involving herself more deeply with Johnny, something she'd been determined not to do. But how could she refuse the longing of her dear friend's heart?

"I'll try." She held little Mary close, somehow drawing strength from her. "I'll do my best."

Leah gathered her clinic materials together, breathing a silent sigh of relief. She'd met with Stacie to turn in her reports, and this time the woman had been almost—well, not friendly, but at least not antagonistic.

As she stood, Stacie looked up from the desk. "Good work," she said curtly.

Leah nodded in acknowledgment. As she started to turn away, Stacie slapped her hand down on the desk.

"What's wrong with you people? Can't you even say thank you for a compliment?"

Leah blinked. "I didn't mean to offend. It's just not our way."

"Why not?" Stacie shoved herself to her feet, both palms on the desk. "A little simple politeness can't be against your rules, can it?"

"It's not that." Although the woman's tone was irritated, she did seem to want to understand, and that was surely a step in the right direction. "The Amish way is that of humility. For me to say thank you would imply that I agreed I had done a good job."

Stacie shook her head. "I don't get it. What's wrong with that? I always figure if I don't think well of myself, nobody else will."

This was like the conversation she'd had with John, which had turned so quickly into a quarrel. Their part of the English world didn't seem to think very highly of humility.

"We believe that God calls us to not think more highly of ourselves than others. To put others first." Trying to explain something that was so fundamental to her beliefs in a way this educated, intense woman would understand seemed impossible.

Stacie shrugged. "You wouldn't get very far in the academic world with an attitude like that."

"I suppose not."

Johnny seemed to have been able to leave that attitude of mind and heart behind. Had it been easy for him to erase the habit of a lifetime?

"Well, I'll see you next week, I guess." Stacie gathered up the forms, tapping them together. "Have a good one."

Nodding again, Leah headed back through the maze of offices. Had Johnny told Stacie that Leah had requested to report to her rather than to him? That might account for the change in her attitude.

But now she had to seek him out for a private talk in order to set up a meeting with Rachel. This could only complicate matters with him, but that couldn't be helped. A little embarrassment on her part was a small price to pay for Rachel's happiness.

She'd just begun to wonder how she'd find Johnny when he came around the corner. His step checked at the sight of her. He nodded stiffly and began to turn away.

"John." This was going to be difficult, given how they'd parted. "May I speak with you?"

His eyebrows lifted. "That's the last thing I expected from you. Had a change of heart, have you?"

She was probably flushing. "This isn't about the clinic. It's about your family."

For a moment she thought he'd walk away. Then he gave a curt nod and gestured toward the door at the end of the corridor.

"Come out on the back porch. We won't be interrupted there."

She followed him, trying to arrange what she needed to say. She'd expect Johnny to be eager to see his twin sister, but did she really know him well enough any longer to say?

The back porch stretched the length of the building, and it seemed to be a repository for things no one had a use for at the moment. Cartons were piled against the wall, and beyond them metal folding chairs leaned against each other.

To her right, someone had attempted to arrange a small sitting area, with a glass-topped table and a couple of benches. John brushed off the seats with the palm of his hand, and they sat down.

She folded her hands and banished the intrusive memory of sitting on the back porch swing with Daniel. How to begin?

"They're all right, aren't they?" The concern in his voice disarmed her. "The family."

"As far as I know."

"Did my parents change their minds? Do they want to see me?" He shot the question at her.

"I'm afraid not. But—"

He planted his hands on his knees as if to rise. "Then there's nothing to talk about."

"There is." She put out a hand to stop him. "Please, Johnny. Just listen to me for a few minutes."

His fingers clenched. Then he nodded, not looking at her.

She took a breath. "It's not that they don't want to see you. You must know that."

"What difference does it make?" He looked at her, and she saw the flash of pain in his eyes. "They won't. That's the bottom line. They're so tied up by the rules of the church that they won't see their own son."

"You're the one who left with hardly a word of explanation." And with no hint of farewell for her. "Can't you see how many people were hurt by that? If you wanted to really come back, we—they—would hold out their arms to you."

"Are you talking about my parents, Leah?" His voice went soft. "Or about you?"

For a moment she couldn't speak. She looked into his face and saw again the boy she'd loved—the boy whose leaving had broken her heart.

She tried to rally her defenses. "This isn't about me."

"Still determined to hide your emotions under that perfect Amish exterior? Can't we talk honestly about it at least once?"

He reached out impetuously to clasp her hand. "Maybe then we can be friends again."

She forced herself to take a deep breath. "The blame is not on one side or the other, I know that. We hurt each other."

His fingers tightened. "I left you. I promised to marry you, and then I left."

The words seemed to wrench open a hole in her heart. Could she, this once, accept the truth about herself?

"And I promised to love you forever." Tears stung her eyes. "But I couldn't go with you. I was afraid."

There. That was the truth, as plainly as she knew how to speak it. She felt as if a brisk wind blew through the hole in her heart, chasing away the last shreds of guilt and bitterness.

"I'm sorry." His voice broke a little on the words, and all the pride seemed wiped out of him in the truth of the moment. "Maybe we were both too young."

"Ja. We were. I blamed you for a long time." She looked at him steadily. "I blamed myself even longer."

It was an astonishing relief to say the words out loud to him after all this time.

"I wish—" he began.

"Don't," she said quickly. "I know you don't regret leaving, no matter how hard it's been."

"No. But I regret hurting people to do it."

She let the silence stretch between them for a moment. For the first time since his return, she felt comfortable with him.

"Can we be friends again, Johnny?"

He squeezed her hand. "Friends."

She nodded. "Then, as your friend, I'm here for Rachel. She wants to see you."

His eyes widened, as if he couldn't believe what he heard. "She does? Really?"

"Really." She smiled, relieved. There could be no doubt about Johnny's reaction to that.

"I'll go right now. I can leave for the day and drive over there—"

"Wait." She grasped his arm to stop him. "Not right away. She'll meet you someplace. She asked me to arrange it."

She felt him stiffen, saw the softness leave his face. "You mean I'm not welcome at my own sister's home. She wants to see me someplace where no one will know, as if I'm a criminal."

He was pulling away, and somehow she had to make him see what he was doing.

"Don't, Johnny. Don't deny the very thing you want out of some foolish, worldly pride. Rachel loves you. She wants to see you again. That's the only important thing, isn't it?"

For a moment it hung in the balance, and she held her breath. Then, a little shamefaced, he nodded.

"You're right." He squeezed her hand tightly, and the bond between them ran so strong that it frightened her. "You set it up. I'll be there."

"*Those* are nice, small stitches, Elizabeth. Your quilt is coming along already."

Elizabeth nodded, not looking up from the patch she was working on. Her brows were furrowed in concentration as she wielded the needle.

Leah suppressed a sigh. She sat in her grossmutter's chair, but she didn't seem to have her gift for drawing out confidences.

Elizabeth's quilt might be progressing, but their relationship wasn't.

Should she be pushing more? She studied the little girl's face, but it gave nothing away, and she feared probing might only make Elizabeth retreat further into her shell.

Perhaps she should discuss it with Lydia again. Her books had been helpful, but talking it out would be even better.

Better yet would be having Lydia counsel the child, but she had no hope that Daniel would agree to that.

She frowned down at her own quilt patch. Her life seemed more like a crazy quilt lately than this neat geometric design. Trying to balance Elizabeth's troubles, her apprehension over bringing Rachel and Johnny together, her tangled feelings for him, her growing closeness with Daniel . . . Maybe they all made some sort of pattern in God's sight, but she couldn't see it.

Guide me, Father, she prayed as she set one tiny stitch after another. *I don't see my path clearly just now, and I need to know where You want me.*

Someone knocked at the front door of the daadi haus. Murmuring a silent *Amen,* she went to answer it.

"Leah, you're just the person I hoped to see." Paula Schatz, the Mennonite woman who owned the bakery where Anna worked, peered past her. "Is your mother here?"

"I'm sorry, but she had to go out—"

"No, no, that's good."

Paula thrust a paper bag with the bakery logo on it into Leah's hands as she came in. With her graying hair pulled back into a bun under her prayer cap and her comfortable girth enveloped in a modest dress, she might have appeared Amish to an outsider.

It was true enough that the Amish and the Mennonites were

cousins in belief, so to speak, though sometimes their differences could be bitter. But she knew Paula nearly as well as she did her own church family.

Paula chuckled. "Listen to me. I'm so distracted that I made it sound as if I didn't want to see your dear mamm. Give her that from me—it's some of my pumpernickel bread."

"She and Daadi will love it, for sure. But if you didn't come to see Mamm—"

Paula clasped her arm. "I thought I'd bring this problem to you, Leah. You'd be the one to handle it, and I didn't want to put another burden on your mamm when she's still recovering."

A problem with Anna, then. Leah's heart sank. She'd just begun to feel as if things were getting back to normal between her and Anna.

Paula caught sight of Elizabeth and blinked. "I'm sorry if I interrupted."

"This is my neighbor Elizabeth Glick. We're making quilts together."

Elizabeth gave a polite nod, seeming to retreat a bit further into herself in the presence of the stranger.

"I'm glad to meet you, Elizabeth." Paula shot a glance at Leah. "Can we talk in private?"

There was nothing to be gained by putting it off, whatever it was. Leah nodded, gesturing toward the kitchen.

"Just keep on with your stitching, Elizabeth. I need to talk with Mrs. Schatz for a few minutes." She went into the kitchen with a silent prayer.

"I'll make a long story short," Paula said, bracing her hands against the back of a kitchen chair. "Seeing as how you have a guest."

Her brown eyes twinkled with curiosity, and Leah knew she was aching to ask about her relationship with the Glick family. Paula, like everyone else in Pleasant Valley, took a deep interest in her neighbors.

"Is there a problem with Anna?" Leah came out with the question before Paula could get sidetracked.

"Now, Leah, you know how much I care about the girls I hire to work in the bakery." Paula's round face, seeming to be made for smiling, grew serious. "They're like my own kin, they are, and I feel responsible for them."

"Ja, I know." That was why Mamm and Daad had felt safe about Anna working there.

"And I don't want to be telling tales on any of my girls, no, I don't." Paula shoved her wire-rimmed glasses up her nose. "But I'm that worried about Anna that I had to talk to someone. 'Teacher Leah's the one,' I said to myself. 'If anyone can get through to Anna, it'll be Leah.'"

Paula couldn't guess how wrong she was about that. Leah seemed to have no influence at all over her baby sister these days.

"What has she done?" She braced herself for the answer.

"Coming late. Leaving early. Not showing up at all sometimes. I tell you, Leah, I'm at my wit's end with her." She hesitated. "It's not my business, but I've seen the boy who waits for her when she leaves—Englischer, he is, with a fancy red car."

Even though Paula herself drove a car, it was a sedate black sedan, with even the bumpers painted black.

Leah let out a breath she didn't realize she'd been holding. She couldn't even say she was surprised. "Have you spoken to her about it?"

"I've tried to talk sense to her, but it's done me no good at all.

I might as well save my breath to cool my porridge. No, you're the one to handle this."

"I'll try." Though she doubted that Anna would listen to her, either. "Thank you for coming to me, rather than Mamm. You're a gut friend, for sure."

Paula patted her hand. "I do my best by those girls, but if ever I saw someone going near the edge, it's Anna. Well, well, we do our best, but sometimes young people have to make their own mistakes."

She headed toward the front door, apparently satisfied that she'd said what was necessary. Leah trailed behind her, impelled by hospitality when she'd rather curl up and weep.

"I'm grateful to you. I'll do my best."

"I know you will." Paula gave her a quick hug. "You're a good, responsible girl, you are. Anna could stand to be a little more like you."

Leah managed a smile. "I don't think she'd like hearing that."

Paula shook her head, chuckling a little as she went out. "No, I don't suppose so. Mind, now, if she doesn't straighten out soon, I'll have to let her go. I wouldn't want to put that burden on your mamm, either. It would worry her."

"It would." Leah's heart sank at the thought of Mamm's reaction to that. She and Paula were old friends, and that would hurt her. Still, what else could Paula do? She had a business to run.

Leah stood watching as Paula drove off, her mind searching for a way to reach Anna. Here was another errant patch for her imaginary crazy quilt, and it threatened to be the most difficult to deal with.

But in the meantime, she was neglecting Elizabeth. She went to look over the child's work before sitting down again.

"Ser gut," she said, picking up her own work. "I'm sorry about the interruption."

Elizabeth fixed her with an apprehensive gaze. "Is something wrong with your mamm?"

Odd, that out of all she must have overheard, that was what she'd fix on. "Not exactly. Mrs. Schatz didn't want to worry her just now, that's all."

"Because she's sick?"

Obviously Elizabeth wasn't going to be content with evasions. Maybe she was relating this to losing her own mother.

"Mamm was very sick last year," Leah said carefully, wanting to be honest without frightening the child. "She's doing much better now, but we still try to keep her from being worried and upset, or from doing too much."

"Is she going to die?" Elizabeth's lips trembled.

Leah's heart clenched. "Everyone will die sometime, but I think my mamm will be with us for a long time."

"My mamm died."

Was this the breakthrough she'd been looking for, coming at her from an unexpected source? She breathed a quick, silent prayer for guidance.

"I know she did. I'm sorry. You must miss her an awful lot."

Elizabeth clenched the quilt patch tightly in her hands. Her face worked. "I was angry at my mamm." Her mouth twisted. "And then she died."

Calm, be calm. Don't overreact. "You got mad at her before she died. We all get mad at the people we love sometimes."

Elizabeth was shaking her head, her face contorted. Leah longed to put her arms around the child, to comfort her and tell her she didn't have to talk about it. But talking about it might be the very thing that would help her heal.

"It's all right, Elizabeth," she said softly. "You can tell me anything you want. I won't tell anyone."

"I prayed to go home again." She seemed to force the words out. "All the time after Mamm took us away, I prayed to go home. But I didn't mean for her to die. I didn't!" Elizabeth burst into tears.

Now Leah did have to hold her. She scooped the child into her arms and settled in the rocking chair, holding her close.

"Hush, hush, now. It's all right. Really, it's all right." She smoothed her hair and stroked her back. "Elizabeth, your prayers didn't bring about your mamm's accident."

"But I prayed to go home." A choked sob punctuated the words. "And after Mammi died, Daadi came to take us home."

Leah rocked back and forth, patting her, trying to find the right words to comfort her. The poor child, carrying a burden like this for months and not telling anyone.

"I know it seems that way," Leah said carefully. "But your mamm was in an accident because she drove a car when she'd been drinking. God didn't make her do that. She decided to do that on her own."

Leah couldn't guess what had led Ruth to the choices she'd made. She could only do her best to deal with the results.

"Her accident was a terrible thing, but you weren't to blame. It's all right to be thankful that you were able to come home."

She felt some of the tension ease out of Elizabeth's body. She seemed to relax against Leah's shoulder, much as she'd done the night she'd burned her hand.

But this was a much deeper, more painful hurt. A professional would know how to deal with it so much better than she did.

Please, Lord. Help this dear child to understand. Take away her burden.

"It wasn't your fault," Leah said again, her words soft. "You weren't to blame."

Elizabeth sighed, hiccoughing a little. "I didn't want her to die. I just wanted to go home again."

"I know. I know. It's all right. God has brought you home, where you belong." She took a deep breath, praying she was saying the right thing. "Maybe you should tell your daadi what you told me. I know he'd want to help you feel better about it."

She shook her head. "I can't. I don't want to say it again."

"Would it be okay with you if I told him?"

At least Elizabeth didn't refuse that entirely. "I . . . I don't know. What if it makes him think I wanted Mammi to die?"

"I promise you he wouldn't think that." She smoothed Elizabeth's hair. "But I won't say anything to him unless you tell me to. All right?"

Elizabeth looked at her for a long moment, as if weighing her trustworthiness. Finally she nodded. "All right," she said.

CHAPTER FIFTEEN

*L*eah was up before the sun the following day. She may as well be—she'd spent a mostly sleepless night with her mind bouncing between the revelation of Elizabeth's feelings about her mother and the visit from Paula Schatz, with her concerns for Anna.

She'd prayed, caught herself worrying, and prayed again.

Why can't I be confident in Your answers to my prayers, Father? I feel so torn. For years I felt so sure that I knew the right thing to do, and now everything seems to be a challenge.

Maybe that was the point. Maybe God was reminding her that only through relying on Him would she find the right path.

I can rely on You for myself, I think. It's so much more difficult to relinquish control when it's a child I love.

Daniel had to know the anguish of guilt that had Elizabeth tied up in knots, but how could she break the child's confidence? If she did, that could destroy any hope of a further relationship between them.

And if she didn't—she didn't want to think about his reaction if she kept this from him.

She couldn't discuss this with anyone else, but she could talk to Lydia. If God had brought Lydia into her life for a reason, this might be it.

And as for Anna—

Sometime in the long night, she had come to a decision. She couldn't deal with this situation on her own any longer. Trying to protect Mammi's feelings was a good thing, but not at the cost of Anna's future.

She would talk to Daad about it. She went softly down the stairs, feeling her familiar way in the predawn darkness. Perhaps Mamm would never need to know how worrying Anna's behavior had been. And if she did, Daadi would know the best way to bring it up.

She went quietly out the back door and across the lawn toward the stable, the dew-wet grass dampening her sneakers. The eastern sky brightened already, and the world seemed hushed, as if it held its breath, waiting for the sun's appearance.

Daadi would be in the stable, feeding the horses, talking to them as he always did. She could have a few quiet moments alone with him before the rest of the house was up and busy.

The stable door stood open, letting out a shaft of yellow light from Daad's lantern. She went in, pausing a moment on the threshold, appreciating the fact that all was just as she'd imagined it.

Daad leaned on Betty's stall door, pouring oats into her feed bucket, talking to her in that same gentle tone that he'd always used with his children as well. He looked up at her step, smiling in welcome.

"You're up early, daughter."

"Not so early as you."

Her father never changed, it seemed to her. His beard might be more white than brown these days, but he still moved with the same quick, wiry strength he always had. His hazel eyes watched her with love and maybe a little question.

She leaned against the stall door next to him, patting Betty's neck. The mare, nose deep in her oats, flickered her ears in greeting.

"Greedy girl," she said, stroking her.

In the next stall Dick, one of the big Percherons, pawed and snorted impatiently. Daad chuckled.

"We'd best get the rest of them fed, if we don't want to hear about it." He handed her a feed pail. "While we're doing it, you can tell me what has you so worried already."

"You noticed that." She took the pail, going to fill it at the barrel that held the oats.

"Ja, I noticed." Daadi poured oats into Dick's feeding pail, glancing at her with a faint trace of a frown between his brows. "Is it Johnny's coming back that has you upset?"

She blinked in surprise. Other people might be talking, but—

"You know me better than that, don't you, Daad?"

"I know you're a levelheaded, responsible girl. But I also know that once you loved him with all your heart."

"That was a long time ago. I don't have feelings for him now." *Do I?* She hoped that was true.

"Are you sure you're not gettin' involved with him again, seeing him as you do?"

"No, Daad." Unless she considered setting up a meeting between Johnny and Rachel getting involved.

He looked at her searchingly for a moment, as if he sensed that she was hiding something. "Ser gut," he said at last. "So what is it then that has you worried?"

"Anna." It was a relief to say it. "I know she has to have her rumspringa, just as the rest of us did, but I'm concerned about what she's doing."

He nodded, leaning his elbow on the top of the last stall. The sound of contented munching filled the stable.

"I know. She's been running with English friends, maybe even a boy, hasn't she?"

She studied his weatherworn face. "Daadi, if you know, why haven't you talked to her about it?"

He smiled a little. "Five times we've gone through this, your mamm and me. Five times we've worried and prayed."

"The rest of us didn't go so close to the line, did we?"

"Well, you were the one we didn't think we needed to worry about, settled as you were on Johnny so early. But when he left, it seemed we should have been more careful with you."

"No one could have predicted that." Not even her, apparently.

"And you don't know what foolishness your brothers got up to." His eyes twinkled a little. "Them I understood a little better than you girls. Your mamm knows you and Anna best."

Maybe that was part of the problem. With Mamm's illness, perhaps they hadn't concentrated on Anna enough.

"I haven't wanted to upset Mamm. But I think you should talk to Anna."

He folded his hands, almost as if in prayer. "We've always believed rumspringa to be a useful time. We give our young people a taste of what life is like on the other side, and then they can make a decision of commitment without regrets."

She didn't have regrets, at least not about that. But still, sometimes she wondered. What would her life have been if she'd gone with Johnny? Could she have thrived, as he apparently had, without family and church?

"You're still worried." He patted her shoulder. "Try to have trust that Anna will sow her wild oats and then come out the other side, just as the rest of you did."

She wished she had his faith. "It's not just the English friends," she said. "Paula Schatz stopped by yesterday to talk to me. She didn't want to upset Mamm, but she says Anna has been coming late, leaving early, sometimes not showing up at all. You know Paula. She wouldn't come to us without cause."

Her father straightened. "That's so?" At her nod, he frowned. "This will not do. It is not right for Anna to be taking her wages without putting in an honest day's work. I'll talk to her."

Leah gave a rueful smile. "I feel as if I've shifted my worries to your shoulders."

He patted her hand. "That is where they belong. I'm glad you care about your sister, but you shouldn't carry the burden for her. It's enough for you to deal with your own concerns." His fingers tightened on hers. "I'm always here for you, Leah."

She nodded, her throat tightening. "I know you are, Daadi."

He was still worrying about her, she could see that. But she couldn't reassure him that everything was all right with her. She didn't know that herself.

"*What* if he doesn't come? Or what if we're late?" Rachel twisted her hands in her lap, peering out the window of Ben Morgan's car. Leah had arranged for Ben to drive them to this meeting with Johnny.

"Calm down already." Leah patted her hand, trying to ignore the fact that her own stomach was tied in knots. "I've never seen you so ferhoodled."

"I haven't seen my own twin in ten years." Rachel transferred her grip to Leah's hand. "Is it any wonder? What if he doesn't come?"

"Johnny wouldn't let you down that way." She glanced toward the driver, but Ben could be trusted to keep quiet about this trip. That was why she'd asked him to bring them.

"I hope not. But ten years with hardly a word . . . I know I'm being foolish, but I can't decide whether I want to hug him or box his ears for him."

"Maybe both," Leah suggested.

Ben slowed the car, peering out at the houses they passed, obviously looking for the number she'd given him. They must be nearly at Lydia's now.

Setting up this meeting had been so difficult that she'd felt at times as if she were negotiating a peace treaty. Rachel didn't want to go anyplace where she might be seen by someone who'd relay the news to her parents, and Johnny had shown signs of getting prideful again about the whole thing.

Finally Lydia had stepped into the breach, offering her home in Mifflinburg, and the time was set.

Leah and Rachel had come early, giving themselves plenty of time to do the fabric shopping that was the stated reason for their trip.

Leah hadn't expected to enjoy the shopping part of the day, but as it turned out, Rachel had found fabric for new dresses for Becky and shirts for the boys, while Leah had bought the lining and backing material for her and Elizabeth's quilts. They'd taken their time, weighing the merits of one bolt against another, but even so, they were arriving at Lydia's place a little early.

"Here we are, ladies." Ben pulled into the driveway of a small white cottage, his gaze meeting Leah's in the rearview mirror with a look of encouragement. "You can leave your bundles in the car. I'll just sit and read the paper."

He slid his seat back a bit and unfurled the newspaper from the seat beside him.

"Ser gut." She opened her door, but Rachel was already out ahead of her.

The yard was tiny but beautifully kept, and several varieties of roses bloomed in a bed across the front of the house. They followed a flagstone path that led to the front door. If it were not for the electric lines running to the house from the street, this might be an Amish home.

"All right?" Leah glanced at Rachel when they reached the stoop.

Rachel nodded, her face pale but determined.

Almost before she could knock, Lydia opened the door. "Welcome to my home. Please, come in. This must be your friend Rachel."

Rachel gave a quick nod, looking around with a certain amount of apprehension in her blue eyes. "It's kind of you to have us."

"My pleasure." Lydia led the way into a small living room, gesturing to the sofa. "John called a while ago to doublecheck the address, so I imagine he'll be along soon." She glanced at Leah. "Perhaps when he comes, you'll join me in the kitchen for a cup of tea."

Leah nodded.

"Maybe you should stay—" Rachel began.

Leah grasped her hands firmly. "You'll be fine. John is still your brother."

"But he's different now. A fence-jumper. Englischer." She glanced at Lydia.

Lydia smiled. "Like me, yes. There's no need for you to feel uncomfortable about it. My situation and John's are similar."

Similar, but not entirely alike. Lydia had already gone over the difficult bridge to establishing a relationship with her family. John had yet to do that, but Leah hoped and prayed that today would be a first step.

A car pulled into the driveway—she could hear the tires crunch on the gravel. Her fingers pressed taut against the skirt of her dress, and her stomach seemed to turn over.

"He's here," Rachel whispered, her eyes wide and apprehensive.

Please, Lord. Leah's throat was so tight that she couldn't have said the words aloud. *Please let this go well. I long so much for Rachel and Johnny to be brother and sister again.*

The knock came at the door, and they could hear the soft murmur of Lydia's voice as she opened it. Rachel gasped, and her hand squeezed Leah's convulsively.

There was the sound of a familiar step, and Johnny appeared in the archway. He stood, hesitant, looking at his sister.

With a strangled sob, Rachel catapulted herself across the room and into his arms. In a moment the two of them were hugging and laughing and crying all at the same time. Leah exchanged a glance with Lydia and followed her into the kitchen.

On the verge of tears herself, Leah sat in the kitchen chair Lydia pulled out for her. She pressed her fingers against her eyes.

Lydia, not speaking, turned the gas on under a teakettle and began rattling cups and saucers, obviously giving her time to calm herself.

By the time Lydia brought the cups to the table, Leah was able to smile at her. "That's kind of you."

"I always think a hot cup of tea does wonders for emotional upset." She poured the brew from a squat brown teapot and then sat down across from Leah.

"I don't think they'll be ready for refreshments for a time." Leah glanced toward the door to the living room.

"I didn't mean them," Lydia said. "I meant you. This surely is emotional for you as well."

"I suppose it is." She held the cup between her hands. "Seeing them together—well, it feels so right. They were always very close, and for a long time, I couldn't get used to seeing Rachel without knowing Johnny was around somewhere."

Lydia nodded, staring down into the contents of her cup. She and her siblings had come to a relationship, she'd said. It must have been a difficult road.

"Everyone's actions affect so many other people," Leah went on. "Rachel just hasn't seemed heart-whole without him. Maybe she'll be better now."

"I hope she's not counting on his coming back." Lydia traced the rim of her cup with her finger. "It would be a nice dream, but it won't happen."

"You think he's too happy where he is?"

"Happy?" Lydia seemed to look at the word. "I'm not sure that describes it. When you fence-jump, you never entirely leave the past behind. How could you?"

"So you never really fit into the English world." That was what Johnny had hinted.

Lydia intrigued her, and she'd like to understand the woman better. Lydia apparently loved her work and was probably very good at it, but she didn't seem entirely to match with the life she'd chosen.

"Something like that." Lydia smiled, her gaze meeting Leah's. "I've told you that sometimes I wonder if I'd be better off right now if I were still Amish, and I can never really leave that yearning behind. But that's not the choice I made."

"You could change." Leah ventured the words tentatively.

Lydia shook her head. "Some can't go back because they invest too much in the English world, like John. Others, like me, might long to return, but there's something they can't give up. For me, it's my work."

Leah nodded. She might not entirely understand what made someone leave, but she could understand why a woman like Lydia couldn't go back.

She hesitated, wondering if it would be intruding to ask the question in her mind. "Do you think, twenty or thirty years from now, you'll have regrets?"

"I'll be alone here in my little house then, you mean. With no family and community to look after me."

Leah thought about Mamm, surrounded by people who loved and cared for her. That was the old age an Amish woman expected to have. They didn't worry about being left alone.

"I didn't mean to offend you," she said.

"I'm not offended." Lydia's smile had a tinge of sadness. "It's an honest concern. Yes, I think about that. But I've made my choice."

Leah nodded. Each time she met Lydia, the woman gave her something new to think about.

"You know, Leah, if you ever left, it would be for reasons like mine. For the work, not for love."

Her breath caught in her throat. She couldn't answer. Couldn't even think about it, because she was afraid Lydia had verbalized something that might possibly be true.

This welcome should go a long way toward convincing his mother that he and the children were fitting in here in Pleasant Valley. Daniel smiled, relaxing a little as he saw that Mamm had settled into a folding chair in the shade of the big maple in the Beilers' backyard.

His mother had arrived on yesterday's bus from Lancaster County, fresh from helping at the birth of his sister's new babe, and already the Beiler family had planned a picnic to welcome her.

"I hope your mamm wasn't too tired from her trip."

Leah paused next to him, a basketful of rolls in her arm that must be intended for the serving table that was filling up with more food as each family arrived once evening chores were done.

"If she was, seeing her grandchildren has more than made up for it." He nodded toward his mother. "It seems like she and your mamm are finding plenty of things to say to each other."

"Ja." The faintest shadow crossed Leah's green eyes at the thought.

Perhaps she still worried about the persistence of the matchmakers who were determined to yoke them together. That didn't seem as annoying to him as it once had.

"It is gut for her to see that we're fitting in and happy here. She can't help but worry."

"That comes with being a parent." Leah smiled, the shadow vanishing. "My mamm certainly hasn't stopped yet, no matter how old we are."

He nodded, looking down at Leah. She'd be that kind of mother, too, he felt sure. You could see that in the care she had for every one of her students.

"When my children were gone—" He paused, his throat tight at the memory. "I don't know how I'd have gotten through it without my family."

"They must have been overjoyed when the children came home at last." She hesitated. "I wonder if—" She stopped, perhaps not wanting to voice the thought.

But he knew what it must be. "They didn't really understand why I wanted to move afterward. They hated seeing me take the children away from Lancaster County, but once they knew I felt it was the right thing, they supported my decision."

"It's hard to let go, for them and for you." Her understanding was as quick as ever. "But I suppose sometimes it's needed. You had to get away from the reminders."

"Getting the children away was the important thing. The older ones, especially. They couldn't seem to settle down after they came home. I felt as if they were always looking for Ruth. They're better here."

Elizabeth raced up to them at that moment, tugging on Leah's skirt. "Did you see that my grossmutter is here for a visit, Teacher Leah?"

"I know." Leah smiled at her. "That makes you both happy, doesn't it?"

The tenderness in Leah's face when she looked at his daughter touched Daniel's heart. Elizabeth darted off again, giving him the opportunity to say something that was on his mind.

"She was happier even before my mamm arrived. She told me—about her feelings over Ruth's dying that way. About feeling guilty over it."

It was difficult even to say the words, but if he'd learned one thing from this, it was that speaking was better than keeping silent. "She said you wanted her to tell me."

Her face filled with the concern she felt for his child. "I did my best to reassure her, but I knew she needed to hear it from you as well. I hope you're not upset that I didn't tell you about it right away."

Maybe he had been, just for a moment, but then he'd realized that Leah had done exactly what she'd said she would. "I can't be, when it's turned out so well. My little Elizabeth acts as if a weight has been lifted from her shoulders."

"That's wonderful gut. I'm so glad." Her free hand moved, as if she'd reach out to him, but then it stilled.

Maybe she was too aware of the people who watched them. No one came near to interrupt them, though. They were being given a chance to be together, even in a crowd.

There was one thing more he had to say—had to admit—to Leah.

"I should have seen long before this that something was eating at her. You tried to tell me, but I thought I knew better."

"Maybe there are times when things are easier seen by an outsider instead of a parent. It won't help Elizabeth for you to be blaming yourself, you know."

"I know. But you're wrong about one thing, Teacher Leah."

She looked up at him, her gaze puzzled. "I am?"

"Ja." He touched her hand lightly, and even that small contact seemed to send awareness of her flowing through his body. "You're not an outsider."

Her eyes darkened as they met his. Was she as aware of the attraction as he was? His grasp tightened, and her fingers pressed his in response. The noise and activity around them receded, and all he could see was Leah.

He took an abrupt step back, dropping her hand as if it were a hot coal. He'd told himself he should think of remarrying, giving his children a mother. And physical attraction was important, wonderful important, in a woman he might think of courting.

But not if it overpowered his common sense. He'd already made a mistake that had nearly cost him his children. He couldn't make another.

That would sound foolish if he tried to explain it to anyone—the idea that he didn't trust feeling too much for a woman he might want to wed. But he couldn't let his head be ruled by his heart, not in something as important as this was to his family's happiness.

CHAPTER SIXTEEN

*L*eah shuffled through her reports for the week, double-checking to be sure she had everything. She'd be meeting with Stacie in a few minutes, and she didn't want to give the woman any reason to criticize her work. Their relationship was difficult enough already, although it had seemed a little better the last time.

She heard a step and glanced up, tensing a little. But it wasn't Stacie—it was Dr. Brandenmyer, coming down the hallway with his long stride.

He paused when he saw her. "Ms. Beiler, how nice to run into you. Are you here to see John today?"

Her fingers tightened on the sheaf of papers as she shook her head. Why would he think that? Did he know about that private conversation between them the last time she was here?

"I'll be meeting with Stacie in a few minutes to go over my interview reports."

She expected him to hurry off, but instead he sat down next to her, his long white coat flapping around his legs. He peered at her over the top of his glasses, his eyes keen.

"How do you feel about the work, now that you've been at it for a while? Is it satisfying?"

She considered. "I like talking with the families, and I suppose I'm satisfied when I draw something out that I didn't expect. But—" She hesitated.

"Go on." He nodded encouragingly.

She smoothed the papers in her hands, staring down at them. "I just wonder sometimes. Is this really going to help the children?"

"You have one particular family in mind?" His voice was warm and interested, giving her the courage to continue.

"I suppose I do, although naturally I'm concerned for all the affected families. But Naomi Miller—hers was one of the first interviews I did. Two of her three children have Crigler-Najjar disease." She forced herself to be honest. "She is a friend. And my brother is marrying her husband's sister, so naturally, that is a personal interest."

"Nothing wrong with that," he said quickly. He reached out, as if he'd pat her hand, and then seemed to reconsider. "Many of us have personal reasons for becoming involved in a particular line of research. My younger sister was a Down's syndrome child, and she died when she was eight."

"I'm sorry for your loss." Her heart filled with sympathy. So that was what drove him—not just science, but love for a small sister.

He nodded. "I don't tell that to many people." He looked a little surprised at himself. "But even though research doesn't bring about instant results, every small step forward brings us nearer the goal of healthy children." He waved his hands, and she saw the light of passion in his eyes. "There are so many things that can make a difference. Genetic counseling, early testing, even organ transplants . . . Those solutions are here already, and there are more to come."

She nodded, moved by his obvious dedication.

"Your brother and his fiancée should come in for genetic counseling, if they're willing. It may not make a difference in their choices, but at least they'll know what the risks are."

That was a positive step, as the doctor said.

"I'll talk with them about it. Perhaps I can persuade them."

"You do that. I imagine if anyone can, it's you."

She blinked. "Why would you think that?"

"Because you are the teacher. You're a person who affects many lives. If you urge your people to have genetic counseling or to have their babies tested immediately after birth, they'll listen to you."

"I'm not so sure of that."

"I am." He touched the forms she held. "Look at the progress you've made already. You're reaching families who would never talk to us. That's important." He did pat her hand then. "I'm not saying that to make you feel prideful, as you Amish would say. I'm telling you that because you are doing good, important work that could touch lives in ways you can't imagine right now."

"I hope what you say is true." Perhaps, as the Scripture said, she was planting a seed, even if she wouldn't be there to see the harvest.

"It's what keeps me going." He stood, giving her a smile that made him look younger than his years.

The door behind him swung open, and John came in quickly, checking at the sight of them. "I didn't mean to interrupt . . ."

"You're not, you're not." Dr. Brandenmyer glanced at his watch. "I must be off. I have patients." He hurried off toward the exam rooms of the clinic.

John looked at Leah with a quizzical expression. "It's not often Dr. Brandenmyer slows down for a private conversation."

"He was asking how I like the work." Actually, the doctor had given her a new image of herself and what she might do, and she wanted to consider that privately. "How are you?"

"Great." He smiled, looking more relaxed and open than she'd seen since he'd returned. "I can't tell you how much it meant to see Rachel again." He shook his head. "Hard to believe she's a wife and mother. I wish I could meet my nieces and nephew."

"Maybe that will come, in time."

"Maybe. Anyway, I owe you, Leah. Not just for making the arrangements, either. For helping me not to let pride interfere."

She smiled in return. "I seem to recall you often needed someone to do that."

"Good thing I had people who cared enough about me to do it."

She suddenly realized that she was at ease with him. With who he was now, not just thinking about who he used to be. That was another step forward, wasn't it?

"*That's* all you managed to get this week?" Stacie's voice was sharp.

Maybe she had honestly expected more interviews from Leah.

Or perhaps her current ill will had been caused by having seen Leah in conversation with Johnny.

"I had other responsibilities this week." She had no intention of betraying to Stacie that some of those responsibilities had involved Johnny. "And now that I'm going to the farther-off homes, I can't do as many in a day."

"If you took a car, you could do more."

Stacie seemed to have forgotten that she was a volunteer. "I'm afraid I can't afford to hire a car each time I make a visit."

Stacie looked momentarily abashed. "No, I guess not."

She frowned down at the forms for a moment, but Leah had the feeling she wasn't really concentrating on them. Her lips were pressed tightly together, as if she were holding something back.

She flipped a page over and slapped her hand down on it. "Maybe if you weren't spending so much time with John, you'd be able to accomplish more."

For a moment Leah stared at her. How open could she be with Stacie? She didn't know anything about Stacie's background or family, and she couldn't imagine how she'd lived her life.

But the emotion she felt now was surely common enough to both Amish and English.

"I'm afraid you have a mistaken idea about the two of us." Leah kept her voice quiet, not wanting to be seen as confronting the woman. "There is nothing between John Kile and me but an old friendship."

Stacie's eyes narrowed. "Is that why he went off someplace to meet you the other day?"

So Stacie had somehow gotten hold of that, but she obviously didn't know that the meeting had been between John and his sister, not between John and Leah. It was easily explained, but if John hadn't chosen to confide in her, Leah could hardly do it for him.

"That was not . . ." She hesitated, not sure what to say. "That was not personal. I'm still close with his family, you know."

Stacie sniffed. "Tell that to someone who might believe it. The only reason you're here is John."

Funny, she was getting the same response from the English at the clinic as she had from some of her own people. But she didn't feel like laughing.

"John is the person who asked me to volunteer, that's true," she said carefully. "But I've continued with it because it's important work, not because he's here."

Stacie slapped her hands down on the desk in the gesture that seemed to be habitual with her. "Maybe you really believe that, or maybe you don't. But I've seen the way John looks at you." Her face twisted a little, and she was suddenly vulnerable. "He has feelings for you."

"No. No, he doesn't." All she could think was to deny it. It wasn't true. It couldn't be, because if it was, her life would be complicated beyond belief.

Stacie ran her fingers through her hair, shaking her head. "Okay, maybe you really haven't seen it. But trust me, he's completely different when he talks to you than he is with anyone else."

Relief washed through Leah. "But that is because we are old friends. The bond between us goes deep. And I am Amish."

Stacie shrugged. "So what? He gave all that up years ago."

It seemed impossible to make Stacie understand, but she had to try. "He left the church, but a person can't stop being Amish so easily. If you met someone who'd grown up in . . . in Africa, for example, you wouldn't expect that person to be able to turn off how he was raised in the flick of a switch, would you?"

"I guess not." The admission was grudging. "But John didn't grow up in another country."

"His life is closer to that than to anything else you might imagine. He didn't learn English until he went to school, for instance. All the things you take for granted"—she waved her hand toward their surroundings—"the computers, the television, the cell phones, the constant information about the outside world. Try to imagine growing up without ever being exposed to that."

"I can't." Stacie's gaze met hers, and for the first time, there seemed to be no antagonism in it. "I guess that means I can't ever really understand him."

"You care about him." Leah said the words softly. "That's all that's important."

Stacie shook her head a little sadly. "I used to think that. But he doesn't seem to see me that way. And nothing you've said changes the fact that he has feelings for you. Not for me."

"No." Denying it might not convince Stacie, but maybe it would reassure her. Because if Johnny really did have feelings for her—

A flicker of panic went through Leah. She couldn't deal with that. Not again.

Daniel smoothed the sheet over Elizabeth's shoulders. Her face was relaxed in sleep, clearly visible in the light of the full moon pouring through her bedroom window.

She stirred a little, as if she felt his touch, and then slipped deeper into slumber. Heart full, he turned and walked softly across the hall to check on his sons.

Jonah slept on his side, one hand under his pillow. But Matthew knelt by the window, a piece of paper in front of him on the sill.

"Was ist letz?" Daniel whispered, tiptoeing to the window. "What's the matter? Why are you still awake?"

Matthew moved his hand over the paper. "The moon is so bright, I couldn't go to sleep."

Daniel knelt beside the boy, resting his hand on Matthew's shoulder. "What are you writing?"

He could feel tension in his son. "It's a drawing."

"A drawing of what?"

Matthew hesitated. Finally he pushed the paper over to Daniel. "For when we bring the hay in next time. To use with the generator, is all. Not electric."

For a moment Daniel struggled to keep from crumpling the paper. Would the boy's interest in mechanics never leave? He took a deep breath, trying to come up with the right thing to say.

Matthew must have sensed his negative reaction. He pulled back. "It's not electric, Da."

He wanted to shut down the idea. But even as his hand tightened on the paper, he seemed to hear Leah's voice in his head, telling him to listen, to talk, to explain instead of order.

He smoothed the paper out, studying the detailed drawing, and his admiration for his son grew. How many ten-year-olds could come up with something like this?

"I see." He tried to sound neutral. "What made you think

about this? Because you like machines?" *Things that pull you toward the English world?*

Matthew eyed him warily. "It's hard to run the farm mostly by yourself, with only me. Jonah's too little to do much. I thought this would help us do more."

For a moment Daniel couldn't speak. His throat was too tight.

He ruffled his boy's hair, feeling the fine strands under his fingers. "That's smart thinking, Matthew."

The tension left the boy's face. "You think so, Daadi? It's not against the Ordnung. Even the Beilers use one, Mahlon says."

"I know." He hesitated. Leah would say this was a moment he should use to teach his son. "You understand why some things are against the Ordnung, don't you? Because they might take us away from our family and our church, or connect us too much to the outside world. The rules aren't meant to punish us, but only to keep us from being worldly. You understand?"

Matthew studied on it for a moment. "It's hard, isn't it, to figure out why some things are okay and some aren't?"

Daniel nodded. "That's why the whole church will talk and talk about a new thing, trying to figure out what God's will is for us, until Bishop Mose helps us come to an understanding."

Matthew nodded slowly, and Daniel had the sense that he was pondering something deeper.

"Daadi—" He stared down at his hands, clasping the window-sill. "Is that why you didn't try to get us back?"

Daniel's heart stopped, as if it had turned to a chunk of lead in his chest. "Is that—" He had to stop and clear his throat. "Is that what you think? That I didn't try to find you?"

He hadn't talked about it when they'd come home, thinking that it would be like probing an open wound. Better to try to forget, he'd told himself. But Matthew, at least, hadn't forgotten.

"Did you?" Matthew glanced at him then.

"I looked," he said, his voice hoarse. "You know that we don't go to the law to settle disputes among ourselves, but that doesn't mean I didn't look. I thought, if I could find you, maybe I could talk to your mamm about coming home."

Should he have done more? Could he have? The questions haunted him.

"Matthew, didn't you know I loved you and would look for you?"

Matthew's gaze met his then, his eyes wide in the moonlight. "I thought so. But Joe—he was one of Mammi's friends—he said you'd have forgotten about us, and when you didn't come—"

Daniel grabbed his son, pulling him tightly against him. "I love you." He muttered the words against the boy's silky-fine hair. "Don't ever think that I could forget you. I never stopped thinking about you for a single moment when you were gone."

Matthew's arms wrapped around him. "I missed you, Da."

"I missed you, too." He kissed his son's forehead. "But now you're here, and we're together." He cupped Matthew's face in his hands, looking at him seriously. "Always. I promise."

Matthew nodded, a smile trembling on his lips. "Always."

Daniel blinked away tears. "Ser gut," he said softly. "Now I think you should be in bed."

Matthew stood and then paused, turning toward the window. "Daadi, that sounds like a buggy on our lane."

The boy's ears, quicker than his, had caught it first, but now he could hear the clop of hooves and the creak of a buggy. Who would be coming at this time of night?

"To bed with you. I'll take care of it." He started toward the door, mind churning. People didn't come calling this late on a summer night. Was something wrong?

CHAPTER SEVENTEEN

A sound woke Leah from the fringes of sleep. She shifted in the bed, puzzled. What had that been? Not one of the usual noises, or it wouldn't have wakened her.

Moonlight still poured through the window, so it wasn't very late. It felt as if she'd just gotten to sleep, in fact. Perhaps it was Anna, coming home. Had Daad talked to her yet? What had he said? More importantly, would it do any good?

She shoved her heavy braid back over her shoulder and settled her head on the pillow again. If it was Anna, Leah wouldn't get any thanks for showing concern.

The sound came again, but this time, awake, she could identify it. Gravel. Someone had thrown a handful of gravel at her window.

She slid from the bed and ran barefoot to the window, her heart thudding. She wasn't a seventeen-year-old, expecting a sweetheart to wake her for a late-night talk. Something was wrong.

She shoved up the window and leaned out. Below her, silhouetted clearly in the moonlight, stood the horse and buggy Anna had taken when she'd left tonight. Anna was a huddled, dark figure on the seat.

A man stood looking up at her window, his face a pale oval in the moonlight. It was Daniel.

If he spoke, she couldn't hear him for the rush of blood thudding in her ears. "What's happened? What's the matter?" She whispered the words, praying no one else would hear.

Daniel seemed to glance at the other windows of the sleeping house, then at the figure on the seat. Anna didn't move. He looked up at her again and gestured for her to come down.

She waved to signify that she understood. Ducking back inside, she grabbed a shawl from its hook and threw it around her. No time to worry about her hair, tumbling in a braid to her waist, or her bare feet and nightgown. Something had happened to Anna.

She fled silently down the stairs, her mind a jumble of prayers. *Please, Father, please, Father, help her. Help us.*

No sound broke the stillness of the house as she hurried through the kitchen to the back door. Levi and Barbara were sound sleepers, and their windows faced the other way. And Mamm and Daadi were staying at Joseph and Myra's tonight to get an early start going to market tomorrow, so the daadi haus was empty.

She swung the door open carefully, mindful of its creak, and hurried across the porch and down the steps to where Daniel waited.

"What are you doing here? What's happened to Anna?" She threw the questions toward him in a hoarse whisper as she hurried past him to the buggy. "Anna—" She reached for her sister.

Anna, slumped against the seat, didn't stir. She turned to Daniel, furious that he just stood there. "She's hurt or sick—"

"She's drunk," he said, his voice low and flat. "Asleep by now, and you won't be able to wake her anytime soon."

Not content with his explanation, she climbed the buggy step to get close to her sister. "Anna," she said again, pulling at her arm.

Anna moved her head a little, seeming to attempt to rouse herself, and then sank back against the seat again, letting out a small snore. With it came the stench of alcohol.

Leah stared at her for a long moment. Then she stepped down again, turning to Daniel. She could only pray that in the dim light, he wouldn't be able to tell how embarrassed she was.

The horse shifted a little, probably wondering why he was standing here instead of being turned into his comfortable stall. The crickets, their noise interrupted for a few moments by the goings-on, began their ceaseless chirping again.

She took a breath. "How is it you're bringing her home?" Daniel would hardly have been wherever it was Anna had been drinking.

"I heard her buggy coming down my lane." He stepped closer, whispering. "She near enough put it in the ditch before I got to her."

Tears stung Leah's eyes—for her sister and the trouble she was in, for herself and her inability to protect Anna. "Denke," she murmured. "It is kind of you—"

"That can wait." He clasped her wrist, holding it loosely in one strong hand. "We're got to get her settled before the whole house is awake. Can we get her to her room?"

Why he was helping, when he so clearly disapproved of Anna,

she couldn't imagine, but she was grateful. She'd never be able to manage on her own.

"No." Her mind raced. "The daadi haus. My parents are away for the night. If we can get her in there, she'll be all right for the moment." She turned, starting to climb into the buggy. "I'll get her—"

Daniel clasped Leah by the waist and lifted her down. "She's too heavy for you." He climbed up in one long stride, leaned over, and slid his arms around Anna, pulling her to the edge of the seat and then lifting her down.

She lolled in his arms like a rag doll, her unbound hair falling to cover her face.

Anna, what were you doing? Where is this going to end?

"This way." She led the way quickly across the grass toward the daadi haus, safely away from the vicinity of Levi and Barbara's bedroom. She was thankful, in a numb sort of way, for his help. She could never have carried Anna's dead weight on her own.

They went quickly up the stairs, with a little less need to be silent here. Leah pushed open the door to the small extra bedroom, thanking God that the moonlight was still so bright. She hadn't had to put on the gas lamps and risk waking anyone.

Daniel carried Anna's inert figure to the bed and put her down. She wore English clothes, of course. Blue jeans and sneakers, with a knit shirt so short it showed a strip of bare skin.

Leah pulled a coverlet over Anna. She'd have to get her changed, but that could wait until she'd gotten rid of Daniel. He'd seen enough of her family's troubles for one night.

She straightened, well aware that it was impossible to look

dignified in her bare feet and nightgown, with her baby sister lying there drunk.

"You've been most kind, Daniel. I'm grateful. I can take care of everything now."

And if he'd just go away home, she could stop wondering what he must think of them.

Not that it was all that unusual for Amish boys to have a drink too much during their rumspringa, but folks were much less likely to turn a blind, indulgent eye when it was a girl.

If Daniel was aware of her embarrassment, he gave no sign. "I'll take care of the horse and the buggy for you. You'll have your hands full enough here."

Was there no end to the things for which she would owe him gratitude?

"It's gut of you," she said, clasping her hands together to still their trembling. "I don't want to keep you away from the children any longer—"

"My mamm is there, remember?" He turned away, giving her the ghost of a smile. "I'll tend to things outside, and then I'll come back to the daadi haus porch. Come down if you can, just to let me know everything is all right."

She managed to nod, managed to smile. But she didn't think "all right" was going to describe anything about her life very soon.

Anna didn't wake as Leah pulled off her clothes, finding the task harder than she'd expected as she fumbled with the unaccustomed fastenings. Finally she got the jeans off and pulled one of Mamm's nightgowns over Anna's head.

How they were going to explain Anna being in the daadi haus, she didn't know, but that was a problem for later. Now she had to see Daniel again and send him off home.

She bundled the English clothes into a pillowcase and stuffed it into the bottom of the chest of drawers. Then she hurried back down the stairs as quickly and quietly as possible.

She peered through the glass of the door to the back porch. A tall form emerged from the darker shadows of the lilac bush.

She opened the door and beckoned to him. "Come into the kitchen," she whispered. They'd been wonderful lucky already, and she didn't want to risk rousing the house when they were so near done.

She was aware of him behind her, a tall, silent shape that sprang to life when she turned up the gas light in the kitchen, thankful that the windows faced away from the main house.

She took her time turning toward him, not eager to hear his disapproval of Anna and her behavior. But when she looked up at him, she didn't see anything but concern in his expression.

"I don't know how to tell you how much this means," she began, but Daniel shook his head.

"It makes no trouble," he said, his voice low, as if the silence around them impelled him to be quiet even if no one could hear. "I cleaned up the buggy as best I could without drawing any attention to the stable."

"There was no damage?"

"None that I could see. I don't think anyone will notice that anything happened." He fell silent, but he looked at her steadily, as if waiting.

Waiting to hear what she would do. He was willing to let her handle it, it seemed, but he probably doubted her ability.

Well, fair enough. She doubted it, too.

"I talked to my daad about Anna." She pulled the shawl tighter around her, needing its warmth. "I hated to burden him, but I couldn't take the responsibility on myself any longer."

"You did the right thing, Leah." His response was quick and comforting.

Her fingers tightened on the soft fabric of the shawl. "Did I? I hoped it would make a difference—that Anna would change once Daad talked to her. And then she goes and does something ferhoodled like this."

Tears welled in her eyes, and she fought to blink them back.

Daniel took a step closer, his hand going out to encircle hers. His grip warmed and comforted her. "As much as you love your sister, you can't take the responsibility of trying to be her mamm."

She resisted the impulse to lean on his strength. "There are so many years between us—by the time another girl baby came along, I was old enough to be the little mother to her. I guess I still feel that way."

"That's only natural. And with your mamm's sickness, you've tried your best to spare her from worry."

"Right now I don't feel as if I've done a very gut job."

His fingers smoothed the skin on the back of her hand, as if he gentled one of the children with his touch. "You've done your best. Anna is old enough now to bear the consequences of her actions herself."

Leah looked up, very aware of how close he was. "Yet you were ready to help me cover for her."

"I was." He looked a little surprised at his own actions. "There seemed no need to let your brother and sister-in-law in on it. Besides, I owe you."

"Owe me? If you're talking about Elizabeth, I just encouraged her to talk."

He shook his head. "Elizabeth, but not only her. There's Matthew, too."

"What about Matthew?" Much as she'd like to help Matthew adjust to his new life, she couldn't see that she'd done much there.

"Things came to a bit of a head with the boy." He looked down at their clasped hands, but he seemed to be seeing something else. "I felt—well, I almost reacted the wrong way, but I thought about what you would do and say. That you'd say it was better to listen, no matter how hard it was to hear what my son had to say."

"And you did?" She had trouble concentrating on his words, too aware of the way his fingers traced circles on the back of her hand.

"Ja." His brows drew together. "It wasn't easy to hear, for sure. Matthew— I guess he thought I didn't care for the children enough to fight to get them back."

Her heart clenched with pain for him. "He must know you love them. Deep inside, I'm sure all three of them have no doubt about that." Now it was her turn to want to comfort him.

His fingers tightened on hers. "I hope so. If I should lose them again—"

That was the fear in his heart, she realized. Deep down, what terrified him was the thought that once his children were old enough to choose, they'd leave.

She clasped his hand in both of hers, hoping he could feel her caring. "It will be all right. They're doing better all the time, really they are."

"Because of you."

Their fingers entangled, and Leah's breath hitched at the sudden passion in his voice. "I haven't done much."

"You've understood. And you've made me see how much they need a mother."

Her heart was thudding so loudly that she could hear it, beating in her ears. A step would close the distance between them. A word of encouragement, and Daniel would propose. She could almost hear the words, and panic flooded her.

She couldn't. She couldn't let him take such an irrevocable step, not when she wasn't ready to give him an answer.

She took a cautious breath and then a deliberate step back. "The children are very dear to me." She loosed her hands, and he let her go instantly. "But it is late now, and I should check on Anna."

"It is late. I must go." But his gaze held hers for a long moment, and the unspoken question seemed to sizzle in the air between them.

He hesitated a moment longer. Then he nodded and went quickly out.

Leah glanced across the crowded kitchen at Rachel's house. The group of women had been there since five this morning, making sandwiches for a hoagie sale to help with medical costs for Naomi Miller's children.

The volume of chatter continued unabated, as it had since before sunrise. White kapps fluttered like so many birds in flight around the long tables that had been set up in the farmhouse kitchen. In all that time, Anna had managed never to look at her.

It had been that way for the entire uncomfortable week. Daad had been upset to hear what Leah had had to say, Anna had avoided speaking to her, and she had been haunted by the memory of what had nearly happened between her and Daniel.

Mamm handed her a hoagie. She rolled it in wax paper and secured it with tape, then added it to the waiting cooler. She stole a glance at her mother's face. It was as serene as ever, her eyes intent upon her task.

At least Mamm didn't know about any of it, so there was nothing to worry her. Daadi had decided that the situation with Anna was best handled by him. And she certainly hadn't confided her thoughts about Daniel to anyone.

"Anna has been very quiet today."

That jerked Leah's gaze back to her mother. Was there a concern hidden in that comment? Or was it her own sense of guilt at keeping something from Mamm that made her feel so?

"Is she?" She wrapped the next hoagie. "She's been busy, I guess." She managed a smile. "And she's not at her best in the morning, is she?"

Mamm shook her head, smiling a little. "Remember how hard it was to get her out of bed when she was little? That must be it."

"I'm sure it is." *I wish it was.*

Mamm sighed a little. "I'd like it fine if she'd just settle down to one sweetheart." She lowered her voice under the chatter of women around them. "Do you think she likes Jonas Stoltzfus?"

"I'm afraid she finds Jonas a little—well, too settled and serious for her." Actually, Anna had said that Jonas was as dull as dishwater, which didn't say much for Mamm's matchmaking hopes.

"Settled and serious are good things in a husband. Anna's trouble is that she doesn't think about what her life will be like a few years down the road, when she has a home and children to care for."

"Maybe in a year or two she'll start looking at it that way."

"Maybe so, but it's time already for her to think of something besides running with her friends." Mamm used a table knife to stuff the sandwich filling into the roll a little more emphatically than was necessary. "A girl her age should be thinking of marriage."

It looked as if Mamm had been worrying about Anna despite all their efforts to shield her. "She might be waiting to fall in love first."

Anna's words echoed in Leah's mind. Anna already thought she might be in love with that English boy.

"Falling in love is wonderful gut, but it's not everything." Mamm's expression grew reminiscent. "Your father and I didn't really understand what love was until we'd been married a few years and gone through some trials together."

"You and Daadi are special. Anna—well, Anna doesn't think of marriage that way."

"And what about you, Leah?" Her mother's gaze probed, seeming to peel away the layers of her protection. "A gut marriage can be made without starting out as boy-and-girl sweethearts."

She could feel her cheeks growing warm. How much did Mamm know, or guess, about Daniel and her? "I ... I don't ..."

"It's all right." Mamm pressed her hand. "I don't mean to

embarrass you, daughter. But think about it. Listen for God's guidance."

"I will." That she could promise, and it seemed to content her mother. She turned back to the sandwiches with a satisfied look.

How could her mother know what had nearly happened between her and Daniel that night? She couldn't, that was all. But Mamm seemed to have an extra sense where her daughters were concerned.

It was fairly obvious what her mother thought she should do. She herself wasn't so sure.

She'd gone over and over every word, every gesture. Sometimes she'd almost convince herself that she was imagining things, but then she'd remember the warmth of Daniel's gaze, the strength of his hands, and she'd be convinced again that she'd been right.

Daniel Glick would propose to her if she gave him the slightest encouragement. And she didn't have the faintest idea what she should do.

She'd decided, after Johnny left, that marriage wasn't for her, and she'd been content with that decision all these years. She hadn't been able to love Johnny enough to have the courage to leave or the strength to convince him to stay. How could she think she could love Daniel enough to be a mother to his children and a wife to him?

"Here is Daniel, come for his order," Mamm said. "You fix it for him, Leah. I'm ready for some coffee." She flitted away.

Mamm wasn't exactly being subtle. Leah could only hope Daniel would attribute her flushed cheeks to the warmth of the kitchen.

Daniel stepped aside to let the Klopp boys hurry past him with the boxes of orders for the men who worked at Bishop Mose's harness shop. Nodding and smiling to those he passed, he came straight to her table.

"Rachel said you'd fill my order." His smile grew warmer when he looked at her.

"Ja, I have it here." She pulled his slip from the pile and began to stack hoagies in a paper bag, trying to find something light to say to him. "You're surely not going to eat all these yourself."

He shook his head, leaning against the table so that he was close to her. "Some of the brothers have come to help with the first cutting of hay today. Mamm wanted to cook for them, but she has enough to do with the children. And they'll enjoy the sandwiches fine."

Since he didn't have a wife to make the lunch. Was that a reminder of his need? He was watching her with such warmth in the deep blue of his eyes that she lost count of how many sandwiches she'd put in the bag and had to start again.

"They'll like these," she said, rallying. "And the money goes to a good cause."

He nodded. "It's a joy to help."

"Ja." It was, wasn't it? That was woven deeply into their way of life, the joy and satisfaction that came from helping your brothers and sisters whenever they had need. And knowing that, in turn, if you needed, they would be there.

It was part of what she loved about being Amish, part of what made them belong to each other.

Maybe, if she were Daniel's wife, she'd lose this disturbing sense she had of never quite fitting. But was it fair to him to marry for a selfish reason?

She glanced at Daniel, and their gazes met. Tangled.

She took a strangled breath. The attraction was there, certain sure, even in the midst of a crowd. That was important to a marriage.

But love?

Daniel had given her the impression, through everything he said about his wife, that if he offered his hand, that didn't mean he was offering his heart.

Still, maybe that was for the best. Maybe, as Mamm had hinted, it was possible to build a good marriage anyway.

Chapter Eighteen

Leah had gone to her room after supper, saying she had to work on her reports. That was true, but a stronger reason was to get away from the tension she seemed to feel everywhere she went lately.

The door opened before she had so much as looked at the first page. Anna stepped into the room, closing the door behind her.

The wave of gladness that swept through Leah was startling in its strength. Anna was ready to talk at last, and for a moment she dared hope that the old, easy relationship between them could be restored.

Anna took an impetuous step toward her. "How can you possibly be friendly with that man?"

It looked as if her hope had been a little premature. She tried to swallow her disappointment. "Come, sit down. If you're talking about John Kile, I've told you already—"

"Not John." Anna dismissed him with a wave of her hand. "Daniel Glick. I saw how you two were talking this morning."

"Daniel." She readjusted her thinking. "Why would you care if I'm friends with Daniel? I should think you'd be happy about it. Everyone else is busy trying to match us up."

"He fits right in with all the rest of the interfering busybodies." Anna's hands clenched against her skirt.

"If you're embarrassed because Daniel saw you . . ." She hesitated, not wanting to say the word. ". . . saw you the other night, you shouldn't blame him."

"I'm not embarrassed." But Anna's cheeks flushed slightly.

Leah longed to grasp the clenching hands in hers, wanted to smooth away the hurt and shame that her little sister surely was feeling. But Anna wouldn't accept comfort from her now, and maybe she needed plain talking more than she needed comfort.

"I would say you owe Daniel your thanks. He found you, he helped you, and more than that, he kept silent about it."

"And now he can look down on me. I hate that he's involved."

When she was six, Anna would have sat in the corner for talking that way. Leah felt her exasperation rising. It was a pity that wouldn't work now.

"You were the one who involved him," she said flatly. "You got drunk, you drove into the wrong lane, you nearly ended up in the ditch. You should be on your knees thanking the Lord that it was Daniel who found you and not someone who'd be quick to spread the news all over the valley."

At last Anna's gaze evaded hers. Her cheeks flushed. "Maybe," she muttered. "But I still don't see why you're so close with him."

"I've helped with the children, as any neighbor would when there are motherless children."

Anna stared at her, eyes widening. "You're not thinking—

Leah, you can't be thinking about marrying him just because his children need a mother!"

Now it was her turn to glance away. "He hasn't asked me," she said, knowing she was equivocating.

"How could you think of it? To marry a man you don't love—sometimes I think you don't even know what love is."

The control Leah had been exercising suddenly slipped away from her. She clenched her hands to keep from grabbing her sister and shaking her.

"And I suppose you know all about love at eighteen."

"More than you," Anna snapped back. "I said it before, and it's true. You don't have any feelings at all."

Leah did grab her then, startling herself as much as she did Anna. Grasping her sister's arms, she held her fast.

"How would you know what feelings I have? You don't spare a thought for anyone's feelings but your own. I know what it is to love and to lose and to spend your days trying to hide the pain. I don't need a child like you trying to give me lessons in what it is to love."

Anna stared at her for a moment, eyes wide in a white face. Then she jerked free and ran out of the room.

She might not feel at ease at the clinic, Leah decided, but at the moment, being here was better than being at home. She settled on a bench in the hallway, planning to go through her list of potential interviewees until her driver returned for her.

But her hands lay idle on the sheet. The days since that dreadful scene with Anna had been so strained that even Barbara, occupied as she was with her pregnancy, the house, and the children, had noticed it. Unfortunately her well-meant attempts to interfere had only made things worse.

Forgive me, Father. I sinned. I expressed anger with my sister instead of trying harder to help her. Now she won't even speak to me, and I fear I've driven her away. Please, forgive me and show me how to help Anna.

"Leah? Is something wrong?"

It was a measure of her distraction that she hadn't even heard Johnny approach. She shook her head, but the lump in her throat kept her from speech.

"I can see—" He stopped when a woman came out of the waiting room, leading a small boy by the hand. He waited until they'd left, then held out his hand to Leah. "We can't talk here. Come out to the back porch."

There wasn't anything Johnny could do. There wasn't anything anyone could do, but Leah couldn't resist the concern in his face. Avoiding his hand, she rose and walked down the hallway with him.

A couple of rocking chairs had been added to the back porch furniture. She sat down, pleating her skirt with her fingers.

"So tell me." Johnny sat down opposite, reaching out to still the nervous movement of her hand. "It must be something bad for you to look that way."

"It's Anna." It was a relief just to say the words. "I'm worried about Anna."

"What has Anna been up to that causes you this much distress?" His voice, warm and gentle, was the voice of her friend, of the person she'd known and cared about her whole life. "Running around too much with her friends? Trying to land you with her chores?"

That coaxed a reluctant smile from her, but almost immediately it trembled from her lips. "If only it were that." She shook her head. "I know I can't expect her to have so tame a rumspringa as I did . . ."

He patted her hand. "No, I'm sure not." There was amusement in the tone.

She pulled her hand away, straightening. "Don't laugh. It's not funny." She looked at him, her eyes welling with tears. "Johnny, she came home so drunk that she was within inches of wrecking the buggy. Only the grace of God kept her from injury."

She was relieved to see that her words wiped the amusement from his face.

"I'm sorry, Leah. She wasn't hurt, though?"

"No. Oh, I suppose my brothers probably did as bad, but this is my baby sister."

"You've tried to talk to her?"

She felt the flood of sympathy, and it warmed her. "Tried and tried again. Daad has talked to her, too, with no results either. I'm afraid she's—"

She stopped, unable to put her fear into words.

"What?" His voice was gently insistent. "What do you think is going to happen to her?"

Her breath caught in her throat, and she had to force the words out. "I think she might leave."

He didn't immediately respond, giving her time to think that maybe Johnny wasn't the best person to talk to about this. After all, that was just what he'd done.

"I'm sorry," he said at last. "I know how scared that must make you."

"It does." The tightness in her throat eased just a little. "I don't begrudge her running-around time. I even understand it. And she's the baby, so maybe she's had her own way a little too much. But this—"

She stopped, shook her head. "I'm sorry. This is probably hard for you to talk about. I shouldn't burden you with it."

"You're not." He smiled slightly. "We're friends. Old friends, no matter what else happened. You can say anything to me, and I promise it won't go any further. You don't have to worry about that."

"I don't." She managed to return the smile. "I know I can trust you." Johnny wouldn't talk. And he wouldn't condemn, either.

"You've been keeping this to yourself. That only increases the worry." He shook his head. "Leah, you're always trying to take care of everyone. Look, what's the worst thing that could happen?"

"I could lose her." She looked at him steadily. *The way Rachel lost you. The way I lost you.* She wouldn't say it, but he must know she was thinking it.

"If she left . . ." He paused. "Maybe I'm not completely impartial, Leah. But would it be such a terrible thing? You could still have a relationship with her. Maybe that's what she needs to do."

"No!" She rejected that with every fiber of her being. "Anna is too young. She's rebellious, and she doesn't really understand what it would be like. Or what she'd be giving up."

He leaned back in the rocker, his gaze intent on her face. "Maybe so. But sometimes, for some people, it's the right thing to do."

"No. Not Anna." She had to cling to that, because the alternative was too frightening.

"Maybe you're right. Maybe Anna is too young, or thinking about it for the wrong reasons. But you're not too young, Leah. Is it possible you're so worried about Anna because you're thinking about it, too?"

She jerked back as if he'd hit her. "No. I'm not."

He brushed that aside with his hand. "Well, maybe you should be."

She started to rise. She didn't want to hear this, and all the comfort she'd felt from Johnny was gone in an instant.

He grabbed her hand. "Wait. Just let me say this one thing. Can't you do that?"

She sat, perched on the edge of the chair, ready to flee. "Go on."

"You're a good teacher, Leah." He leaned toward her, hands braced on his knees. "I know that. But think how much more you could do if you were able to develop your teaching gifts to the fullest. You could get a degree, you could learn all the latest methods, you could—"

She stood, shaking her head. "No. Don't. You have no right to say that to me, John."

"Why not?" He stood, too, and passion filled his voice. "I'm the person you said you loved once. Doesn't that give me a right to be concerned about you?"

Still shaking her head, she hurried to the door. "That was a lifetime ago."

"It's still true." His voice roughened. "Leah, let yourself think about it. Don't you fear that you aren't preparing your scholars for the world they have to live in? Haven't you thought that maybe the right place for you isn't here?"

She couldn't listen. She hurried through the hallway, out the front door, and down the steps to the parking lot where her driver was waiting.

But she couldn't outrun his words. They echoed in her heart, and she knew what she was afraid of. She was afraid they were true.

He'd been on the verge of proposing marriage to Leah. Daniel frowned down at the road disappearing under the wheels of his buggy. The night that he'd taken Anna home, those quiet moments in the kitchen together . . .

Leah had been the one to draw back. He could only be grateful for that. He'd known, in the clear light of day, that he'd almost acted on impulse, something he'd vowed never to do.

He should have been able to think the situation through and come to a sensible conclusion. That was the only way to approach marrying again. Practical. Logical. Make a decision on what would be best for himself and his children.

Unfortunately, every time he tried to do that, the memory of Leah's caring face, her vulnerable eyes, got in the way.

There was the lane leading to the schoolhouse, and sure enough, Leah's buggy stood at the hitching post. He'd stopped by the Beiler farm, and Barbara had been delighted to tell him that Leah had gone to the school to do some work on her teaching materials. Barbara had obviously hoped there was a romantic reason for his visit.

Romantic wasn't the word he'd have picked, he guessed. He had to talk to Leah, had to make a decision, one way or the other.

And then, of course, she'd have her say. He smiled ruefully as he stopped at the hitching post and climbed down. Maybe he was kidding himself even to think that her answer would be yes.

He went quickly to the open door and hesitated on the threshold. Without the children, the schoolroom was a little forlorn, as if it waited for their return.

Chiding himself for his fanciful thoughts, he stepped inside. Leah stood at her desk, a stack of books in front of her, watching him.

"Daniel. What brings you here?" She brushed a strand of hair back from her face and came around the desk toward him.

"I wanted to ask how things are going with Anna." He went toward her and rested his hand on the corner of the desk. "Each time I've seen you since then, there have been so many other people around that I didn't want to bring it up."

"I'm grateful for your silence. I told Anna she should be, too. There are others who'd have been hard put to hold their tongues if they'd found her that night."

"Judging by the cold shoulder she's given me each time I've seen her, I don't guess she feels very grateful about it."

"No. But she should." Leah's eyes darkened with worry, making her look vulnerable. "I don't understand her anymore. I never thought I would say that."

"Is she not sorry for what she did, then?" He'd think the embarrassment alone would be enough to bring the child to her senses.

"If she is, she's doing a fine job of hiding it." She smoothed the errant strand of hair back again. "All she seems to think about is going out with her friends."

"English friends." He filled in the word.

"I suppose so. She doesn't confide in me." A spasm of pain crossed her face as she said the words.

It made him want to put his arms around her, comfort her, tell her everything would be all right. But he couldn't. Because he didn't have the right, and because he couldn't be sure it would. He barely knew Anna, but he feared for her.

Leah sighed, shaking her head. "I'm sorry. I shouldn't have poured all that out to you. It's not your burden. It's ours."

True enough. But if he did ask her to marry him, Anna would become his problem, too. And there was something—something he felt driven to say, even if it made Leah angry.

"I'm sorry for your troubles. I wish I could be of more help."

She managed a smile, but the life seemed to have gone out of it. "You've already helped more than you know."

"If I have, I'm glad of it," he said. He hesitated. "There's something that's been on my mind since that night. And I don't know what to do except just to say it."

Her eyes grew wary. "I don't think—"

He shook his head, knowing he had to blurt the words out before he could change his mind. "Are you sure your work at the clinic isn't setting the wrong example for Anna?"

Leah's eyes widened with shock and pain, and the look cut him to the heart. But it had to be said, didn't it?

"I don't want to hurt you. But isn't it possible that she sees you spending time with the English, working with them, and thinks it's all right?"

"That's completely different!" Leah had recovered, and now it was anger that flashed in her green eyes. "I volunteer at the clinic because I want to help the children, and for no other reason."

"You didn't go there until John Kile came back." It couldn't be jealousy he felt when he said the fence-jumper's name.

"I didn't know that there was anything I could do until John told me about it." She threw the words back at him.

"You're there often, working with those people." He pushed doggedly on, even knowing he was antagonizing her with every word. "Maybe you've started enjoying it."

"And maybe you're talking about Ruth, not me." She looked shocked that the words had come out of her mouth.

No more shocked than he felt. For a moment he could only gape at her.

But he owed her an honest answer. "I guess what happened between me and Ruth affects how I look at it. But can you be sure I'm not right?"

She hesitated, her hands straining against each other. She took a deep breath. "I'd like to say that it's not your concern."

"That wouldn't be true, would it?" He took her tense hands in his. "We both know we've been moving toward something, Leah, even if no words have been spoken."

She stared down at their clasped hands for a moment. "You're saying that my work at the clinic is a barrier between us."

"I guess I am." He didn't want to draw a line between them, but what else could he say? No one could go through what he'd been through and come out unchanged.

She drew her hands away slowly. Her shoulders straightened. "I don't think I can be the woman you want, Daniel."

Her words, her voice, her expression all told him that that was an end to it.

Chapter Nineteen

When she saw the headlights coming down the dark lane to the farmhouse, Leah knew deep in her soul that something bad had happened to Anna. Maybe it was that instinct, stronger than words, which had kept her awake this night.

Pulling her shawl tight around her, she pressed her face to the living room window. The lights belonged to a police car. She could make it out now, see the dome on its roof and the reflective letters on the side.

Her heart thundering in her ears, she ran toward the door that led out to the daadi haus, but before she could reach it, Daad was already there, pulling suspenders over his shoulders. His face was bleak.

"Anna," he said.

"She's not home." Leah's voice broke, and she clutched his arm. "She's not here. It must be—"

"Ja." His face tightened until the skin seemed stretched over the bones. "You should go and stay with your mamm."

Before Leah could move, her mother came in, clad like Leah in a nightgown and holding a shawl tightly around her, as if it would protect her from whatever was coming toward them.

"No need," she said. "I'm here."

Daadi patted her shoulder. "Go back, now. Let Leah stay with you until we know what is wrong."

She shook her head, her graying braids swinging. "I must hear it, Elias. She is my baby."

Footsteps echoed on the porch, heavy and authoritative. The knock on the door hammered against Leah's heart.

Mamm clung to Daad now, so Leah went to open it. The tall state trooper was young—young enough to look embarrassed at the sight of her in her nightgown.

"Is this the home of Anna Beiler?"

She stepped back, opening the door wide and gesturing for him to enter. "Yes." She struggled to catch her breath. "I am Leah Beiler, her sister. Our parents, Elias and Martha Beiler." She clutched her hands together, framing a wordless prayer. "Anna— how bad is it?"

He frowned, looking as if he were trying to remember whatever he'd learned about how to break bad news. "There's been an accident out on the Fisherdale Road—a car and a buggy. Anna—"

He stopped as Levi thudded down the stairs, followed by Barbara, voluminous in her nightgown. Mahlon came last, stumbling and rubbing his eyes.

"Was ist letz?" Levi said, face white. "What's the matter?"

"It's Anna." Leah was astonished that the words came out so calmly. "An accident."

"How bad?" Mahlon clutched the railing, looking young and scared.

She turned back to the officer.

"Anna Beiler was injured," he said stiffly. "And three other people were hurt, too. They've all been taken to the county hospital. I have instructions to drive you people there."

"How bad is she hurt?" she said again. *Please, Lord, please don't take our Anna away.*

His official mask slipped a little, and she saw the conscientious young man beneath it. "I don't know, ma'am. Honestly. They didn't tell me that. Just to break the news and drive you." He glanced at her nightgown and then away. "I'll wait while you folks dress and take you in."

"Ja. We all go," Levi began, but Daadi shook his head at the words.

"No, no. Leah will go with us, to talk to the doctors. She'll understand better how to deal with them. Mahlon, you must hurry to tell Joseph, so they don't hear from someone else. And Levi, you fetch Bishop Mose and ask him to come to the hospital."

Mahlon looked as if he'd argue for a moment, but then he nodded. He ran upstairs.

"I'll dress and then help Mamm—" Leah began.

"I'll do that," Barbara said quickly. She gave her a gentle push. "You just get ready."

Nodding, Leah ran for the stairs, her mind spinning more rapidly than she could believe. She tried to grab on to something reassuring.

Injured. Anna was injured. It might not be serious—maybe nothing more than a broken bone.

And the others who were hurt—three, the policeman had said. What other families were getting a visit like this one right now?

Praying, the words tumbling over one another in her haste, Leah pulled her clothes on, fumbling with the straight pins that secured her dress.

Hurry, hurry. The words echoed to the thud of her heart. *Hurry.*

In moments she was racing back down the stairs again. Mahlon and Levi had already hustled out the back toward the stable. Better, as Daad said, to send them off to tell folks—better that than have them all tripping over each other at the hospital, waiting, not knowing . . .

Barbara came in with Mamm, and together they walked her out to the waiting police car. Barbara urged Mamm into the middle of the backseat, so that she'd have Daad on one side and Leah on the other.

Leah shot her a look of thanks. Barbara had her faults, maybe, as they all did, but she was steady and calm in a crisis.

The doors slammed, and the car pulled out. Mamm's hand closed tightly over Leah's. She wrapped it warmly in hers, wanting to say something encouraging, unable to think of anything.

All she could think of was Anna—of all that bright, eager life tumbled into a ditch someplace in the wreckage of her buggy.

Leah glanced toward the front of the police car. The dim lights on the dashboard showed her the young policeman's profile, his hands on the wheel.

"Do you know anything else about the accident? Were you there?"

"No, ma'am, I wasn't. All they told me was what I've told you." They reached the road, and the vehicle seemed to spring forward. "We'll be at the hospital in a few minutes, ma'am. The investigating officers will be there. They'll be able to answer your questions."

The car passed the turnoff to the Glick farm, and she could see that the house was dark and still. Daniel would be a tower of strength at a time like this. But Daniel wasn't there. Wouldn't be there.

Her father reached over to wrap his hands around theirs. "We must pray."

Nodding, Leah closed her eyes, letting the sound of her father's voice roll over her as he led them in prayer for Anna.

"The doctors are still running tests." The emergency room nurse gave them a look of such sympathy that Leah's courage failed her. She wouldn't look that way unless it was serious.

Please, Father. Give me Your strength, for I have none of my own.

The Lord must have heard her, since she didn't crumple to the tile floor, although her hands gripped the counter's edge so hard that it cut into her fingers.

"Can we see her?"

The woman consulted her computer. "It looks as if she's just been taken to a patient room. You can go up, and the doctor will tell you what they know so far."

Leah forced herself to ignore the stares of the English who sat in the waiting room. The nurse checked the room number and then pointed out the direction to the elevator. Putting her arm around her mother's waist, Leah led the way.

When they reached the proper floor, she had to urge Mamm

forward out of the elevator. How long was Mamm going to be able to hold up? Her face was gray and drawn, and the hand that gripped Leah's strained.

She glanced at her father. Daad, always so strong and controlled, looked almost frail in this setting.

My parents are old. The thought shocked her. *They have grown old, and I didn't notice.*

Leah checked the room numbers and led the way down the hall. As they neared the room, a doctor strode out and then stopped at the sight of them.

"We are Anna Beiler's family." Leah spoke, because her parents seemed unable to do so. "Can you tell us how she is?"

He shot a glance over his shoulder into the room and then turned back to them. "We're still waiting for the results of some of the cranial tests we've run—an EEG, CAT scan . . ." He paused, looking at her doubtfully. "Do you understand what I mean?"

It wasn't the first time she'd encountered the assumption that the Amish were ignorant, and it probably wouldn't be the last.

"Yes, doctor. My sister has a head injury, and you are trying to determine the extent of the damage."

He nodded, looking relieved. "She's unconscious but stable right now. We're hoping surgery won't be necessary, but a lot depends on the results we see and on how she does during the next few hours."

He stepped to one side, clearing the doorway for them.

"You can go in and sit with her. Don't touch any of the equipment."

She bent her head in obedience and ushered Mamm and Daadi into the room.

Anna lay in the high metal bed, as still as if she lay in her coffin. Her head was bandaged, her face scraped and bruised. Machinery hummed and buzzed, and what seemed like dozens of tubes snaked around her. A nurse in blue scrubs appeared to be checking a monitor.

Leah felt her mother sag and grasped her waist, supporting her. "It's all right, Mammi. Look, we'll pull a chair over so you can sit right next to Anna."

The nurse gave a sympathetic smile and pushed a green plastic chair across the floor. "That's right, honey," she said. "Sit down right here. Don't try to wake her, but you can talk quietly to her. It might comfort her to hear your voice."

Mamm, given something positive to do, straightened and walked to the chair. Leaning forward, hand on the bed as if she wanted to touch Anna but didn't dare, she began to talk softly in the dialect that Anna would know, even if the nurse wouldn't understand.

Daad moved to the other side of the bed and clasped his hands, eyes closing, lips moving in prayer.

The nurse gave Leah an assessing look. "You'll make sure no one touches or bumps the equipment?"

She nodded.

"I'll have a couple more chairs brought in for you."

"Is there anything else we can do?"

The nurse shook her head. "Just wait, I'm afraid." She glanced at Leah's father. "And pray." She went out, leaving the door open.

The chairs arrived, and Leah persuaded Daadi to sit. Minutes ticked by. Anna didn't move.

Leah's heart seemed almost too full to pray, and she struggled to find the words.

Gracious Lord, extend Your hand to my little sister. Guide the doctors, and give her Your healing.

Her hands clasped tightly together, and she began to murmur the words of the Twenty-third Psalm, reaching for the comfort of the familiar, beautiful words.

Someone would come. Sometime, someone would come to tell them if Anna would live. If Anna would be whole again.

Finally a footstep sounded in the hall outside the door. She glanced up to see a uniformed figure peering in—the township police chief, face somber. He caught her eye and gestured.

With a murmured explanation, she went out to him, faintly relieved to see a face that was at least familiar. The People knew and respected Chief Walker—he was said to be both fair and kind.

"Teacher Leah, I'm sorry for the trouble that's come on you folks." He pushed his hat back on his head, his lean, weathered face worried. "How is your sister doing?"

"We don't know anything yet. The doctors are waiting for some test results."

He nodded. "Well, that's something. The other three young folks got off with minor injuries—a broken wrist, some cracked ribs."

She was ashamed to realize she hadn't given them much thought. "I'm glad of that."

"The folks in the buggy got off light, too. Lucky to escape with bumps and bruises."

For an instant his words didn't seem to register. She frowned, shaking her head a little. "I'm sorry, but what you do mean? Was someone in the buggy with Anna?"

His face changed, and he looked at her with what must be pity. She seemed to freeze. Something bad was coming. She knew it as surely as she'd known there was trouble when she saw the lights.

He cleared his throat. "I'm sorry. I thought you knew. Anna wasn't in the buggy. Anna was driving the car."

An abyss seemed to open before her. She reached behind her for the stability of the wall, pressing her hand against it as she tried to make sense of this.

"That . . . That can't be. I'm sorry, but someone has gotten it wrong. Anna left home in her buggy."

He shook his head, sorrow carving deeper lines in his face. "I'm sorrier than I can say for this, but Anna wasn't driving a buggy. I don't know where she left it. She was behind the wheel of the car when it sideswiped the buggy."

Leah grasped for sanity in a world gone askew. "But she doesn't know how. She doesn't have a license. Who would let her drive a car?"

"We both know she's not the first Amish teen to drive a car. It belonged to one of the other kids, so I suppose he let her drive it. I haven't gotten the whole story from the other teenagers yet, but you can be sure I'll keep after them until I have the truth."

He was trying to reassure her, she supposed, but she still grappled to get her mind around it all. "The buggy—who was the family?"

"Aaron Esch, his wife and two children. They live over toward Fisherdale. Not in your district, I guess, but I reckon you'd know them."

She nodded numbly. Before their district had gotten so large that it had to be split into two, the Esch family had been part of their church. Aaron was first cousin to Jonah Esch, whose children were her scholars.

"They were all right, you said?" She grasped for something hopeful in this dreadful situation.

He nodded. "Seems like Anna swerved, trying to avoid them, and lost control. The driver's side hit a tree. She had the worst of it."

"Ja." She glanced toward the room.

"I'm awful sorry," he said again. He shifted from one foot to the other. "I sure don't want to add to your troubles, but . . . well, maybe you should think about hiring a lawyer for Anna."

A wave of dizziness swept over her, and she fought it off. She had to hang on. The family depended on her.

She had to clear her throat before she could speak. "You know that it is not our way to go to the law."

"This time the law's going to come to you, I'm afraid. It seems like Anna's been doing a lot that's not your way. Now, you know I'm not one to come down hard on Amish youngsters who are just having fun during their rumspringa. But this time folks got hurt."

Pain had a stranglehold on her throat. She forced out the words. "What will happen to Anna?"

He shrugged. "Not really up to me. I just investigate it. The district attorney will have to decide whether he wants to prosecute."

Prosecute. The word had a terrifying sound.

The chief patted her hand. "You take my advice and talk to your folks about getting a lawyer for Anna. That's the best thing they can do right now." He settled his hat firmly on his head and walked off toward the elevator.

Leah sagged against the wall. She had to have a moment to gather herself before she could go back into the room. Had to think, had to decide.

But she knew that no matter how long she thought, she wouldn't come up with any satisfying way to tell her parents.

CHAPTER TWENTY

Daniel stepped off the elevator at the hospital. It wasn't hard to figure out where to go—a waiting room was spilling folks out into the hallway, as most of the church district seemed to be here to give support to the Beiler family.

That was the strength of being Amish. The People were always there for one another. Not saints, just ordinary folks with their share of faults, but when one was hurting, all were there to lend a hand.

He halted in the doorway, returning muted greetings and nods as his gaze searched the room for Leah. There she was, making her way from one person to another, probably expressing her parents' appreciation for their kindness.

Bishop Mose Yoder clapped him on the shoulder, a smile lighting his gentle face. "Have you heard the good news? Anna has been waking up, even talking to her mamm and daad. Praise God, it looks as if she will be well."

"That is good news." Daniel murmured a silent prayer. Both of them knew that even if Anna recovered physically, she'd have other troubles that needed praying for.

His gaze followed Leah's progress through the room. He'd had his final answer from her, but that didn't keep him from wanting to help her, as a friend and a neighbor, if nothing more.

She turned toward him, and he sucked in a sharp breath. Suffering had drawn her skin taut. Her eyes were dark and shadowed with it, and she looked as if she couldn't manage another word.

He slid through the crowd and took her arm. "Komm," he murmured, and led her out of the room, not caring what anyone thought of that.

The hallway wasn't much better, with people moving back and forth, soles squeaking on the tile floor. He steered her down the hall and around the corner. There was a small, empty room with benches, a sort of chapel, he supposed. He steered her inside and led her to a seat.

She sank down with a sigh and then looked at him with a question in her eyes. "Did you need to talk with me, Daniel?"

"Not as much as you needed to sit down and be quiet for a bit."

That startled the ghost of a smile from her. "They are being kind, but you're right. It is tiring to keep saying the same things over and over."

"I won't make you say them again to me, but I understand from Bishop Mose that Anna is waking up. That's wonderful gut news."

Her eyes lightened. "It is. She knows us, that's the important thing. The doctors say it looks as if she won't have to have surgery." She brushed away a tear that had spilled onto her cheek. "I know it's foolish of me, but I can't help wondering what people are saying about what she did."

He leaned toward her to take her hands in his. "It doesn't matter," he said firmly. "Whatever Anna did, once she confesses she will be forgiven and loved."

She nodded, her gaze downcast, as if she looked at their hands. "I know. Just as I know that everyone is helping. Mahlon told me that you'd been over to do the milking. Matthew, too."

"It's gut for the boy. It helps him to remember what it means to be Amish."

If it made her feel better to talk about that, he would oblige, but he couldn't help but see that thinking of Anna's confession before the church distressed her.

"The horse and buggy are back safe, too," he went on. "One of the Esch boys showed up with them this morning."

"Ser gut," she murmured, but he thought her mind was elsewhere.

"If you want to be by yourself—" he began.

Her fingers tightened on his. "No." The word came out quickly, and then she bit her lip. "I'm sorry. I shouldn't impose on you."

"You are not imposing." He cradled her hands in his, wishing he knew some way to ease the burden she carried. "You can say anything you want to me, Leah. It will go no further."

"I know." She looked at him then, her eyes dark with misery. "The police chief talked to me last night. He said that Anna may have to face charges in a court." Tears spilled over again. "I don't know what to do." Her voice dropped to a ragged whisper. "I don't know how to help her."

Her pain pummeled his heart. He moved to the bench next to her. Tentatively, he put his arm around her, intent only on giving comfort.

She turned into his shoulder, her tears wetting his shirt. Her whole body shook with the sobs.

He stroked her back, murmuring softly to her as he would to one of the children. "It will be all right."

That was the best thing to say right now. The only thing. He just prayed that it was true.

Leah frowned down at the quilt patch she was piecing as she sat in Anna's hospital room. She'd have to take those erratic stitches back out again. It was surely true that they reflected her state of mind.

She glanced at her sister. Anna napped, face turned away from her. In the three days that had passed since the accident, things had settled into a more normal routine. She, Mamm, and Daad had taken turns being here at the hospital, but it had been a battle to convince Mamm that she didn't have to be with Anna twenty-four hours a day.

The plain truth was that every time Leah heard a step in the hallway, she feared it might be the police. The prospect of her sister being charged hung over her, and she still didn't feel they'd gotten from Anna a complete story of what had happened. If the worst came, somehow they must try to protect Mamm.

Leah couldn't think about that trouble without remembering

weeping in Daniel's arms. He'd comforted her without question when that was what she'd needed. She'd never realized before how much it meant to have someone to lean on.

She stared down at the quilt patch. Her life still resembled a crazy quilt rather than this neat arrangement of geometric shapes.

Was her volunteer work at the clinic really so important that she couldn't give it up for the sake of marriage to a good man? For the sake of those children she already loved?

Maybe the truth was that she was afraid. Afraid she'd fail at loving, as she had with Johnny.

Not that Daniel was offering love. Everything else—a stable life, children, a home, support, and security. But not love.

Anna moved slightly in the bed. Her eyes flickered open, then shut again at the sight of Leah.

Leah touched Anna's hand, shaking off her own perplexities. This time, perhaps, she could get the full story from her sister. Anna couldn't keep escaping into sleep. She had to face the situation.

"How do you feel?"

"Tired. I need to sleep some more." Anna kept her eyes closed. She'd done that as a child, refusing to face doing something she didn't want to do.

"You've slept enough," Leah said briskly, pushing the button to elevate the head of the bed. "The nurses say you should be getting up more now. You need to get your strength back."

"I don't want to." Her eyes snapped open, and she frowned at Leah. "Where's Mamm?"

"Home, getting some rest, I hope."

Anna had grace enough to look a little embarrassed at the reminder. "Is she all right?"

"As all right as she can be under the circumstances." They both knew that Mamm was troubled by more than Anna's being hurt.

Anna's fingers pleated the edge of the sheet. "What about— what about the other people in the accident? How are they?"

It was the first time Anna had seemed willing to have a real conversation about what had happened. That was a good sign, surely.

"The Esch family is fine, they say. Just some bumps and bruises. Daad is making arrangements to have their buggy fixed."

Anna smoothed out the pleats. "And the others?"

"Your English friends were not badly hurt. They've all gone home from the hospital."

"Have any of them come to see me?"

"No." Better the plain truth than soft evasions. None of the English teens who'd been with her that night had come to see her.

"They—they want to. I know that."

Leah couldn't say the words that trembled on her lips about the kind of friends who had led Anna into such trouble and then left her there. That would only make her sister more defensive.

"Maybe so," she said, her tone neutral. "Everyone from the church has been here, though, at one time or another. And brought food to the house, and took over the chores for Daad and Levi so they could be here."

Anna nodded, head down.

Leah felt exasperation mixed with the love she had for her sister. "Anna, why did you do it? Did the others talk you into driving that car?"

"Nobody talked me into it." She stared at Leah, her face set.

"I wanted to. It's not so bad. I'll bet the boys drove cars lots of times."

"If they did, at least they never had an accident. That buggy—" Her throat tightened. "Anna, don't you see how dangerous it was? If you'd hit the buggy full on, that family would be having a funeral right now. You of all people should know what to watch out for."

Anna's lips trembled, and her eyes filled with tears. "I didn't mean to drive too fast. The car just went so easy when I touched the pedal. All of a sudden I saw the reflector on the buggy, coming up so fast. I swerved to avoid it, Leah. I did."

In that instant she was Leah's baby sister again. Leah bent over the bed, putting her arms around Anna in a fierce hug. "I know. I know you're sorry for what you did."

For an instant Anna clung to her. Then she stiffened and pulled away.

"Well—I'm sorry they got hurt. But I bet lots of people have accidents when they're learning to drive."

In other words, she wasn't sorry about driving the car. Leah grasped the bed railing. "You're not lots of people, Anna. You're Amish. We don't drive cars."

Anna didn't respond. She averted her face, staring out the window.

The closeness Leah had felt with her sister disappeared as quickly as leaves blown by the wind. With her face set and averted, in her print hospital gown, Anna looked like a stranger.

Leah should talk to her. Should try to impress on her how wrong she'd been, how much trouble she might be in.

She looked at the sister she no longer seemed to know. Would anything she said reach her? Or was it too late?

. . .

With Anna taking refuge in sleep again, Leah headed for the elevator. Maybe a cup of hot coffee and a few minutes out of the hospital room would ease some of the tension.

She rounded the corner and came to a stop. John Kile stepped off the elevator. He carried a tissue-wrapped bunch of flowers in one hand.

"I know." He smiled with a touch of regret. "You're going to say that it's not a good idea for me to visit Anna."

"No. I was just going to say that I'm surprised to see you here. But it is kind of you." Her throat choked with tears. What was wrong with her that she allowed simple gestures of kindness to affect her so? "I'm sorry—" The rest of the words wouldn't come out, not without tears, in any event.

John grasped her elbow and piloted her through the nearest door. It was the same meditation room where Daniel had brought her for refuge. John took her to the nearest bench. The same bench.

He sat down next to her, laying the flowers aside and taking both her hands in his. "Don't take it so hard. Please, Leah. I know Anna is your baby sister, but she's not your responsibility."

For a moment she just took comfort from the gentleness of his touch and the caring that was obvious in his voice. Then the words penetrated, and she shook her head.

"That's what makes her my responsibility, no matter how old she is." Her voice might be wavering a little, but she was sure. She looked at Johnny, the tears wet on her cheeks. "Don't you know that?"

He blinked. "I didn't mean— Well, of course you love her and want to take care of her. But Anna's eighteen now. You have to let her make her own choices."

Part of what he said was right. But part of it was wrong. Anna was and would always be her baby sister, and she could never stop trying to protect her and take care of her. That was what siblings did.

If she said that to him, it would be the same as telling him that he'd let his sister down, and she couldn't do that, not when he and Rachel were just beginning to restore their relationship.

He seemed to take her silence for agreement. "You'll see. She'll come out of this a stronger, better person."

Anna needed to come out of it a humbled, repentant person, but Johnny had gone far from that Amish viewpoint, it seemed.

He stroked her hands gently. "Leah, I didn't really come here because of Anna. You must know that. I came because of you."

"Because you're my friend."

"Because I have feelings for you." His grip tightened, and he leaned toward her, face intent. "Maybe the timing's bad, but I can't hold this back any longer. I still care about you. I knew that the minute I saw you again. We were always meant to be together. You know that, don't you?"

She could only stare at him, her mind spinning hopelessly out of control.

"You feel the same way, I know you do." He sounded exactly like the young, impetuous Johnny of ten years ago. "I was going to give it more time, but I can't. Dr. Brandenmyer has offered me a two-year contract, and I have to give him an answer. I know you wouldn't want to stay here, but we can go away together. We can get married, you can go to school, we can travel—we can do all the things you've always just dreamed about."

The spinning stopped. Certainty pooled in her heart and mind. Somehow, in these past difficult days, she'd come to know where she belonged. She knew the place to which God had called her.

Maybe Johnny understood before she even spoke, because the eagerness faded from his eyes.

"I'm sorry," she said gently. "I'm sorry."

Anger flashed in his face. "You're still afraid."

How could she explain it so that he would understand? It was so clear to her now.

"I'm not afraid. I'm just sure."

"Is there someone else? Is that why?" He drew his hands away.

Sorrow was a weight on her heart. There might have been, but Daniel had made that impossible.

"No. At least, not the way you mean." Words weren't enough for this, but they were all she had. "You told me that I wasn't doing enough for the children I teach, but you're wrong. I'm not teaching them just by the subjects they learn. I'm teaching them by my life and my actions."

"You can't live your life for other people's kids. You deserve more."

"There is nothing more than this." She shook her head. "I am being a part of the community where no single piece is more important than any other. What anyone does affects everyone, especially the children."

He sat with his face averted, like Anna had.

"Johnny, I'm not blaming you for the choice you made." She

wanted to comfort him, as she would one of the children. "I just know that if I left, ripples would spread out from that action, affecting so many lives. You were right, in a way. I suppose at some level I was thinking about what the English world would be like, the way a child wonders what it would be like to be a bird. But I couldn't leave. I would be lost if I did."

"I'd take care of you." But there was no confidence in his words.

"I know you'd try." She took a breath, feeling the peace that settled into her. "I'm sorry I've never been able to give you what you want. Ten years ago I refused to go with you out of fear. But now—now the answer is the same, but the reason is different. I can't go, because I know where I belong. It's here."

CHAPTER TWENTY-ONE

Leah would never have imagined that she'd be dreading seeing her baby sister. But as she walked down the hospital corridor the next day, she realized that *dread* was exactly the right word for what she felt.

She'd spent the night praying for Anna and praying for guidance. Her newfound peace about who she was and what God intended for her life didn't seem to extend to her relationship with the sister she loved.

Why, Father? Why can't I reach her? Why can't I show her what is right?

To that, there didn't seem to be an answer.

Leah pushed the door to Anna's room open. She froze, fingers gripping the edge of the door. The room was empty, the bed stripped, the cards and flowers Anna had received gone.

She forced herself to cross the room to the small closet. The dress, cape, shoes, and kapp she'd brought yesterday in anticipation of Anna coming home soon were still here. Only Anna was gone.

The door swished behind her, and she whirled. The smile died on her face when she saw it was one of the nurses, a plump, comfortable, middle-aged woman in blue print scrubs.

"My sister." She nearly stammered the words. "Where is she?"

The woman's gaze slid away from hers. "She's gone. She checked herself out of the hospital first thing this morning."

"Gone!" Leah's mind spun dizzyingly. "How can she be gone? Where did she go? We were told that we might be able to take her home tomorrow."

"The doctor wanted her to stay another day, but she was very insistent." Faint sympathy crossed the woman's face. "Your sister is eighteen. Legally she's an adult, and she could check herself out."

Leah gripped the bottom rail of the bed. "But where did she go?"

"I'm sorry. I'm afraid I can't give out any information without the patient's permission." The nurse looked as if the sorrow was genuine—surely that was pity in her face.

Leah took a breath, trying to calm herself, trying to frame the words that would convince the woman to tell her where Anna was. "Please—she's my baby sister. You have to tell me where she is."

She shook her head, lips pressed together as if she wanted to speak but couldn't.

Please, Lord...

"She was still so weak. How could you just let her walk away?" Leah tried to keep her voice steady, but it wobbled despite her best efforts.

The nurse glanced behind her at the closed door and then turned back to Leah.

"We wouldn't let her walk, of course. I took her out myself in a wheelchair, and her young man brought his car right up to the sidewalk and helped her in. They drove away together."

The woman looked at her meaningfully. Leah's hands clenched. The English boy. Of course. For a moment her mind was blank, and then it came to her, as clearly as if she heard Anna speaking.

Jarrod, Anna had said. *His name is Jarrod Wells.*

"Thank you." Her eyes filled with tears as she pressed the woman's hand.

The nurse gave her a quick hug. "Don't thank me," she said. "I didn't tell you a thing."

"This is it." Ben Morgan, who'd come at once when Leah called from the hospital, pulled to a stop in front of a large, elegant home set back from the street in a suburban neighborhood. He patted Leah's shoulder as she started to slide from the car. "I'll wait for you. Good luck."

She nodded. Murmuring a silent prayer for guidance, she started up the walk.

She felt—small, she supposed. Out of place. Surely every one of these fancy homes looked in disdain at the sight of a Plain woman disrupting the modern style of their neighborhood.

She rang the doorbell, half expecting Anna or the boy to come. But when the door opened, she found herself facing a woman who must surely be the boy's mother, even though her carefully styled blonde hair and flawless makeup made her look too young to be the parent of a boy that age.

"I am here to see my sister." There seemed little point in beating about the bush. They both knew why she had come.

The woman stiffened. "I don't think she wants to see you. She's made a choice of her own free will. Why don't you people just leave her alone?"

She made it sound as if they were persecuting Anna.

"Anna is my baby sister. I will not go away without seeing her." She stepped boldly into the hallway, the woman stepping back as she did.

She flushed. "You can't—"

"It's all right. I'll talk to her." The voice was Anna's. But the young woman who stood in the archway wasn't Anna—not the Anna she knew.

Blue jeans, sneakers, a bright knit top that clung to her body and a dangling necklace that hung between her breasts. Makeup drew attention to her delicate features, and—Leah's breath caught—her hair. Anna's hair was cut to her chin in a shining bob that swung when she moved her head.

"All right," the woman—Mrs. Wells, she supposed—said doubtfully. "If you're sure. Go in the sunroom. You'll be private there."

"Thanks." Anna gestured to Leah. "This way."

Wordlessly, Leah followed this new Anna down the hallway. The sunroom had tile floors and glass all around, with plants blooming so profusely that it looked like a greenhouse.

Anna swung to face her, not offering her a seat. "I'm not going back, so there's no point to your saying anything." She flicked her hair with her fingers. "Cut my hair first thing. You like it?"

"I liked it the way it was." Leah took a step toward this girl who was and yet wasn't her beloved sister. "Anna, don't do this. Come home with me. It's not too late. Everyone will welcome you—"

"Everyone will be glad to see the last of me, you mean."

"You know that's not true. We only want you to come home."

"And be exactly like everyone else." Something that might have been hurt flickered in her blue eyes. "I can't. I don't want to. Jarrod's mother says I can stay with them until I figure out what I want to do."

It seemed incredible that the boy's mother would encourage this. Surely she must think that her son was too young to form a lasting attachment.

"I know you think you love him, but this is only going to bring unhappiness. You're both so young—"

"You wouldn't say that if I were talking about marrying Eli Stoltzfus or Martin Brand." She shrugged. "Anyway, it's not like that. They're just helping me because they think I have a right to make my own decisions."

"I will not argue that. But what about the police? The chief said—"

"That's taken care of. Mrs. Wells got a lawyer for me. I just plead guilty to driving without a license, and I'll be put on probation for a few months. See? My friends are taking care of me."

"It's gut of them to help you." Anna was getting off easy, Leah felt. Because of the Wells family involvement? She didn't know.

"It is." Anna's face was stony.

Leah reached out a tentative hand toward her sister. "But we love you. How can you decide to leave us this way? Don't you love us anymore?"

For a moment she thought Anna wouldn't answer. Then her lips trembled a little, and her eyes filled with tears.

"I love you." She blinked rapidly. "That's what makes it so hard. But this is right for me. Really." She flung out her hands. "Don't you see? I have to find out what the world is like. I have to see for myself. I can't just settle down and get married and never know anything else. Can't you understand that? Sometimes I feel as if I'm going to explode if I don't get away from here."

"I know things have been upset, with Mamm's health and Mamm and Daadi moving into the daadi haus—"

"It's not that." She shook her head decisively, her hair flaring out and then fluttering against her cheek. "I admit that's pushed me along, but this has been coming for a long time." She smiled a little sadly. "You just didn't notice. Leah, please, try to understand. Try to forgive me for hurting Mamm and Daad. I'm sorry. But I have to go and see what the world is like. I have to."

Leah didn't want to understand. She wanted to take Anna's hand, the way she had when Anna was little, and lead her back home. But she couldn't.

Leah was meant to stay, she knew that now. But it seemed that Anna was equally convinced that it was her time to go.

"I will miss you. More than you know."

Relief flooded Anna's face. "You understand."

"No, not entirely. But I accept that you feel you have to go." She opened her arms to Anna, her heart full of love and pain. "Da Herr sei mit du. The Lord be with you."

Anna threw her arms around Leah in a fierce hug. "I love you, Leah." Her voice cracked with emotion. "Thank you."

Leah stroked the silky hair. "Just don't disappear, the way Johnny did. Don't forget us."

"I won't." Anna pressed her cheek against Leah's.

Pain ricocheted through her, and she remembered the first time she'd held her baby sister, her heart overflowing with love.

Please, Father. Please. Bring our Anna back to us one day.

She was almost home already, and she still hadn't figured out what she was going to say to her parents. Leah reached across to touch Ben's sleeve, knowing he was unlikely to hear her with his favorite country music blaring from the radio.

"Just drop me here. I'd like to walk the rest of the way."

His eyebrows lifted. "You sure of that?"

"I have some thinking to do."

He pulled up at the edge of Daniel's pasture. "I'm sorry about this business with Anna. Hope everything works out all right."

"I do, too." Her throat thickened, and she couldn't say more. But Ben was a good friend to the Amish, and he'd understand.

She slid out, raising her hand in a wave as he drove away.

Walking along the road, even in the heat of the summer sun, was better than being cooped up in an automobile. She took her bonnet off and let it dangle from her fingers.

Tiger lilies had begun to open along the side of the road, their orange blossoms unfurling, and Daniel's cows surveyed her from the other side of the fence. It was beautiful, and peaceful, and

Anna was rejecting it. Rejecting the life she'd always lived in favor of the unknown.

Mamm and Daadi wouldn't take her word for Anna's decision, of course. They'd insist on trying to talk to her themselves, sure that they could make her see sense.

But Anna wouldn't change her mind. She was set on this course. One day, if God chose, she might realize that here was where she belonged.

Leah's vision blurred with unshed tears, and she closed her eyes for a moment. When she opened them, she saw Daniel, working on the fence at the corner where his lane met the county road.

Maybe that was why she'd had that urge to get out of the car, if she were truthful with herself. She'd hoped to see Daniel. Hoped to borrow a little of his strength for the ordeal ahead of her.

He saw her coming and straightened from his work, watching as she approached. "Was ist letz?" he asked as soon as she was close enough. "What's the matter?"

She stopped, finding it harder than she'd expected to answer the question.

He touched her hand gently, drawing her closer. "Anna? She's not coming home, is she?"

So he'd guessed. The tears spilled over before Leah could stop them. "She's gone to her English friends."

"She might change her mind once she's thought about it a bit." He brushed away the tears on her cheek, and his fingers were warm against her skin. "Maybe it's not too late."

"I don't think so."

Anna wouldn't come home. She wouldn't kneel before the

congregation, confess her sin, and receive their forgiveness and love. Leah fought back tears so she could speak.

"Maybe for now, that's the right thing. It seems she'll never be happy unless she's seen some of the world. Maybe, once she's seen it, she'll realize her place is here."

He took her hands in his. "Is that what you believe?"

"It's what I hope and pray."

"Then I will hope and pray that also." His fingers tightened on hers. "Has she left it to you to tell your parents?"

She nodded. "I wish I could find the words to break it to them gently."

"They will not be surprised."

She looked up at him, startled at the comment, and realized he was probably right. She longed to protect them, but they wouldn't be surprised. They knew Anna.

"What makes you so wise?"

He smiled, shaking his head. "I'm not so wise. But I care." The smile faded, and his blue eyes grew very serious. "This is not the time or the place, but I cannot wait any longer to ask this. Leah, will you be my wife?"

Her breath caught in her throat, and the waving meadow grass blurred. She looked at him—at the strong column of his neck, the firmness of his jaw, the kindness in his eyes.

Looking at him, she seemed to see the life that would be hers if she said yes. The children, the laughter, the sharing. It was all there within her grasp. But she couldn't take it.

"I'm sorry." The words came out in a whisper, and she took a deep breath and lifted her chin. She wouldn't be a coward about this. "I thought I could do without love, but I've learned something about myself in the past few months. I can't marry without it. You can't offer me your heart, Daniel. So I'll have to settle for being your friend."

"Leah." His voice was husky, and his fingers tightened on hers when she tried to pull free. "Knowing you has turned all that I thought I knew upside down. I've been so foolish, comparing you with Ruth and thinking that if you were around the English, you'd want to be one. I see now that the gut work you do at the clinic has only made you stronger."

He let go of her hands then, but only so that he could cup her face between his palms. "I love you, Teacher Leah. With all my heart. I believe that God led me to this place because we are meant to be together, and I will never try to change the strong, faithful woman you are, if only you will be my wife."

Her heart was so full that she could not speak, but he must have read the answer in her eyes, because he bent his head and kissed her. After the first surprised moment she put her arms around him, secure in his warm embrace.

He lifted his head after a long moment.

A smile trembled on her lips. "Are we really standing at the end of your lane, kissing in broad daylight? The People will think for sure we are ferhoodled."

He drew her closer, his lips brushing her cheek tenderly. "There is no one to see but the cows, and they don't mind. You haven't answered me, you know."

"I thought I had." For a moment she pushed away all thought of the troubles yet to be faced. "I love you, Daniel, with all my heart. Ja, I will marry you."

Here was the answer she'd been seeking, even without really knowing it. In all she'd done, God had been preparing her for this role—Daniel's wife, the mother of his children, the woman who could fill a role at the Englischer clinic without compromising being Amish.

She lifted her face for Daniel's kiss. God had chosen this role for her from the beginning. He was just waiting for her to be ready to step into it.

GLOSSARY OF PENNSYLVANIA DUTCH WORDS AND PHRASES

ach. oh; used as an exclamation

agasinish. stubborn; self-willed

ain't so. A phrase commonly used at the end of a sentence to invite agreement.

alter. old man

anymore. Used as a substitute for "nowadays."

Ausbund. Amish hymnal. Used in the worship services, it contains traditional hymns, words only, to be sung without accompaniment. Many of the hymns date from the sixteenth century.

befuddled. mixed up

blabbermaul. talkative one

blaid. bashful

boppli. baby

bruder. brother

bu. boy

buwe. boys

daadi. daddy

denke. thanks (or *danki*)

Da Herr sei mit du. The Lord be with you.

Englischer. One who is not Plain.

ferhoodled. upset; distracted

ferleicht. perhaps

frau. wife

fress. eat

gross. big

grossdaadi. grandfather

grossdaadi haus. An addition to the farmhouse, built for the grandparents to live in once they've "retired" from actively running the farm.

grossmutter. grandmother

gut. good

hatt. hard; difficult

haus. house

hinnersich. backward

ich. I

ja. yes

kapp. Prayer covering, worn in obedience to the biblical injunction that women should pray with their heads covered. Kapps are made of Swiss organdy and are white. (In some Amish communities, unmarried girls thirteen and older wear black kapps during worship service.)

kinder. kids (or *kinner*)

komm. come

komm schnell. come quick

Leit. the people; the Amish

lippy. sassy

maidal. old maid; spinster

mamm. mother

meddaagesse. lunch

mind. remember

onkel. uncle

Ordnung. The agreed-upon rules by which the Amish community lives. When new practices become an issue, they are discussed at length among the leadership. The decision for or against innovation is generally made on the basis of maintaining the home and family as separate from the world. For instance, a telephone might be necessary in a shop in order to conduct business but would be banned from the home because it would intrude on family time.

Pennsylvania Dutch. The language is actually German in origin and is primarily a spoken language. Most Amish write in English, which results in many variations in spelling when the dialect is put into writing! The language probably originated in the south of Germany but is common also among the Swiss Mennonite and French Huguenot immigrants to Pennsylvania. The language was brought to America prior to the Revolution and is still in use today. High German is used for Scripture and church documents, while English is the language of commerce.

rumspringa. Running-around time. The late teen years when Amish youth taste some aspects of the outside world before deciding to be baptized into the church.

schnickelfritz. mischievous child

ser gut. very good
tastes like more. delicious
Was ist letz? What's the matter?
Wie bist du heit. It's nice to meet you.
wilkom. welcome
Wo bist du? Where are you?

Dear Reader,

I'm so glad you decided to pick up this book. I hope that you enjoyed Leah's love story as much as I enjoyed writing it. These characters have been living in my heart for some time now, and it's a delight to see them on the page and to share them with you.

I would love to hear your thoughts about my book. If you'd care to write to me, I'd be happy to reply with a signed bookmark or bookplate and my brochure of Pennsylvania Dutch recipes. You can find me on the Web at www.martaperry.com, e-mail me at marta@martaperry.com, or write to me in care of Berkley Publicity Department, Penguin Group (USA) Inc., 375 Hudson Street, New York, NY 10014.

Blessings,
Marta Perry

An Excerpt from

RACHEL'S GARDEN

Pleasant Valley
BOOK TWO

by Marta Perry

A flicker of movement from the lane beyond the kitchen window of the old farmhouse caught Rachel Brand's eye as she leaned against the sink, washing up the bowl she'd used to make a batch of snickerdoodles. A buggy—ja, it must be Leah Glick, bringing her two older kinder home from the birthday party for their teacher already.

Quickly she set the bowl down and splashed cold water on her eyes. It wouldn't do to let her young ones suspect that their mamm had been crying while she baked. Smoothing her hair back under her kapp and arranging a smile on her lips, she went to the back door.

But the visitor was not Leah. It was a man alone, driving the buggy.

Shock shattered her curiosity when she recognized the strong face under the brim of the black Amish hat. Gideon Zook. Her fingers clenched, wrinkling the fabric of her dark apron. What did he want from her?

She stood motionless for a moment, her left hand tight on the door frame. Then she grabbed the black wool shawl that hung by the door, threw it around her shoulders, and stepped outside.

The cold air sent a shiver through her. It was mid-March already, but winter had not released its grip on Pleasant Valley, Pennsylvania. The snowdrops she had planted last fall quivered against the back step, their white cups a mute testimony that spring would come eventually. Everything else was as brown and barren as her heart felt these days.

A fierce longing for spring swept through her as she crossed the still-hard ground. If she could be in the midst of growing things, planting and nurturing her beloved garden—ach, there she might find the peace she longed for.

Everything was too quiet on the farm now. Even the barn was empty, the dairy cows moved to the far field already, taken care of by her young brother-in-law William in the early morning hours.

The Belgian draft horses Ezra had been so pleased to be able to buy were spending the winter at the farm of his oldest brother, Isaac. Only Dolly, six-year-old Joseph's pet goat, bleated forlornly from her pen, protesting his absence.

Gideon had tethered his horse to the hitching post. Removing an object from his buggy, he began pacing across the lawn, as if he measured something.

Then he saw her. He stopped, waiting. His hat was pushed back, and he lifted his face slightly, as if in appreciation of the watery sunshine. But Gideon's broad shoulders were stiff under his black jacket, his eyes wary and his mouth set above his beard.

Reluctance slowed her steps. Perhaps Gideon felt that same

reluctance. Aside from the formal words of condolence he'd spoken to her once he was well enough to be out again after the accident, she and Gideon had managed to avoid talking to each other for months. That was no easy thing in a tight-knit Amish community.

She forced a smile. "Gideon, wilkom. I didn't expect to be seeing you today."

What are you doing here? was what she really wanted to say.

"Rachel." He inclined his head slightly, studying her face as if trying to read her feelings.

His own face gave little away—all strong planes and straight lines, like the wood he worked with in his carpentry business. Lines of tension radiated from his brown eyes, making him look older than the thirty-two she knew him to be. His work-hardened hands tightened on the objects he grasped—small wooden stakes, sharpened to points.

He cleared his throat, as if not sure what to say to her now that they were face-to-face. "How are you? And the young ones?"

"I'm well." Except that her heart twisted with pain at the sight of him, at the reminder he brought of all she had lost. "The kinder also. Mary is napping, and Leah Glick took Joseph and Becky to a birthday luncheon the scholars are having for Mary Yoder."

"Gut, gut."

He moved a step closer to her, and she realized that his left leg was still stiff—a daily reminder for him, probably, of the accident.

For an instant the scene she'd imagined so many times flashed yet again through her mind, stealing her breath away. She seemed to see Ezra, high in the rafters of a barn; Gideon below him; the old timbers creaking, then breaking, Ezra falling as the barn collapsed like a house of cards . . .

She gasped a strangled breath, like a fish struggling on the bank of the pond. Revulsion wrung her stomach, and she slammed the door shut on her imagination.

She could not let herself think about that, not now. It was not Gideon's fault that she couldn't see him without imagining the accident that had taken Ezra away from them. She had to talk to him sensibly, had to find out what had brought him here. And how she could get him to go away again.

She clutched the shawl tighter around her. "Is there something I can do for you, Gideon?"

"I am here to measure for the greenhouse."

She could only stare at him, her mind fumbling to process his words. The greenhouse—the greenhouse Ezra had promised her as a birthday present. That had to be what Gideon meant.

"How do you know about the greenhouse?"

The words came out unexpectedly harsh. Ezra was gone, and plans for the greenhouse had slipped away, too, swamped in the struggle just to get through the days.

He blinked, apparently surprised. "You didn't know? Ezra and I went together to buy the materials for your greenhouse. He asked me to build it for you. Now I'm here to start on the work."

The revulsion that swept through her was so strong she could barely prevent it from showing on her face.

Perhaps he knew anyway. The fine lines around his eyes deepened. "Is there a problem with that?"

"No—I mean, I didn't realize that he had asked you. Ezra never said so."

"Perhaps he thought there was no need. I always helped him with carpentry projects."

True enough. It wasn't that Ezra couldn't build things with his own hands, but he was far more interested in the crops and the animals. Since his childhood friend Gideon was a carpenter, specializing in building the windmills that had begun to dot the valley, Ezra had depended on him.

But that was before. Now—

Now the thought of having Gideon around for days while he built the greenhouse that was to have been a gift of love from her husband . . .

No, she couldn't handle that. She couldn't. It was, no doubt about it, a failure on her part, one that she should be taking to the Lord in prayer.

"Rachel?" She had been silent too long, and Gideon studied her face with concern. "Was ist letz? What's the matter?"

"Nothing," she said quickly. "Nothing at all. It's just that I hadn't thought about the greenhouse in months." Her voice thickened—she couldn't help that.

Gideon heard it, of course. A spasm of something that might have been pain crossed his face.

"It gave Ezra great pleasure to think about giving it to you." His deep voice seemed choked.

She blinked, focusing her gaze on the barn beyond him, willing herself to be calm. Think. What could she say that would not hurt Gideon, but would get him to go away?

"I haven't—I haven't decided what to do about the greenhouse." As she hadn't decided so many things in the past few months, lost as she'd been in grief. "Will you give me a little time to think?"

"Of course."

But his voice had cooled, as if he knew something of what she was feeling. His gaze was intent on her face, probing for the truth, and all she could think was that she wanted him to leave so that she didn't have to talk about the bittersweet nature of Ezra's last gift to her.

The creak of an approaching buggy broke the awkward silence between them. She glanced toward the lane.

"Here is Leah, back with the children." She probably sounded too relieved as she turned back to him. "Perhaps we could talk about this some other day."

His expression still grave, Gideon nodded. "Ja, another time, then." He turned away, but then glanced back over his shoulder. "I promised Ezra, ain't so? I have to keep that promise."

He walked toward his waiting buggy, back stiff.